Esmahan Aykol was born in 1970 in Edirne, Turkey. She lives in Istanbul and Berlin. During her law studies she was a journalist for a number of Turkish publications and radio stations. After a stint as a bartender she turned to fiction writing. *Divorce Turkish Style* is the third of the Kati Hirschel series. The first two are *Hotel Bosphorus* and *Baksheesh*, also published by Bitter Lemon Press.

D1490999

Also available from Bitter Lemon Press
by Esmahan Aykol:

Hotel Bosphorus
Baksheesh

DIVORCE TURKISH STYLE

A Kati Hirschel Mystery

Esmahan Aykol

Translated by Ruth Whitehouse

BITTER LEMON PRESS
LONDON

BITTER LEMON PRESS

First published in the United Kingdom in 2015 by
Bitter Lemon Press, 47 Wilmington Square, London WC1X 2ET

www.bitterlemonpress.com

First published in Turkish as *Şüpheli Bir Ölüm*
by Merkez Kitaplar, Istanbul, 2007

Bitter Lemon Press gratefully acknowledges the
financial assistance of the Arts Council of England
and of the TEDA Project of the Ministry of Culture
and Tourism of the Republic of Turkey

A CIP record for this book is available from the British Library

ISBN 978-1-908524-577
eBook ISBN 978-1-908524-584

Typeset by Tetragon, London

Printed in EU by Pulsio SARL

Supported using public funding by
ARTS COUNCIL
ENGLAND
LOTTERY FUNDED

DIVORCE
TURKISH STYLE

1

Istanbul had become a dangerous place, especially in and around İstiklal Street. I only had to mention that I was going out to the bank and Fofo would start fussing over me and wishing me luck. Not only that, he'd recently started rising early to prepare me wonderful breakfasts, saying how young and beautiful I looked, and embracing me before I set out as if we were seeing each other for the last time. But he was right. Anything could happen. There was a constant danger of disappearing down one of the many holes in the pavement that the council had opened up, or of being pushed under one of the huge trucks that sped along our street, despite its being officially closed to traffic.

In my attempts to stay alive, I'd taken to wearing cargo pants and comfortable shoes. I'd also stopped carrying a bag over my shoulder because it slowed me down, so now the roomy pockets of my cargo pants were filled with all sorts of items, including my mobile. Despite the initial embarrassment at venturing out in trainers, I soon found them to be invaluable for comfort and safety.

Actually, I'd made considerable progress. When the council started replacing the paving stones the previous year, I was barely capable of remaining upright when picking my way through the squelchy mud. Who'd have thought it now possible for me to jump over a two-metre pothole and land safely the other side? My previous limitations now seemed amusing. However, it was difficult to believe that İstiklal Street was really meant to be a traffic-free area for pedestrians to stroll about in comfort, because it was constantly filled with machinery, diggers, trucks and winches. Suitable attire, reliable reflexes, strong muscles and alertness – and bad enough manners to elbow other pedestrians out of the way – were essential.

It was incredible but true that the paving stones were being replaced for the second time in a year. Fofo told me that roads in Spain were constantly being dug up because it enabled successive governments to create newly rich contractors who were then beholden to them. Turkey seemed to be going the same way, judging by the number of men who had abandoned public transport and were now driving their wives around in shiny new Range Rovers.

Since moving to Kuledibi, I'd started going to the bank in İstiklal Street once a week on Fridays, and that was more than enough. I'm not as young as I was, and one's calamity avoidance coefficient inevitably reduces over time.

That Friday, I went into Şimdi Café in Asmalımescit Street after visiting the bank and, as I sipped a Turkish coffee, quietly congratulated myself on having negotiated the toughest part of the journey. Provided I managed to make my way past the Swedish Consulate and down the slope in front of the German High School without mishap, I knew that I'd be safe and sound with Pelin and Fofo within five or six minutes.

Any readers who remember how Fofo had infuriated me by going off with his lover might wonder why I keep mentioning his name. Well, the affair was soon over and, after a few days in a cheap and nasty hotel, Fofo finally plucked up the courage to ask if he could come back to live at my place. Naturally, soft as I am, I couldn't bear to see him living like that, and gave in.

Okay, I admit that describing myself as soft is a bit of an exaggeration. However, I don't consider myself a bad person. After all, it didn't even occur to me to fire Pelin when Fofo returned and threw himself so eagerly into working at the shop. I made her promise to complete her university course that year, and indeed trusted her to do it. There had been the usual explosion of summer visitors to Turkey, and I suspected that Pelin had ideas about training as a tour guide in order to prey on this influx of rich tourists. She needed telling that the gains to be made in Turkish tourism were small and that being a tour guide was a risky business. However, I wasn't the person to do that. It wasn't my business to wreck a young girl's dreams.

My business was selling crime fiction. With my shop in Kuledibi, I became, and indeed still am, the first and only specialist seller of crime fiction in Istanbul. I'm always being asked what made me think of doing this, but what could be more natural than selling a product I love? And I adore reading crime fiction.

Readers who have followed my progress through life will know that, after considerable difficulties, I'd succeeded in buying a bargain-price apartment close to the shop. Having raised a few loans to have the place refurbished, I'd now moved in. Thanks to Atakan, my friend Candan's cousin, the work was completed sooner and more cheaply than expected, which of course was a lovely surprise. I now took great pleasure in recommending Atakan to everyone. After all, he'd handed the keys back to me on the agreed date as promised, making me ashamed of my assertions that the construction industry was rotten to the core and totally untrustworthy. I didn't normally make such generalizations, but I'd had a few bad experiences with contractors and architects. Atakan reminded me that there are good and bad guys in every situation. That's how the world is.

However, one generalization that I considered to be true was summed up in that depressing film *Gentlemen Prefer Blondes*. That men like blondes is beyond dispute. Take my friend Lale.

She went blonde and found herself a new lover even before her first retouch! Was that coincidence? And, would you believe it, the guy was none other than Erol, the bearded man living on the top floor of my new apartment block. Actually, he no longer had a beard because Lale didn't like it, and he certainly looked better without it. He and Lale had been together for over a year.

And me? I was still without a partner, as I had been for ages. I'd been thinking of going blonde too, because I felt that my appearance didn't conform to the Turkish perception of a German woman. However, I decided instead to spread the word that Germany was not a nation of blonds. Research apparently shows that only fifty-one per cent of German women and fifty-four per cent of German men are blond.

When I reached the shop, Pelin hadn't yet arrived and Fofo was in a flap.

"Where were you?" he cried.

Fofo's habit of watching third-rate TV series had taught him that Turkish was a language to be spoken with a succession of screams accompanied by exaggerated gestures and facial expressions.

"I thought something had happened to you!" he yelled.

"Stop shouting, for goodness' sake! My head's already pounding from the roadworks in İstiklal Street," I said.

"Look at this," said Fofo, pressing a folded newspaper into my hands.

You may remember that I wasn't in the habit of reading newspapers. I preferred to read a good detective story rather than waste my time reading press rubbish. However, this piece of news, or at least the headshot of the smiling blonde, immediately caught my attention. It was as if she'd been created to support my theory about the allure of golden-haired females. She was utterly and unbelievably beautiful. What's more, I recognized her from somewhere. Her face was the sort that, once seen, was unforgettable. I wondered if I'd seen her at one of the crowded clubs full of cigarette smoke and noisy music that Fofo dragged me to on Saturday nights.

"Where do I know that face from?" I asked.

"Take a good look. Don't you recognize the place?" said Fofo.

"Stop winding me up and tell me."

"It's the little restaurant we go to for lunch."

"But her hair... that woman isn't blonde," I said, sitting down in the rocking chair, my eyes still glued to the photo.

"No, she used to be brunette."

"So she's had it dyed."

"Dyed to this year's colour."

Since our decision to eat more healthily, we'd been lunching at a restaurant in the Tünel area, where we'd even shared a table with this woman a few times owing to lack of space. Whenever I'd seen her, she was picking at a minute salad. I glanced at the newspaper article and saw that she was Sani Ankaralıgil, aged thirty-two.

Sani Ankaralıgil had married into the renowned Ankaralıgil family, one of Turkey's richest. Six months previously, she'd left her husband, and subsequently applied for a divorce. She'd been found dead around noon the previous day at her luxury villa in Paşabahçe, where she lived alone. Sani Ankaralıgil had apparently died as the result of a tragic accident. The police had taken a statement from her grief-stricken husband Cem Ankaralıgil, who had last spoken to her the previous week.

"So? What of it? It's nothing to do with us," I said.

"Don't you think her sudden death in the middle of a divorce case is of interest?"

"If you really want to know, struggling to pay off my bank loan is a lot more interesting to me right now," I replied. "Tell me, how many books have you sold this morning? Hmm?"

"What's happened to your bloodhound nose? A woman divorces her rich husband—"

"I keep my nose for sniffing out financial matters," I interrupted. "Not that it seems to have any effect on my staff."

"What if she was murdered?" persisted Fofo.

"Do you know how many women are murdered every minute? Things like that are handled by the police, whose salaries are paid for out of my taxes, and by women's associations, to which I give financial support despite my current material straits. It's none of my business."

"You're impossible today. Sorry for taking up your time," said Fofo reproachfully, rising to his feet with a bitter smile.

He went out to the small kitchen area behind the orange- and green-striped curtain and picked up a duster, which he started flicking randomly over the bookshelves. Meanwhile, I sat down at the computer to go over the previous week's accounts.

Business on Fridays was always erratic. Sometimes, there'd be a constant flow of customers and barely time to breathe, while at other times we'd squabble with each other just to pass the time. However, that Friday was very busy. Our customers ranged from foreign tourists taking a look at city life to locals wanting to arm themselves with books before setting off to spend the best days of autumn on an Aegean boat trip. It was a profitable day. If only every day could be like that.

After paying Pelin and Fofo's salaries, I was finding it difficult to keep up the repayments on my bank loan, never mind putting money aside for retirement.

"From now on, we'll be opening at the weekends," I'd announced at the start of summer, ignoring the way Fofo and Pelin looked at each other as if I was out of my mind. "Not only is Kuledibi much nicer when all the trashy shops are closed, our target customers mainly come here at weekends, either just to have tea or to see Istanbul from the Galata Tower."

Fofo and Pelin remained silent.

"Any objections, either of you?"

"We'd have to make up a new rota," said Pelin.

"Of course we'll have a new rota. Since you'll be at university during the week, you can open up at the weekends. Fofo and I will take care of the other days."

"Fine," said Pelin.

Fofo nodded reluctantly. He was a dear friend, but wouldn't so much as move his little finger unless compelled.

So Pelin and Fofo started running the business without me at the weekends. In return, I'd come in early on Monday mornings. That Monday, I'd opened the shutters and was waiting for the water to boil to make green tea when the telephone rang.

"Are you online?" shouted Fofo down the line.

"Yes," I replied, holding the receiver away from my ear.

I'd opened up the computer as soon as I arrived, as always.

"Go to Skyrat. Our Sani is headline news!" cried Fofo.

Skyrat was a popular website for gossip and rumours in Istanbul. For security reasons the website owners didn't reveal their names, but the word was that three men ran it: a couple of journalists who had lost their jobs while investigating the police, and the editor of a society magazine.

From this website, for instance, we'd learned that Turkey's self-styled most beautiful woman, the singer Binnur Baran, had discovered her husband in bed with their Romanian maid, and the identity of the person who supplied drugs to the beautiful young model Gül Arkan, whose corpse had been found in the street the previous year. The website provided all kinds of source material: from pre-fame nude photos of a well-known actress to secret sex tapes of a university professor who was familiar as a TV news commentator.

With the phone wedged between my neck and shoulder, I typed in the website address.

A page of flashing headlines came up and invited me to click for more details. I clicked.

Investigations are continuing into the sudden and mysterious death of Sani Ankaralıgil following an accident at her villa in Paşabahçe. She was in the process of divorcing her husband Cem Ankaralıgil, a familiar face in society and the only son of Tamaşa and Bahri Ankaralıgil, the well-known shipping magnate and owner of the Ankaralıgil group of companies. A few days before her death, Sani Ankaralıgil is known to have dined at the famous Shining Sun restaurant with a close friend of her husband.

What was discussed at this meal?

Bookmark skyrat.com.tr for breaking news!

"So, what about it?" I said.

"It's hotting up!" said Fofo, his voice ringing with excitement. "We're not the only ones who've refused to let this go. Why don't we go and speak to the people who run this website? We might find out what's behind it all."

"You're full of good ideas today, aren't you, Fofo?" I retorted. "But I can't be running after killers. I need to concentrate on running the shop, paying off my debts and putting money aside for a rainy day."

However, I was beginning to weaken. This could be another chance to prove my skills at sniffing out a murderer. As you'll appreciate, dear reader, it wasn't every day that a seller of crime fiction was presented with a murder waiting to be solved.

"Anyway, suppose we decided to pursue this," I said, still putting up a defensive front, "where are you going to find the people who run this website? No one knows who they are."

"Oh, Kati, how naive you are," interrupted Fofo cheerfully. "Don't tell me you really think something like that can be kept secret in Istanbul."

"What do you mean?"

"I mean that I know the two journalists. I see them cavorting around on the dance floor whenever I go to Pakize's. You've seen them too. Remember the guy with brown hair and horn-rimmed glasses?"

"Uh-huh," I said in a non-committal way, finding the description pretty unhelpful.

"You know, the one who dances like a lunatic?" continued Fofo. "He removed his shirt once and started waving it about. He's tall, with—"

"Yes, I think I remember," I said.

An image was beginning to form in my mind, not of a face but a trim, muscular body, the type I'd swear spent at least four days a week at the gym, weightlifting in front of a mirror and watching his muscles swell. How did he find time to stretch out this one-line piece of news like a piece of chewing gum?

"Well, it's him," said Fofo with a deep sigh. "They say he's totally straight, but if you ask me, there's a bit more to him than that."

This was nothing new. Fofo was always claiming that men were naturally bisexual from birth. His belief in this theory was quite unshakeable.

"Could you find this guy?" I asked.

"I can do more than that," he said, brightly. "I don't have his number, but I know who he hangs out with, and one of them is my friend Taner. How about that?"

"You're a marvel! Call him immediately," I said, suddenly feeling ready to pursue a murder case with the energy of a panther preparing to pounce on its prey. Never mind the shop and the endless loans!

"Old habits die hard, I see," laughed Fofo. "Isn't that what you used to say?"

"Why break the habit of a lifetime?"

"Indeed. But what about the shop?" said Fofo, suddenly sounding serious. "Can we get hold of Pelin? If this man works near here, we might be able to see him straight away."

"I'm calling Pelin now."

"And if you can't reach her?"

"Don't worry, I'm not missing this for anything," I said.

"Yeah, I like it!" said Fofo.

I called Pelin and used various threats to get her to come to the shop immediately. Then, as I was going over the piece on Skyrat again, the telephone rang. It was Fofo.

"Sweetie," he said. "We're on! Be at Cactus Café in fifteen minutes. Don't be late! I worked hard to persuade him to meet us."

Rather than attempt the hazardous walk, I jumped into a taxi and was the first to arrive at Cactus Café. By the time Fofo rushed in, all out of breath, I was settled at a table on the street, flipping through a magazine and sipping lemonade.

"I told the guy that we're private detectives," whispered Fofo, pulling a chair up to mine. "I also hinted that his help wouldn't go unrewarded."

"You hinted what? Do you think I've got money to throw away?" I replied, probably too loudly, because a little girl, who'd been waiting for a chance to sell me a packet of tissues, glared and walked away. "You do realize I haven't paid off my loans yet, don't you? And there's all that interest! I'll go bankrupt at this rate."

"Oh, Kati. This isn't like you. Stop being so melodramatic."

"Fine," I said, and thought for a moment. "There's a hole in my pocket, I'm skint, I'm running on empty, and I've left everything to the cat! Is that good enough for you?"

"Money never brings happiness," grinned Fofo.

We stopped arguing and looked up as the journalist approached us. I scrutinized his face to see how else Fofo might have described him other than saying he was brown-haired with horn-rimmed glasses. Actually, he could have been taken for a student. There was a penny-pinching air about him, and I hated him instantly.

"Fofo Bey?" he asked, checking that he was sitting down at the right table, and appearing to be seeing Fofo for the first time in his life.

"We've met before, at Pakize's," said Fofo, looking most impressed by all the designer gear the man was wearing.

"I don't set foot in Pakize's unless I'm stoned, so I never remember faces from there," he said, as if anyone who frequented Pakize's was not even worth remembering.

"But we remember seeing you dance until dawn. In fact, I'd even say that your style is quite unforgettable," I commented, making no effort to hide my contempt.

Fofo and the journalist looked taken aback.

"What do you mean by that?" asked the journalist, scratching his sideburns.

"Nothing," I said, patting a strand of hair into place.

"We haven't been introduced," said the journalist, clumsily pushing his glasses into place on his nose.

"This is my business partner, Kati Hirschel," said Fofo.

When did we become partners?

"His boss, actually," I corrected. "I'm Kati Hirschel."

"Do you have a private detective company? Your name seems familiar, but I can't think why."

"It's a sideline of mine," I said, as if I owned a company, or even a chain of companies.

"What is it you want from me?" he asked, this time looking directly at me. Actually, his eyes weren't bad. Brown, flecked with green, which wasn't obvious unless you looked carefully behind the glasses. I prefer good looks that aren't immediately obvious, like a fine Riesling that's best after a few sips. Not that I understand much about wine, but I enjoy it.

"Did you write the piece on the website?" asked Fofo. "The one on Sani Ankaralıgil?"

"Maybe. Why do you ask?"

"Can we keep this off the record?" whispered Fofo to the journalist, sounding like someone in a TV crime series and making me wonder if I was too harsh on him about his Turkish.

But what was he up to?

"The situation is this," continued Fofo. "We're conducting an investigation on behalf of Sani Ankaralıgil's family."

"Yes?" said the journalist.

"We believe there's something suspicious about the poor woman's death."

I sighed inwardly at the inanity of what Fofo was saying.

"Yes?" said the man again, before turning to me and saying triumphantly, "I know why your name's familiar! Don't you sell crime fiction in Kuledibi?"

"Maybe. Why do you ask?" I replied, imitating his earlier reply.

"I know you. You're a friend of Lale Hanım, aren't you?"

Fofo and I exchanged glances.

"A German film director was killed in Istanbul five or six years ago. Remember that?" asked the journalist.

Fofo and I exchanged glances again.

"Lale Hanım engaged some of our investigative staff to get information for you," continued the journalist. They said one of your friends was mixed up in it."

"Yes, that murder was never solved," I said, with feigned regret.

Officially, it was recorded in the statistics as "unsolved murder". However, you dear readers will remember that... But of course, I'm not one to boast.

"You'd be amazed at the number of crimes that go unsolved," said the journalist.

I nodded in agreement.

"I'm going to be open with you," he said.

I'd been about to ask for his name, because I was warming to the way he spoke, as I had to his eyes. However, not wanting to interrupt, I remained silent.

"It's thanks to Lale Hanım that I got into this business," said the journalist. "It's impossible to get into media without a *torpil* to put in a word for you. It's the same at every level. Even a tea boy is related to someone's uncle. This business of *torpil*s is the shittiest part of the media world – excuse my language. Everyone, right down to the lowliest reporter, is someone's man, brother, daughter or son. But Lale Hanım never bothers with *torpil*s. She just demands that people do their jobs properly. She's a law unto herself, and as straight as a die."

As you might imagine, I was delighted to hear these words spoken about my closest friend. I liked this man more by the minute. My first impressions had turned out to be wrong again.

"Yes, you're absolutely right," I said.

There was silence for a moment. When I say silence, I mean the silence of daytime Beyoğlu, where the constant drilling was mixed with the cries of people fearing for their lives as they tried to make their way on foot down İstiklal Street.

"When I started working for *Günebakan* newspaper, I'd just graduated from university in Anatolia. I was no more than a kid, and knew no English. You're no one in the media business without English, so my chances of finding work that involved using the phone were zero. As my dad would say, who wants a one-armed mechanic? Anyway, to cut it short, it was all thanks to Lale Hanım that I got a job, and I'll never forget what she did for me. So, since you're a friend of Lale Hanım, ask whatever you want. I'll tell you what I know, and what I don't know I'll find out."

He spoke like a grateful and excited student addressing an elder.

"So did you learn English later?" asked Fofo, making it sound like a silly interview question.

"What?" I said, giving Fofo a withering look. "What's that got to do with anything?"

"Nothing. I was curious," said Fofo. "It's just that I've read his interviews with foreign models on Skyrat, that's all."

"Of course I learned English. I also spent time in the UK to improve it, so I can speak enough to get by. But then the work dried up, because when Lale Hanım was fired they got rid of me too. As I said, no one survives without a *torpil*. Anyway, my best friend was also out of work, so we went off to the UK together and set up Skyrat on our return. Internet businesses were still relatively new then, and we decided to go for special-interest items and stories that no one else covered. For two years, it was just the two of us running the website, then my older brother joined us. We've started employing other people now because we can't keep up with the work. So that's it, Kati Hanım."

Since he'd just told us everything about himself that we needed to know, I launched straight into asking questions about what was of real interest to us.

"It said on the website today that Sani went out to dinner with someone. Who was it?"

"Demir Soylu. He was Cem Bey's lawyer, as well as a child-hood friend. We learned that from another source, not Demir Bey. However, he didn't deny that they had dinner together."

"Did you wait for Demir Soylu to corroborate that before putting it on the website?"

"No. We called him the moment we got the story, and had it confirmed straight away. Our policy is to release a headline and follow with information a bit at a time. That way we keep people logging into our website throughout the day. It's common practice in Internet journalism."

"Do you know what they discussed over dinner?"

"Demir Bey didn't give us any details, but he said that the couple had signed a prenuptial agreement and that he and Sani had been discussing the implications of this agreement in the light of her application for a divorce."

"Was it a financial agreement?"

"Of course. It concerned alimony, lump sum settlements and so on. Inheritance too, probably. Though Cem Bey would be Sani Hanım's legal beneficiary, anyway."

"Who leaked that information to you?"

"Someone dining at the Shining Sun at the same time. But I'm sure you're not expecting me to reveal my sources."

"Is that how you get all your information? Or was this an exception?"

"No, ma'am, it was no exception. It's called gossip journalism. You obviously don't follow our website or media journal. Most of our news items are based on information received from people who've spotted a couple dining out together, or maybe a married man dancing with another woman at a nightclub."

"Hmm, from now on, I'm going to be more careful about where I go, who with, and what I do," said Fofo. "Or, if you like, I could be a volunteer reporter for you."

The journalist looked distinctly unexcited by Fofo's offer.

"We could go to my office, if you like," he said, glancing at his watch. "It's not far from here, in Süslü Saksı Street. We can talk more comfortably there. Also, there's no one in it at the moment, and I don't really like leaving it empty."

I suddenly thought of my abandoned shop. Hopefully Pelin would have kept her promise to be there.

"Won't you have anything to drink?" I asked, seeing the waiter coming towards our table.

"Okay, I'll have a lemonade," he said, without any hesitation.

The office was light and spacious. As soon as we entered, the journalist, whose name I finally learned was Murat, disappeared to make coffee. Fofo and I settled into armchairs and started looking through some gossip magazines lying on the table.

I picked up a particularly dog-eared magazine in which, among some pictures taken at a fairy-tale wedding at Esma Sultan Palace, I noticed a photo of Tamaşa and Bahri Ankaralıgil. The caption beneath the photo read "Tamaşa Hanım, one of society's best-dressed women, dazzled us in a purple evening gown by Valentino".

I showed the picture to Fofo, who studied it carefully.

"Definitely not my type," he said eventually. "Too much Botox.

I can't stand it when Botox is used to raise the eyebrows, especially if they have lines between them."

"How do you know about Botox treatments?" I asked in amazement.

"Through Mustafa, my doctor friend."

I nodded. I'd met Mustafa once when I went to his house to collect Fofo.

"He does Botox. All the skin specialists do nowadays. He explained it all to me."

"Does it work?" I asked, thinking I might pay him a visit one day.

"Mustafa goes for a very natural look. He doesn't create masks like that."

"Tell me, why do people have their eyebrows raised?"

"Because if you raise the eyebrows, it tightens the area around the eye," replied Fofo, using one hand to demonstrate. "That's why you see so many people going around with such arched eyebrows."

When Murat returned, we were both engrossed in magazines.

"Please, ask whatever it is you want to know," he said, pulling up a wheeled office chair.

This time, I didn't even allow Fofo time to open his mouth.

"Actually, we don't know much about what happened. We only know what we read in the press."

"Is that so?" said Murat.

I began biting my nails.

Fofo glared a silent order at me to remove my hand from my mouth. Bless him – he's like a mother to me. However, I paid no attention and continued gnawing at my nails. Why should I pay attention to that halfwit Fofo?

"You said Sani Ankaralıgil's family hired you as detectives," said Murat.

"Well, that's not entirely correct. Nobody hired us. But we knew Sani Ankaralıgil. Or rather we used to see her almost every day."

"I don't understand what you're saying."

"There's a small restaurant at Tünel, where we have lunch. Everything there is home-cooked. The food's simple and there's little choice, but it's tasty," I said, simultaneously realizing that I was famished. "Our lunch break often coincided with Sani Hanım's, though she only ever ate salad. We often ran into each other, but we had no idea who she was. It was only when we saw her picture in the paper that we realized—"

"Is that all?" said Murat, shuffling in his chair.

"That's it," I said.

"Excuse my curiosity, but why are you interested in this? I mean, if the family didn't contact you—"

Fofo frowned and moved his lips as if silently saying, "Well done!"

"For the same reason as you," I said. "Out of curiosity."

Murat laughed gleefully.

"Curiosity killed the cat!" muttered Fofo, taking courage from Murat's laughter.

"In that case, let's see what I can do for you," said Murat. "But first we'll have coffee."

Murat went out and soon returned with a tray of coffee. It was terrible. It tasted like tar, and I abandoned it after a couple of sips. Fofo and I watched as Murat took his coffee over to his desk, where he pulled up a chair and sat down.

"I'm looking up some files on people we consider news-worthy," said Murat. "We search magazines that aren't online, and anything that might be useful goes into this archive. Like Sani Hanım's marriage to Cem Ankaralıgil, for instance. Ah yes, I see she had an office on the fourth floor at the Tünel Business

Centre, so it's not surprising that you saw her around there. I'll give you the short biography used for news items about her. She was born in 1974 in a village called Kayacık, outside Lüleburgaz. Her maiden name was Kaya, and she was born into a farming family. She went to the village primary school, where she was a brilliant student, and was sent to middle school in Istanbul, where she stayed with an uncle. After attending a high school that specialized in science, she went on to graduate in industrial engineering from Istanbul Technical University and was awarded a scholarship to the USA, where she did a PhD in economics. Apparently, she met Cem Ankaralıgil while over there, and they returned to Turkey together in 2003. Cem took over his father's business, and a few months later, despite family opposition, he married Sani. His mother Tamaşa was particularly opposed to the marriage, and even issued a statement, which caught our eye because this family rarely speaks to the press."

Murat took his eyes off the screen to look at us.

"There are two types in society life," he continued. "One type talks incessantly, while the other never gives interviews, rarely accepts invitations and wants no one to know what they're doing. Tamaşa belongs to the second type. She normally hides from the media, yet on that occasion she was actually prepared to make a statement concerning her son's marriage."

"What did she say?" asked Fofo.

"What did she say?" repeated Murat. "It was one sentence: 'Saniye Hanım is undoubtedly an admirable person, but I do not consider her right for our family.' That was it."

"Saniye Hanım?"

"Yes, Saniye Hanım. Sani is an abbreviation."

"Like Kati," grinned Fofo.

"Katharina is a long name, and difficult to pronounce," I said. "But Saniye isn't."

"Saniye wasn't considered appropriate for society. It sounds too rural. Sani is more modern," said Murat.

"Hardly modern, but it sounds more trendy," said Fofo. "But never mind the name, what did Tamaşa Hanım mean when she said that Saniye wasn't right for their family? Who do these wealthy people think they are?"

"Well, of course, it wasn't just a question of wealth. Tamaşa Hanım is a sixth-generation descendant of the exiled Vezir-i Azam Abdullah Pasha. The family has a long pedigree. Her father's the great scientist Professor Lütfullah Mısırlı, who established the first gynaecology faculty in Turkey and later became Health Minister. When her parents divorced, Tamaşa Hanım was sent to a Roman Catholic boarding school in Switzerland. She knows French, English, German and Italian. She's also a collector of antiques. Definitely not a member of the nouveaux riches, if that's what you were thinking."

"I think you have a degree of sympathy for this Tamaşa Hanım," I commented.

"Sympathy? No, but I think she's unusual. She's not the sort to be seen out with her arms full of designer shopping bags or being pursued by the paparazzi. The world is full of Paris Hiltons, but Tamaşa Hanım strikes me as different."

"So what happened? Did Tamaşa Hanım sever relations with her son because of his marriage?" I asked.

"No, I don't think so. But she didn't talk to the press again. Perhaps the prenuptial agreement put her mind at ease. Or maybe she realized that the couple were truly in love and that she would never make Cem change his mind. Anyway, for whatever reason, she made that one statement and then said nothing more. If you ask me, given that they were about to divorce, I think she'd probably been manipulating her son. As you know, mothers and sons—"

"Don't I just!" I said. "Especially Turkish mothers and sons."

One of the reasons I'd settled in Istanbul was that my lover's mother couldn't accept her son being abroad with a "foreigner". To her dying day, the poor woman did her best to prise us apart, and then pegged out before seeing us separate.

"What did Sani Hanım do? I mean at the office in Tünel," I asked.

"People with loads of money never know what to do with themselves," said Murat sullenly, possibly out of jealousy. "Cem was into extreme sports like bungee jumping, skateboarding, mountaineering and so on. I think Sani tried to keep up with him. You know, 'anything you can do, I can do better'."

"You mean she organized extreme sports tours? In her office at Tünel?"

"Tours? No, no! Sani organized trips for people interested in environmental issues. She set up an environmental association called GreTur to fight against pollution in Thrace."

"Interesting. Did they have any success?"

"You heard what happened to the Ergene Basin, didn't you?"

"Of course," I said. "Leather workshops and factories were set up there without proper clean-up facilities, causing an unbearable stench and the destruction of first-class agricultural land."

"Well, at least Sani achieved something," said Murat. "A few years ago, hardly anyone could have placed the Ergene Basin on the map."

2

As soon as we left Murat's office, I called the shop to see if Pelin was there. She said a group of Spaniards had just been in and bought up our entire stock of Spanish crime fiction.

"Hey, Fofo! You missed a group of Spanish tourists at the shop," I said.

Fofo loved having opportunities to chat to his compatriots.

"Never mind Spanish tourists. What do you think about Sani?" he said.

"What can I say? It's interesting. As an industrial engineer with an American PhD, she could have had a marvellous career, yet—"

"Having married into the Ankaralıgil family, she probably didn't want to work for a rival company, but at the same time didn't want to work under her husband."

"Very likely," I said, my attention more on the rumblings of my empty stomach than Sani Ankaralıgil.

"What do you say to calling in at her office?"

"Let's eat something on the way," I said.

"It'll only take two minutes. Two more minutes of hunger won't harm you," persisted Fofo.

"Okay, but let's avoid the main road and go by the backstreets."

"Do you really think the backstreets are any better? At least on the main road there's room to escape if a truck comes along. Come on, let's go!" said my dear friend, tugging at the sleeve of my cashmere sweater.

*

The Tünel Business Centre was like a labyrinth. We lost our way twice in its dark corridors before finding the GreTur office.

"I wonder what GreTur means?"

"Probably an abbreviation of Green Turkey or something."

"Aren't you the smart one?" remarked Fofo.

Was he mocking me?

After passing rows of brown doors, we finally came to one with a small GreTur plaque on it.

"We should have eaten something first," I said despondently. "Anyway, we've found the office. Now what?"

"How often does Professor Langdon eat in *Angels and Demons*?"

"How should I know? Do you think I count every mouthful consumed by Dan Brown's heroes?"

"He drinks a glass of hot chocolate on page three and has his first meal on page 710. There are pages and pages without even a mention of hunger. The man even parachutes out of a plane on an empty stomach. This business takes discipline and professionalism."

"Okay, but I don't subscribe to puritan self-denial," I protested.

"Nor did Professor Langdon. Now ring the bell and let's get this over with," said Fofo.

I reached out for the doorbell, but my hand stopped in mid-air.

"Oh, that's just great!" I exclaimed, elbowing Fofo back out of the way.

Fofo's expression changed from bewilderment at my apparent hesitation to wide-eyed apprehension on seeing that the door latch was broken and dangling uselessly.

"Someone's been here before us," I whispered.

"Didn't I tell you?" whispered Fofo in reply.

"What?"

"That it was hotting up."

Deciding not to argue with him, I knocked at the door.

It immediately swung open and a young woman, her eyes red from crying, stood before us as if she'd been waiting for someone to knock. I instantly assumed that she was a secretary, though I was later to question why I'd jumped to that conclusion so quickly. Perhaps it was the air of transience about her. Something was odd. She didn't look as though she belonged there, and would certainly never have been a contender for an office manager prize. Giving the appearance of being a visitor at one's place of work isn't exactly the best way to advance a career. At my shop, the situation was quite the opposite, because my employees were so involved that I was almost redundant. But that's another matter.

The state of the office looked no more promising than the woman. Files, papers, folders and general office paraphernalia were strewn all over the floor. The woman looked me, as if expecting me to say something.

I cleared my throat, in preparation for telling a little white lie.

"We've come to enrol as members of GreTur," I said, peering into the office as if I'd only just noticed the chaos, and asked with feigned concern, "What's happened here?"

"I thought you were the police," said the woman.

Even the humblest of employees should have recognized that Fofo and I were not the police. Still, our appearance was irrelevant.

"I'm waiting for the police," she said. "We're not allowed to touch anything."

"Looks like a break-in," said Fofo, "but what would anyone steal from an office?"

"What do you think? They've taken the computers."

"There was a security guy downstairs when we entered the building," I said, craftily nudging the woman inside. "Isn't anyone on duty during the night?"

"I don't know if it was night or day when the burglary happened. We weren't open on Saturday because it was our president's funeral that day, God rest her soul."

"Why do things all happen at once like that?" I mused sympathetically.

"Was your president elderly?" asked Fofo, with an air of innocence.

I had difficulty suppressing a smile.

"No, she was young. You must have read about her in the papers – Sani Ankaralıgil," replied the woman.

"Ah yes, of course. My condolences. We obviously couldn't have chosen a worse time to apply for membership," said Fofo.

"We don't take members, anyway."

"What do you mean?" said Fofo. "All associations are out to increase their membership, collect subscriptions and encourage members to outdo each other with voluntary work like organizing dinners, giving tea parties, holding sales of hand-knitted socks and home-made paper lampshades—"

"Why don't you take members?" I asked, interrupting Fofo's foolish patter.

"There are three of us working here. Sani Hanım is president, Aylin Hanım is vice-president, and there's me. I answer the phone and deal with correspondence. You know, general office work."

"Yes, but that doesn't explain why your association doesn't have members."

"Well, that's what I was told," she said with an air of finality, obviously hoping to close the subject.

"Didn't you ask why?"

"It's illegal for an association to have no members," said Fofo, almost threateningly.

The woman looked hard at Fofo, then me, before collapsing

onto a chair. She seemed truly distressed by the idea that the association might have been operating illegally, yet her reaction seemed altogether too naive and extreme for the twenty-first century.

"I don't know what I'm saying any more. I've been all over the place since yesterday, so why don't you come back later?"

"We can wait with you until the police come. That is, if you don't like being here alone..." I said, with an angelic expression.

The woman's face lit up.

"Oh, would you? I've got a terrible headache," she said, and tears started rolling down her cheeks right on cue. "I'm scared they'll think I did it. No one had a key to the office apart from us three."

"You mean Sani, Aylin and you?" I asked.

She nodded.

"But they didn't enter with a key. They broke the lock. Why would anyone think you did it?"

The woman was clearly very ingenuous. No one could put on such a convincing act.

"You're right," she said, brightening up. "They didn't come in with a key, so why would they think I did it? Rich people always make me feel so guilty. If they have anything you don't have, they act as if you're about to run off with it. Oh, I don't know, I just panicked when I saw the place had been burgled."

"It obviously had nothing to do with you, so stop worrying," said Fofo, placing a comforting hand on her shoulder. "But I know exactly what you mean. My boss rules my life with an iron rod."

"Women bosses are the worst," said the secretary.

Fantastic! Not only was she anti-rich, she was also a misogynist.

"So it was your bosses who told you not to register members?" asked Fofo, trying to coax a bit more out of the secretary.

"Yes. But they're right, whatever you're thinking. I've worked for other associations and I know what it's like. Friends and relatives start turning up and wanting to make changes. They register as members and then, before you know it, they've formed a majority, overturned the board of directors, and are running it themselves."

"Like political parties," I commented and, since the woman obviously had no idea what I meant, I turned to Fofo and continued, "It's the members who elect the delegates and delegates who elect the chairman. Therefore, the chairman surrounds himself with delegates who support him. That way, he remains in the chair until he dies. How do you think third-rate people keep getting themselves elected?"

"Yes, that's how it works. But how else can it be done?" said the woman.

"What was on the computers that were stolen?"

"Everything. We kept everything on the computers."

"What kind of things?"

"Lists of the factories and workshops polluting the Ergene Basin, letters to factory owners and petitions to attorneys. Sani Hanım was preparing court cases against many of the factories and went round speaking to the villagers, often a couple of times a week. Her father and sister, who live out there, are both environmentalists too. She put a lot of effort into it."

"So the names and addresses of villagers who supported her were on those computers."

The woman nodded.

"Was it difficult to persuade the villagers?"

"That was the hardest part. Even though Sani Hanım grew up there, she still found it difficult. Villagers either just don't care, or their children work at the factories and are bringing in steady money. They don't want to get into a fight with the factory boss, even if their land and farm equipment are being affected. They're right, of course, if you think about it, because the rich always come out on top."

"Who's the lawyer for your association?"

"Aylin Hanım's husband Remzi Bey was going to take care of everything. As I said, Aylin Hanım is our vice-president."

"I suppose Aylin will look in today, since there's been a burglary?"

"No, she won't. She went abroad after the funeral. I let Remzi Bey know about the burglary, but he's busy with other work and isn't likely to show up here."

"What's Aylin Hanım's surname?"

"Aköz. It was Aylin Hanım who introduced Sani Hanım to her husband. I overheard them say that once. When Aylin Hanım's father was living in America..." said the secretary, tailing off at the sight of two uniformed policemen.

The policemen looked us over as if we were all suspects.

"Did you call the police?" asked the shorter of the two policemen.

"What a mess! You have quite a job on your hands here, madam," said the other.

I think the term "madam" was intended for me, but I pretended not to notice.

"It was me who called you," said the secretary, jumping up from her chair. "There's been a burglary."

"Sorry to hear that. What did they take?"

"They took the computers, messed up all the files, and threw things about so it's impossible to tell what's here and what isn't."

"What about money? Or gold?"

"No. What would money and gold be doing here? This is an association."

"What kind of association? I've never heard of it before."

"An environmental association. We fight environmental pollution."

"No offence," said the short officer, covering his mouth to hide a smirk, "but wouldn't you do better to fight poverty and let environmental pollution wait its turn?"

"Each to their own," said the secretary stiffly, obviously in tacit agreement. Everything about her demeanour suggested that she regarded environmental issues as no more than an amusement for the rich. "But it's my bread and butter. I work here."

"Whoever's in charge here needs to come to the station and make a complaint," said the tall policeman. "Then forensics will be sent to take fingerprints. But don't get your hopes up. We rarely get a result."

"Because most burglars take the precaution of wearing gloves," said the other, still smirking.

"But there's something unusual about this," I said, despite my intention to remain silent. "There could be evidence of a possible homicide on those computers."

"Does this lady work here too?" asked the short officer, addressing the secretary.

For some reason, nobody had yet asked who I was.

"I came to sign up as a member of the association," I said.

"Are you an environmentalist?" asked the officer.

"Yes," I replied.

Both officers looked at me as if that explained everything.

"What's the homicide that the lady referred to?" asked the short one, again addressing the secretary.

"I know nothing about any homicide," said the bewildered woman.

"Possible homicide," I corrected. "This is the head office of an association of which the late Sani Ankaralıgil was president."

"Ankaralıgil? You mean of the industrialist Ankaralıgils?"

"She's the daughter-in-law. The press said on Friday that her body had been found at her house."

The two officers exchanged glances, then the short one looked at me as if to say "Bingo!" and the other took out his mobile.

"Police Constable Gündüz here. Put me through to the superintendent," he said, his voice becoming more serious as he continued. "Good day, Commander. Police Constable Serkan and I visited the scene of the incident, sir. The perpetrators had fled... Yes, sir. But there's a matter I'd like to discuss with you, sir. A lady here..." The officer turned towards me and asked, "What's your name, lady?"

"Kati Hirschel," I said, wondering how I'd managed to get mixed up with such matters yet again.

"Ms Kati Hirshem—"

"Kati Hirschel," I corrected.

The officer waved his hand as if to indicate that it was of no consequence.

"She said that the crime scene here is the office of Sani Ankaralıgil, whose body was found at her home the other day. It's an environmental association, sir." Turning to the secretary, the officer asked, "What's the name of this association?"

"GreTur. Short for Green Turkey," said the secretary.

"The name is GreTur, short for Green Turkey, sir," repeated the policeman. "The computers have gone, sir. And some documents may also have been taken. There's one employee here, sir." He paused and nodded as if he was listening to instructions in full view of his superintendent and continued, "Yes sir. Will do, sir."

The policeman then hung up and said, "My superintendent will inform the officers investigating the death of Sani Ankaralıgil. We must all remain here until they arrive."

"Us too?" asked Fofo, anxiously. I hadn't heard a peep out of him for a while, and was missing the sound of his voice.

"We must all remain here," repeated Constable Serkan.

"Would it be okay if I moved the papers off this chair and sat down?" I asked.

"Nothing is to be touched," said both officers in unison.

"Sorry, I wasn't thinking. Sit here. I'll send out for some tea," said the young secretary thoughtfully, offering me her chair.

"If they do toasted sandwiches, could you order some? On me, of course," I said. "When do you think the other officers will arrive?"

"It'll take a while," said Gündüz.

It was almost an hour before the officers investigating the death of Sani Ankaralıgil arrived. We waited in silence, trying not to touch anything. Every so often, the secretary looked at me as if wanting to ask a question, but when our eyes met she looked away and continued staring out of the window. Was it because she didn't want to speak in front of the police officers? Or was there some other reason?

As for me, I spent the time watching the two policemen chain-smoke. Having given up the habit eight months previously, I couldn't decide whether to ask for a cigarette or convince myself that smoking was no remedy for the boredom I was experiencing. Unfortunately, I hadn't thought of putting a book in my bag when we rushed out of the shop.

We were all just about at the end of our tether when the door opened.

"Oh no!" I thought.

Was it good luck or misfortune that out of all the detectives in Istanbul who could have been leading the murder investigation, it had to be him?

Yes, you've guessed correctly. It was Batuhan.

I hadn't seen him for about four years, but he looked as fit as ever. He had a few grey hairs around the temples, which was only to be expected, and a slight paunch, but only very slight. Islamic Turks wear wedding rings on their right hand, secular Turks on their left, so I looked at both hands, in case unbeknownst to me Batuhan had undergone a religious conversion. Neither hand sported a wedding ring.

"Kati Hanım, so you're here too. You've beaten us to yet another incident in the Tünel district," he said, and laughed out loud.

Fofo, the police officers and the secretary looked at us in amazement.

"Is this *the* Superintendent Batuhan?" asked Fofo.

"Homicide Detective Commander," said Batuhan.

"So you've been promoted," I said. "Congratulations."

Since it was me rather than him who'd solved the two murder cases on which we'd collaborated, I couldn't help thinking that, had I been a member of the police force, I too might have been promoted to a senior rank at Police HQ by now.

Supposing I had been promoted, what then? Would I have been a happier person? I didn't think so. I could never forget the police raids in Berlin, when they tried to force us to vacate the properties we'd occupied. However, I had to admit that Batuhan was an exception.

Homicide officers were different anyway. Even in films it was obvious that the smartest and most proficient candidates were cherry-picked for this department.

"You haven't changed at all," said Batuhan. "It must be over three years since we last saw each other."

"I believe so," I said.

Batuhan turned towards the other officers, who were still

gazing at us in bewilderment, and asked, "Are you from Karaköy Police Station?"

"Yes, sir," said Gündüz.

"You can send me your report. Return to your duties now," said Batuhan. Then, looking at Fofo and the secretary, he asked, "Do you work here?"

"Fofo works at my shop," I said, placing a proprietorial hand on my friend's shoulder.

"I work here," said the secretary, the colour draining from her face.

"What's your connection with this incident, Kati?"

"We have no connection. We just read about it in the press."

"You read about it in the press and thought, 'Ha, I'll bag that one. Another murder waiting for me to solve.' Is that it?"

"Who said anything about murder?" asked the secretary. "It was an accident, wasn't it? Sani Hanım slipped, didn't she?"

The three of us pretended not to hear her.

"Wait outside, all of you," ordered Batuhan. "We need to conduct a search of the place. I'll speak to you when we've finished."

"We haven't touched anything," I said.

"Maybe. But you've been walking about, drinking tea, opening windows, smoking, and so on."

"I've given up smoking," I said.

As we filed out, Batuhan leaned into the corridor and summoned three men wearing jackets with "incident scene analysis" written on the back.

We lined up in the dark corridor of the business centre like a row of suspects.

"What makes you think Sani Hanım was killed?" whispered the secretary in my ear.

"I didn't say she was killed. I said she might have been. There's a big difference."

"Okay, but what made you say that?"

"We're just talking about a possibility. Why are you so upset?"

"I liked Sani Hanım," she said. "It's terrible if she's been killed. Of course I'm upset."

Not only was she not an aggrieved secretary, she was actually on good terms with her employer. It certainly wasn't my day for character assessment.

Batuhan reappeared with a small notebook in his hand, and addressed the secretary.

"What's your job at the association?"

"I'm the secretary. I take care of all the calls and correspondence."

The poor woman spoke as if her role as secretary was indispensable, when all she did was answer the phone and write a few letters.

"Your name?"

"Sevim Mercan."

"Can you tell us what's been stolen, Sevim Hanım?"

"They took the computers. But I don't know what else has gone, because everything's been scattered all over the place."

"What was in the computer files? Did you make backups?"

"It was all stuff to do with the association. Sani Hanım didn't go anywhere without her laptop. She never wrote anything by hand, even claimed to have difficulty signing her name. All correspondence was put on her computer."

"So Sani Hanım had a laptop."

"It might be at her house," said Sevim, giving Batuhan a questioning look. When Batuhan didn't respond, she added, "It's a Toshiba."

Batuhan remained silent as he wrote something in his note-book, and then asked, "What happens at this association? What does GreTur mean?"

"It's an abbreviation of Green Turkey," said Sevim, and continued as if reciting a memorized text. "We're fighting environmental pollution. As well as planting trees, we seek to have penalties imposed on factories that pollute the environment and to make the installation of purification plants compulsory. We're trying to get parliament to pass an environment bill that complies with European standards. The main focus of our work has been against the pollution in the Ergene Basin."

"Is that so? What about Yatağan and Dilovası? Why the Ergene Basin?" asked Batuhan.

Sevim stopped her little speech to think of an answer, then replied, "Probably because Sani Hanım's from Lüleburgaz, and her family still lives there. She used to say the Ergene Basin would become as bad as Dilovası."

"Was it just you and Sani Hanım working at the association?" asked Batuhan.

"Sani Hanım was president, and there's Aylin Aköz, our vice-president. There are three of us."

"Can I have Aylin Aköz's phone number?"

"Aylin Hanım went abroad after the funeral. I'll give you her number, but I don't know it from memory. I need my handbag."

"Recep, bring me the lady's bag, will you?" called Batuhan to one of the officers working in the office.

"It's on my desk," said Sevim.

When the bag arrived, Sevim gave Batuhan mobile numbers for both Aylin Aköz and her husband.

"Where do you live, Sevim Hanım?" asked Batuhan.

"In Bakırköy."

"I need your full address, for the report."

"Altıkuyular Road, Mektep Street, number 21/6."

"And would you also give me your phone number? Then you can go."

Since I couldn't take notes under Batuhan's watchful eye, I memorized the secretary's phone number. At some point, I'd need to talk to her without any police hovering over us. The numbers for Aylin Aköz and her husband could always be found through directory enquiries.

"Now it's your turn," said Batuhan, turning to us as soon as the secretary entered the lift to leave the building. "How long have you been here?"

"Oh, ages. I've lost all track of time," I laughed.

Batuhan laughed too. He looked very handsome when he laughed. Some things never change. However, other things do. He was clearly not quite as well disposed towards me as he'd been in the past.

"How did you get mixed up in this?"

"Ask Fofo. It was his idea," I said with a grin that I hoped would melt the ice between us. But this time Batuhan did not smile.

"We haven't met," said Fofo.

"Go on," said Batuhan, reluctantly shaking Fofo's outstretched hand and barely glancing at him. "You were about to tell me how you got mixed up in this."

"I saw a news item in the Friday papers," said Fofo. "The sudden death of a woman who was about to divorce a rich husband seemed suspicious. And then when I found that I knew who the woman was—"

"You knew her?" said Batuhan, his interest in what Fofo was saying suddenly aroused.

"We used to see her, but we didn't really know her," I intervened. "There's a restaurant on the ground floor of this building where we go for lunch and we used to see her there. When we read that she'd died, we decided to visit her office."

"And when you saw her over lunch, I suppose she told you exactly where her office was," said Batuhan mockingly.

"We did our own research when we learned of her death," I said, standing my ground.

"...through open sources," added Fofo.

"That's right. We did some googling and asked a few questions."

"And what did you learn by googling and asking a few questions, apart from the office address?" said Batuhan.

"That before she died, she had dinner with her husband's lawyer and they discussed a prenuptial agreement."

"Prenuptial agreement?" said Batuhan, looking at me through narrowed eyes, which I knew to be an indication that it had caught his interest. "Who is the husband's lawyer?"

"You first," I said, with mischievous pleasure. "What does the autopsy say? Does it confirm that it was murder?"

"You don't really expect me to reveal the content of confidential documents that are vital to the investigation, do you?"

I did, actually. But I wasn't so naive as to think he would sing like a canary the moment he saw me. It would take time.

"If the laptop was stolen then... Well, you could at least tell us if anyone forced their way into her house," I said, knowing that I was pushing my luck.

"No one forced their way in," said Batuhan.

"She had dinner with a lawyer named Demir Soylu last Monday," I said in return as a gesture of goodwill.

Unfortunately, my gesture was not reciprocated. I didn't get another word out of Batuhan.

*

Busy days at the shop, when I had to talk incessantly about crime fiction with a never-ending flow of customers, should have accustomed me to spending time with so many people, but that day had been too much. When we left GreTur's office, all I wanted to do was stay in and stare at the ceiling.

"I'm going home," I said to Fofo, as we made our way down Galip Dede Street.

The descent was by no means easy, of course. Indeed, was anything easy in Istanbul, especially Beyoğlu? The narrow pavements were filled with stalls, so we had to walk down the middle of the street, darting to left and right along with all the other pedestrians to avoid being mown down by traffic.

"Don't go home," said Fofo. "We need to make a plan of action and work out who we're going to talk to."

"We'll discuss it this evening."

"Let's have a look at Sani's house first."

"What would we do at Sani's house, since we can't get in? We could go to Lüleburgaz, but—"

"I wonder who found the body. Maybe it was the porter, or a nosy neighbour. Your Batuhan didn't say anything about that."

"Never mind Batuhan," I said. "We need to strengthen our hand a bit. Then he'll move heaven and earth to find out what we know. People don't go running straight to the police to tell them what they've seen. Our position is much better than his."

At least I knew enough about the business to realize that being a police officer in a homicide investigation was not always an advantage.

3

We rose the next morning with a plan of action. After much huffing and puffing, Fofo had agreed to open up the shop for me and had taken on the task of finding a car to take us to Lüleburgaz. Unfortunately, I'd had to sell all my valuables, including my beloved Peugeot, when I bought my apartment.

Tuesday was cleaning day and I was obliged to have breakfast with Fatma Hanım, who talked endlessly about her cute grandchildren and her husband, who had recently retired and now spent all his time dozing at home. The new shop rota meant that normally I'd already left for work by the time she arrived, so before I went out she took the opportunity to get me to help her turn the mattress, which proved to be laced with spiderwebs. Why I needed such a large bed if I was destined to sleep alone for the rest of my life, I'd no idea. But there it stood in the middle of the room, like some sort of omen. Then, because I was taller, Fatma Hanım sent me up the stepladder to lift down the rugs we'd stored on top of the wardrobe for the summer. After that, I dressed quickly and left before she could find anything else for me to do.

Fofo was waiting for me at the front door, grinning from ear to ear.

"I've got a Renault Clio from a friend who lives in Cihangir. How about that?" he said before even saying hello, and as if we were in a position to choose the brand of car we took.

"When will we have it?"

"Whenever we want," said Fofo. "I called Sevim, the secretary. She'll meet us early this evening to tell us about Sani's family and how to find them."

"All we have to do is go to Kayacık village, outside Lüleburgaz, and ask for the Kaya family. It's simple," I said, patronizingly.

"Kayacık? How do you know that?"

"Murat mentioned yesterday that Sani was born there, smart-arse. You need to keep your eyes and ears open in this business."

Fofo looked apoplectic, but managed to shrug it off and said, "Oh dear, I forgot."

However, I knew what he was thinking: one–nil.

"It's still a good idea to go and see Sevim," I said. "Just a moment, how did you find out her number?"

It might have been normal for me to memorize a phone number, but not for poor muddle-headed Fofo.

"Yesterday, when she gave the phone number to Batuhan, I filed it away in a corner of my mind," said Fofo, his self-confidence restored.

"Well done," I said, giving him a pat on the shoulder, which only seemed to make him tense up again. "But it's better if I meet Sevim on my own."

The tense look on Fofo's face turned to one of total dismay, and not without justification. I was getting him to make all the arrangements and then excluding him from the action. I wasn't being fair.

"It's for the sake of our investigation," I persisted. "A woman always opens up more easily to another woman. But if you want to come…"

Fofo stared out of the window.

"Do you really think she'd be more comfortable speaking to you?" he asked.

"That's the way it is. People who've grown up in conservative environments always connect more easily with people of their own gender."

"It was the same in Spain. My mother and aunt always had women friends," muttered Fofo. "Fine. Go on your own. But you will tell me everything, won't you? Promise?"

"Of course. You know you can trust me, don't you?"

Peering at me closely, as if he believed it was possible to read a person's soul by looking into their eyes, Fofo finally said, "No, I don't trust you."

Was it possible to read a person's soul by looking into their eyes?

"Don't be silly, Fofo. We're not in competition. We're a team."

Was that convincing, I wondered?

Sevim and Fofo had agreed to meet at Simit Sarayı in Taksim Square at five o'clock. It was a five-storey building selling *simit*s and other pastries, and was frequented by all sorts of people, mostly from Istanbul's outlying suburbs. I'd never set foot in the place before. It wasn't my sort of thing, but lots of these eating "palaces" had sprung up in Istanbul recently. In the old days, of course, *simit*s were baked in brick ovens, piled on to trays and sold cheaply in the street.

I'd been to an identical Simit Sarayı in Kottbusser Tor on my last visit to Berlin. It had been Christmas time, and nowhere else was open. I couldn't speak for other cities in Germany, but the Turks who settled in Berlin had shown great enterprise in the field of gastronomy by bringing with them native specialities like doner kebabs, *simit*s, nuts, dried fruits and jacket potatoes to sell alongside their halal versions of pork-based Berlin specialities like *currywurst*.

I'd just started to worry that I might not recognize Sevim among the crowds in Simit Sarayı, but relaxed when I saw a

drably dressed woman approaching me with the glee of someone greeting a close relative. Maybe I'd been too hungry or my
mind had been completely occupied with Sani, but I suddenly
realized I'd paid no attention whatsoever to Sevim the previous day. I certainly hadn't remembered how unprepossessing
she looked.

Before making our way to the non-smoking area on the third
floor, we went up to the self-service bar and bought ourselves
tea and stodgy orange-flavoured cookies of the sort that were
only edible if dunked. I've already mentioned that I'd given up
smoking, haven't I? I wasn't yet an anti-smoking fanatic, but
preferred to sit in a smoke-free environment if possible. However,
I refused to acknowledge Fofo's claims that I was just trying to
avoid remembering my happy days as a smoker.

"We didn't get the chance to speak much yesterday, but I
wanted to ask you a few questions, Sevim Hanım."

"I'm sorry, I didn't catch your name."

"Kati."

"Kati Hanım, first let me say something. You might not believe
this, but I couldn't sleep a wink last night. I spent the whole night
tossing and turning, wondering how to get hold of you. I felt so
much better after your friend phoned. I have the feeling that
when you talked about becoming a member of GreTur, it was
just an excuse to come to the office. Am I right?"

Should I have been humbled by this woman's ability to see
through my stupid ruse?

"You could say that," I said. "But I do care about the environment, and I support projects like that."

I was being truthful. For instance, I avoided buying gold on the
grounds that cyanide is frequently used to separate it from the ore.

"You said yesterday that Sani Hanım had been killed," said Sevim. "Were you at the funeral? It was so crowded that it was impossible to see who was there and who wasn't, but I don't think I saw you."

I shook my head, indicating that I hadn't been there.

"At the funeral they said that Sani Hanım died in an accident. I checked the papers and they said it was an accident as well. I was very upset when you said yesterday that she'd been killed."

"Look, I only said it was a possibility. That might not be the case at all."

I suddenly realized that, all the time I'd been referring to Sani's death, I'd no idea how the poor woman died.

"What kind of accident did they say it was at the funeral?"

"They said that she fell over."

"Fell?"

"Yes. It's tragic, isn't it? She caught her foot and slipped. Fell over. She probably hit her head. Did you know her?"

"I'd spoken to her a few times, but I wouldn't say I knew her."

"If you'd known her, you'd have liked her a lot. Who'd want to kill a person like that?"

"Did you know the police have taken her husband in for questioning?"

"Is Cem Bey under suspicion?" she said, covering her mouth as if it was a shameful question to ask.

"In the case of a suspicious death, the first task is to determine who might benefit from that death. Spouses come into that category."

"But it's impossible. Cem Bey wouldn't hurt a fly. He's such a polite person. A real gentleman. And anyway, how would Cem Bey benefit from Sani Hanım's death? They were about to get divorced."

"Well, I'm sure you know that some people are awarded alimony or compensation after a divorce. The civil law's been changed, so that any assets acquired during a marriage are shared between the couple. Cem Bey probably acquired a substantial amount of wealth during their marriage. In fact, more money than you and I will ever see in a lifetime."

"Shall I tell you something?" asked Sevim, looking very serious.

"Go ahead," I said, matching her seriousness.

"Cem Bey would never kill anyone, even if billions were at stake. As I said, he's a real gentleman. And so courteous. He really loved Sani Hanım. It's just not possible."

Sevim was making me feel almost ashamed for having even entertained such a thought.

"I only mentioned it as a possibility. It's not even certain that Sani Hanım was killed."

"A possibility all the same," said Sevim, rolling her eyes. "But why were the police like that yesterday? I phoned them to report a burglary, and the murder squad turned up. What was the name of your policeman friend?"

"Batuhan."

"Yes, Batuhan. I suppose you're old friends. I sensed a closeness between you. I have powerful intuition, being a Pisces. Are you interested in astrology?"

"Not really, but I know my star sign."

"Don't tell me. Let me guess," said Sevim eagerly. Then, pointing her forefinger at me as she thought for a moment and said, "You're Aquarius."

"Not bad at all. My rising star is Aquarius, but I'm actually Scorpio."

"Sani Hanım was Scorpio too," she said, withdrawing her finger as if I was going to bite it. "But Aquarius balances you out because its rising star is Scorpio. It's a very dangerous sign. Scorpios end up in trouble, as you know."

Since I didn't know what to say, I broke a piece off the orange cookie and put it into my mouth.

"If Sani Hanım was killed, then of course you'll have to investigate her private life," said Sevim.

"What private life?"

"You know, her private life. Lovers and so on."

Lovers? I hadn't managed to even find one so far. Did Sani have a collection of lovers?

"Kati, it couldn't be anyone other than a lover," Sevim blurted out.

I choked on the cookie I was chewing, and started coughing.

"Which lover?" I asked, when I was able to speak again.

"Your face is all red," she said, looking pleased.

"It's just from choking. You didn't tell me who her lover was."

"Sani Hanım's lover? Well, you didn't hear this from me, but there was someone else in her life."

"Do you know who it was?"

"Sinan. He's the vocalist in a group called Sniff."

It was the first time I'd heard of this group, or Sinan, which of course said nothing about the fame or quality of him or his group. But what would I know, since I listened to nothing but classical music?

"What kind of music do they play?"

"Rock music. My sister goes to all their concerts. She's mad about them, especially Sinan. Even *I*'ve been to one of their concerts."

We sat in silence for a while. A multitude of thoughts were going through my mind. Given the situation, Cem might have killed his wife out of jealousy. He certainly hadn't been taken off my list of suspects just because of Sevim's claim that he wouldn't hurt a fly.

51

Or maybe Sinan pushed Sani down the stairs during a row.

"You just said that Sani fell while she was at home. Did she fall down the stairs?" I asked.

"Does her house have any stairs?" asked Sevim.

How come this woman knew about Sani's lover, yet didn't even know if there were stairs in her house?

"Who knows about Sinan apart from you?" I asked.

"No one."

"Aylin Hanım is a close friend, isn't she?"

"Yes, but she doesn't know."

"How do you know she doesn't know?"

"I just know. What do you think I am?"

Not again! I obviously didn't have a clue about my fellow humans. However, I still thought I'd much rather share a secret with my closest friend than with my secretary.

"I wondered why she told you about her lover and not Aylin Hanım. That's all."

"She didn't tell me. But when you work with someone from morning till night, you can't help picking up certain things."

Sevim suddenly started crying, as if a button had been pressed, just like the previous day. Was it only nerves?

"I didn't mean to tell you that," she sniffed.

"You did the right thing," I said. "You're clearly in no fit state to talk to the police, but you needed to tell someone."

"That's what I thought. But when you treat me as if I'm to blame—"

"Why should I blame you? We're just talking."

I placed my hand over her stubby fingers as a gesture of sympathy and in the hope of getting her to say a little more.

"She may have told someone else other than Aylin Hanım," I ventured.

"Sani Hanım said no one knew about Sinan except me, and I

didn't tell anyone," said Sevim, taking a tissue out of her handbag and wiping her nose.

"Not even your sister?"

"I swear I didn't. Sani Hanım made me promise not to tell anyone. But my sister... Well, she found out I knew Sinan and—"

"Knew him?" I interrupted.

"That's how I found out that something was going on."

"How did you find out?"

"One evening, I realized I'd left my mobile at work, and had to go all the way back to the office. When I opened the door, I saw... Well, I suppose they had to meet there because they had nowhere else to go. Sani Hanım was terrified that her husband would hear about it, so I promised not to tell anyone. I gave her my word, but now that she's dead... And Sinan didn't even come to the funeral. That's shameful, isn't it? He broke up her marriage and then didn't come to her funeral. Men – they have their way with you, and then it's over. We definitely live in a man's world."

"Tell me about Aylin Hanım."

I sensed that she would have preferred to carry on discussing relationships and how men use and discard women like dirty linen, as she probably did with her sister. However, she began talking about Aylin without any further encouragement.

"What can I say? She's a society type. She squeezes in visits to the association when she has time between shopping sprees. Her father used to be the Turkish ambassador to America, and it was at one of his receptions that Cem Bey was introduced to Sani Hanım. Aylin Hanım isn't beautiful like Sani Hanım, but she takes good care of herself. She buys all her clothes abroad, which of course you can if you have the money."

"I didn't write down Aylin Hanım's phone number when you gave it to Batuhan yesterday. Would you give it to me?"

"I wonder when Aylin Hanım will be back from her trip," pondered Sevim. "She has bad migraines and goes to see a doctor about them every month."

"What a coincidence," I said. "I have a migraine starting now."

Which was true.

It was not every day that I ventured outside the city, so I was excited when we set out the next morning. Most of the route consisted of a lovely broad motorway, lined on both sides with fields of sunflowers. We reached Lüleburgaz after two hours and parked opposite the town hall. I immediately started looking for a place to eat. It's strange, but I only have to travel out of the city for half an hour before visions of food start floating before my eyes, yet a journey within Istanbul can take two hours and I don't have a single pang of hunger.

Lüleburgaz was full of small cafés specializing in tripe soup, obviously a local delicacy. Tripe soup was a favourite of mine, but I refrained from even tasting it. Nor would I let Fofo have any, because I didn't want us to be breathing out garlic fumes when talking to Sani's grieving family. We took the advice of an old man drinking tea in a run-down café and ate braised lamb at what was probably the poshest restaurant in town, before setting off on the road to Kayacık.

What first caught our attention was that everyone was able to give us directions. Anyone who has got lost trying to venture out of Istanbul's suburbs would understand. It was easy enough getting someone to sit next to you as far as the main road, but almost impossible to find anyone with the wit to give plain instructions like "Straight ahead, turn right before the lights, then left after fifty metres". However, thanks to Lüleburgaz locals, we found the road that led out of the city without difficulty and were soon on our way to Kayacık, enjoying the Turkish countryside.

"We've got it all wrong," said Fofo. "We're much too stuck in Istanbul."

"I've never even been to Ürgüp or Pamukkale," I said.

"And I haven't seen Izmir yet."

"If Pelin were to become a tour guide, she could take us to all Turkey's—" I suddenly broke off and held my nose because of a terrible stench. "Can you smell that?"

"Impossible not to," said Fofo, also holding his nose.

"What is it? Is that the notorious Ergene Basin?"

I took a right turn. The narrow asphalt road was completely empty apart from some miserable-looking storks and crows floundering in the mud by a pitiful stream. We got out of the car. The stench was hard to describe. Imagine the smell after thousands of rotten eggs and animal corpses have been thrown into a cesspool and left in the sun for months on end. Well, this smell was even worse than that.

The stench pursued us for the twenty minutes it took to reach the village. I slowed down as we passed some dilapidated tents just outside the village.

"What's this? A refugee camp?" asked Fofo.

"I don't know. Maybe they've come to work in the fields."

We sat down in the most central of the three cafés overlooking the village square. After a few minutes, the owner came up to us.

"Welcome," he said. "Are you looking for someone?"

Clearly this wasn't a village that attracted tourists.

"Your village headman's surname is Kaya, is that right?" I asked.

"Are you looking for Rıfat Bey? I'll get him for you."

"And we'll have two teas," I added.

After a while, a skinny man wearing a cap approached us.

I noticed that his cheeks were hollow and his face was etched with lines of sadness.

"Welcome. You were asking for me."

"We've come from Istanbul. We'd been thinking of launching a project with Sani Hanım against the pollution at Ergene and, since we were in the area today, decided to call on you."

Sometimes I amaze even myself at the ease with which I'm able to tell lies.

"Oh yes," said the poor man.

"My condolences," I said, shaking his hand.

"Thank you. May she rest in peace. It's true that there's no pain like that of losing a child. I wouldn't wish it on my worst enemy."

"They say it was an accident," I said.

"They do indeed say it was an accident," repeated the poor man. "Yes, just an accident."

I studied his face as carefully as I could, which wasn't easy because he kept his head bowed over his clasped hands even while talking to me. Did he suspect something, I wondered?

"The police are looking into it," I said.

He nodded, without altering his expression or stance. Rıfat had no interest in either the police or their investigation. He was just a father overwhelmed by grief, and in no state to have suspicions about anything.

At that point, a few people sitting at nearby tables pulled up their chairs to join us. All men, of course. There wasn't a woman to be seen.

"Welcome. It's a pleasure to have you here," said a plump, blond man. "I hope there's nothing wrong."

He had a way of swallowing his h's and spoke with a Thrace accent, which I found rather attractive.

"We're doing some research into the pollution at Ergene," I said.

Fofo had fallen silent again, as was his way when he was with people unlike those in his immediate circle.

"Are you a journalist?" asked the blond man. "We've given countless statements to journalists, but nothing's been done. I wish them well, but they don't do anything."

"We're not journalists, we're environmentalists," I said.

"A lot of environmentalists have been here too. But nobody seems to have enough clout," said another man.

"Sani, God rest her soul, did everything she could to find a solution to this problem," said the blond man.

"How many years have we put up with this terrible smell?" said Rıfat, his eyes welling up.

"I'm affected more than anyone," said the café owner, coming over to our table. "I open up at five in the morning, when the smell is at its worst. The factories let their dirty water out into the stream at night when there are no patrols about."

"Can you smell it now?" asked the blond man.

"Can't smell a thing, thank God," said the other.

"We're so used to the stench we don't smell it any more," said the blond man.

"Which is why the report says 'the smell is at an acceptable level'. It's just that the people who live here have got used to it," said a man, seating himself at a table just near enough for him to be able to hear everything that was being said.

"Never mind the smell. It's the land. The land's completely ruined," said the blond man.

"We saw fields of sunflowers on our way here," I said.

"Sunflowers, wheat, barley, corn. Yes, we grow those because the land's arid. We grow anything that doesn't need water."

"This land used to be very fertile. Perfect for rice. In the past, we used to grow sugar beet, beans, cabbages and leeks. But the soil's ruined now and those crops won't grow any more."

"The water even burns our feet when we're working on the land."

"Is that because the River Ergene is polluted by factory effluents?" I asked.

"Thrace has exactly 1,406 factories, of which over a thousand are unlicensed and operating illegally. They draw water from underground wells, pollute it and then release it into the river. Not only are they contaminating the river and the basin, they've almost used up our underground water reserves," said a young man coming towards us. "Are you journalists?"

"No, they're not," replied the blond man on our behalf.

"How many years has this been going on?" I asked.

"Twenty years. It started in President Özal's time," said the blond man, pointing to a stream which we could smell but couldn't see. "In the past, there were turtles and frogs in that water. Catfish as plump as your thigh. Then one day we noticed some of them floating unconscious in the water. We all ran out and started collecting them up like fallen apples. The doctor at the health centre told us not to eat them on any account. Some people did, of course. Later, the water was sent to Ankara for analysis. What was the name of that doctor, Rıfat? You know, the young one."

Rıfat didn't reply.

"Selçuk, wasn't it?" said someone else.

"Hah, Doctor Selçuk. He sent water samples all the way to Ankara for analysis, but when the report came back it stated that the water was clean. The doctor said, 'This land's being ruined. Don't waste your energy for nothing, because everything's in the hands of the rich nowadays.' Not a single living creature has survived in that river. They've all died. If we irrigate the land with that water, the land dies too."

"So what happens if you water the land?"

"It goes all slimy and mushy."

"I watered the ground to grow beets, but after six years the land still hasn't recovered."

"It doesn't produce anything nowadays. In the old days, we'd get over a hundred tons of beet per hectare, but nobody grows beet any more."

"We used to have three thousand hectares of beet, but this year, only two out of 200 families grew it on a plot of less than half an acre, just to retain our quota. If we stopped growing it completely, the quota would be lost."

"How do you live under these conditions?"

"We live on thin air, because the water's certainly no good," said the blond man in his attractive Thrace accent.

Everyone at the table laughed.

"But how do you water your crops?"

"With rainwater. They only get watered when it rains. We owe everything to Mother Nature."

"There's water lying nine to fifteen metres below ground here that we could use, but the diesel costs for extracting it are so high it's not economic."

"And that water, which we can't access, is drawn off by industry. Then, just before dawn, when there's nobody around to check, they release the dirty water into the stream."

"They don't do any checks anyway. All that stuff about doing it at dawn is a myth. They release dirty water all the time."

Fofo and I looked at each other in horror.

"Why don't the factories have purification facilities?" I asked.

This time all the villagers looked at me as if I was either naive or stupid.

"Purification costs money, which is why even the factories that have purification plants don't use them. After all, it costs nothing to release dirty water into the river," said the young man who had recently joined the table.

"But they won't be able to pollute the water any more," said a man at a far table. "A commission's been set up in parliament to draw up an environment law and establish a team of environmental police. They came out here to tell the industrialists how to get purification plants if they didn't already have them. They can't still be polluting the river. I don't believe it."

"Why not?" shouted Rıfat, joining in the discussion. "All those laws were introduced in order to enter the EU. It was just for show. Which of those laws actually benefited us? As we said, there are more than a thousand unlicensed factories. Leather, paint, textiles, glass, pharmaceuticals – everything you can think of. And what does the government do? Nothing. The industrialists get rich and the governor drives a Mercedes. Matter closed. I'm all right, Jack. The businessman who creates the most pollution gets elected industrialist of the year. What don't you believe? It's all there before your very eyes!"

"The governor has a Mercedes?" I asked.

"Yep. The industrialists got together and bought a Mercedes for the governor of Kocaeli so that he would leave them in peace to pollute the environment. It was in all the papers. Didn't you read about it?"

Obviously not. That's what comes of not reading the papers.

"Can't the villagers get together and do something?"

"That's what our dear Saniye was trying to do," said the blond man, his hand resting on Rıfat's shoulder.

"Our villagers are timid and inactive. They're scared of falling out of favour with the government, and it seems to be impossible to shake them out of their passive way of thinking. They believe they'll lose their land or get sacked if they stick their necks out. What do you do with people like that?" said Rıfat angrily.

Once started, there was no stopping him.

"But you've already lost your jobs," said the man sitting at the far table, who seemed to take Rıfat's comments as a personal threat.

"Everyone complains about the factories and pollution," said Rıfat, "but most of them have children working in those factories. If the villagers hadn't sold their land to the industrialists, there wouldn't be any industry here. They sold fertile land for a handful of gold and became factory workers. Eventually they were sacked, and now they go hungry and spend all their time hanging around in cafés. It's too late for regrets now."

"Were you with Sani when she visited the villages?" I asked, with a growing suspicion that these industrialists might have arranged to get rid of Sani because they feared she'd be able to get the villagers organized. If industrialists could collectively organize the purchase of a Mercedes for the Kocaeli governor, it was surely not beyond the bounds of possibility that they could cooperate over a murder.

"We went from door to door, village to village, explaining the problem," said Rıfat. "The environmental pollution created by industry isn't our only problem. There's also population growth, or the migrant issue."

"We noticed some tents outside the village on our way here."

"They're not migrants," said Rıfat with a rueful smile. "They're Gypsies. They live in Lüleburgaz and come here as seasonal labourers to work in the fields. The other villages won't let them set up their tents. Our village is the only one they can persuade to let them stay. People say Gypsies steal, yet our government deprives our unborn children of bread. If a Gypsy goes stealing, at least it's for a chicken. And good luck to him! But we've seen no sign of them stealing anything so far."

"Do they work in the fields for cheaper rates?"

"Of course. What else can they do, poor wretches? Around here, both our Bulgarian kinsmen and the Gypsies get taken for a ride. Bulgarians get twenty lira a day, while Gypsies get fifteen."

"So why do you complain about the rise in population, then?"

"The government wants to make this area completely industrialized. The papers say the population of Thrace will rise to four million within a decade. They're going to build ten thousand new houses in Gebze and Çorlu and send Istanbul's surplus population out to us. Everyone knows that Thrace can't even cope with its present population, so what would it be like if four million more come?"

It was indeed a very bleak prospect. I remained silent, deciding not to order another tea, or even finish drinking what I had, for fear that the poisonous effluent had got into the tap water.

"Would you mind showing us around?" I murmured to Rıfat eventually. It had become too crowded around our table for talking to him about Sani.

"I'll come with you," said the plump blond man at once.

"I'd rather we were alone, if possible," I whispered to Rıfat. "I want to talk to you privately."

"What about?"

"I wanted to talk about Sani."

"About Sani?" said Rıfat, looking flustered as he straightened his cap and put his hands in his pockets.

"Yes," I said.

"Wait here. I'll go and get my car."

"There's no need. Mine's right here," I said, pointing to the Renault Clio.

"In that case, let's go," he said.

"We have to pay for the teas," I said.

"No, no, my girl. You're our guests here," said Rıfat, indicating with his hand that he would hear no more about it and turning to the blond man, saying, "Ahmet, wait here, I'll be back soon."

*

I indicated to Fofo to sit in the back.

"You aren't environmentalists, are you? Who are you?" asked Rıfat.

"We're—" I started.

"If you don't mind, I'd like to see your IDs," he interrupted.

It was a strange and pointless request. What could he learn from our IDs?

I asked Fofo to pass my handbag from the back seat.

"We're not the police or anything," I said, holding out my birth certificate.

"Who said anything about you being the police?" said Rıfat, which was just as well because I hated being likened to the police.

"Kati Hirschel," he read out aloud. Turning to Fofo, he said, "And you?"

"I'm Spanish," said Fofo, giving him his passport.

Rıfat read out his name too.

"What do you want from us?" he asked.

"We want to find out whether or not your daughter really died as the result of an accident," I said.

"Why?"

Not having a sensible answer to this sensible one-word question, I turned on the ignition and asked, "Which way are we going?"

Rıfat indicated a track to the right.

"Why are you so interested in Sani's death?" he asked, clearly making a superhuman effort to maintain his composure.

"We're private detectives," I said, hating myself for this pretence, which was against everything I'd been brought up to believe, but there was no other option.

"Who hired you?" he asked and, without waiting for an answer, added, "Was Sani murdered?"

"There's a possibility that she was murdered, which is what we're looking into," I said.

"Do the police think she was murdered?" asked Rıfat, frowning.

"The police are pursuing their own investigations, so they must have their suspicions."

The track came to an end, and I stopped in the middle of a field.

Rıfat took a packet of cigarettes from his pocket and offered them round. Fofo and I declined.

"So you're telling me that my daughter was murdered," said Rıfat as he opened the window and lit a cigarette for himself.

"It's a possibility."

"Who would do such a monstrous thing?"

"She was preparing a court action against the industrialists who are polluting the environment here. We have our suspicions about them."

"Has someone hired you to investigate this?"

"No," I said.

"No one's paying you?"

"No."

"Were you a friend of my daughter's?"

"No," I said again.

"Why are you getting mixed up in this if there's nothing in it for you?"

"Does anyone pay you to fight against the industrialists and environmental pollution?" I asked.

Rıfat said nothing, but looked directly at me. I saw a gleam in his eyes, and felt that he recognized a kindred spirit in me. Neither of us were the sort to give up. We shared a steely determination that enabled us to fight against anything that offended our sense of justice or values, whether it was a suspicious death or an illegal factory polluting the environment.

"My youngest daughter Naz is a doctor at Lüleburgaz State Hospital. Talk to her before you go back to Istanbul," said Rıfat. "She was interested in the environment before the rest of us. It was Naz who got Sani involved. She'll tell you what you need to know."

With his head bowed, he walked back towards the village with a stooping gait.

4

"This stink makes me feel ill," moaned Fofo, closing the window that Rıfat had opened when he was smoking.

"It's just the smell of 'an acceptable level of pollution'," I said.

"I can't imagine how anyone finds it acceptable. I certainly don't. Poison seems to be oozing out everywhere. And we drank that tea!"

"I don't think we'll die from drinking one glass of tea," I said, ignoring the fact that I'd glared at my tea glass as if it were full of cyanide. After all, I had to set an example to Fofo.

"Nothing will happen to you, because you're like a real Turk, but I'm still very Spanish," said Fofo, holding his nose.

He was right, of course. But should Turkish robustness be expected to withstand physical assaults comparable with the Chernobyl disaster, radioactive farm produce, bird flu, or even AIDS?

Needing to digest what we'd learned, we didn't speak again until we reached Lüleburgaz.

I approached a nurse sitting behind a glass partition marked "Patient Reception", and asked to speak to Naz Kaya.

"Doctor Kaya is on leave until the end of next week. The doctor covering her is—"

"I need to speak to Naz Hanım in person," I said. "Her father, Rıfat Bey, sent us."

"You might find her at home."

I'd made the mistake of not getting Naz's number from Rıfat, but going all the way back to the village would have made it impossible to get back to Istanbul before the evening rush hour.

"Could you please phone her at home?" I pleaded.

"I'll try," said the receptionist. "Who shall I say you are?"

"Say that we spoke to her father. My name's Kati."

I arranged to meet Naz an hour later in Nehir Café, opposite the Kubbealtı Mosque.

Naz Kaya resembled the press photos of her older sister in her heyday, and she was just as beautiful.

"People have said we look very similar," she said with a trace of irony, the significance of which I didn't fully understand, but I let it pass.

"Your father obviously told you we were coming. He should have given us your phone number," said Fofo.

"He rang me after you left him. He was worried you wouldn't find me as I'm on leave. Lüleburgaz is such a small city you can always find people, but try telling that to someone who's spent his whole life in a village."

"I suppose your father told you that we're investigating your sister's death."

"I gather that you believe the factory owners had my sister killed. Is that right?" said Naz, lowering her voice even though all the nearby tables were empty.

"We're actually considering a number of possibilities. But what do you think of that theory?" I asked.

"My father says you're from Istanbul," said Naz, ignoring my question. "Are you Spanish, too?"

"Your father looked at both our IDs," I said.

"He actually checked your IDs?" she said, shaking her head in disbelief. "Did you notice how frightened he is? They're all afraid of their own shadows. Even my father."

"Who are they afraid of?"

"Who? The factory owners, of course. Who else? It just takes one to cause an upset and everyone is ruined."

Fofo and I looked at each other in alarm, sensing the intimidation that engulfed those people.

"What would you like?" asked a grinning waiter.

We ordered three mineral waters.

"I'm from Lüleburgaz, but my parents are Albanian," said Naz, as the waiter moved away. "They're both Macedonian Albanians. They were born here, but we still have relatives there. In other words, we're not originally from here. As you know, there are lots of migrants from the Balkans living in Thrace."

We made no comment, in the hope that she would explain why she was telling us this.

"People suffered terribly when they were turned out of their country, both during and after the Balkan War," continued Naz. "Anyone who lived through that time has it etched on their memory for ever. The last of them were forced to leave Bulgaria during the religious and ethnic oppression of the late 1980s and many settled in Thrace."

"Where they had kinsmen, you mean," said Fofo.

"People are forever referring to kinsmen. I use the term too, but I don't like it," said Naz.

I took a sip of the mineral water that the waiter had put on the table, and prepared to return to the main topic.

"You were asking if the industrialists could have had my sister killed," continued Naz. "I'm only a cardiologist. An oncologist would be better placed to give an accurate picture of the situation in Thrace, but I'll give you a few simple statistics. In this region, 30 per cent of deaths are from cancer, which is three times the national average in Turkey. The majority of cases are stomach and liver cancers caused by environmental pollution."

"Three times the national average?" said Fofo, his eyes widening.

I started to bite my nails.

"It's incredible, isn't it?" said Naz. "Yet we still can't persuade the villagers to unite against the factories, which just goes to show how much fear has been instilled into them. But coming back to your question... My view is that the unchecked development of industry in Thrace means that the industrialists are, in one way or another, committing murder every minute of every day. People have been, and still are, dying from the pollution already created. However, future generations will also die because the factories are depleting the supply of water in the underground wells and contaminating the River Ergene, which is in turn destroying the agricultural land and the forests. You asked me if the industrialists killed my sister. What do you expect me to say?"

I felt mesmerized by her words and unable to respond.

"I don't understand the business about the underground water," said Fofo.

"We're told there's a six-hundred-cubic-metre table of water in central Thrace that's been there since time immemorial. In recent years, four hundred cubic metres of this water have been used, mainly for industry but also for agriculture and drinking water, and they're continuing to extract the remaining two hundred cubic metres. Therefore, within a very short time, there's danger of serious drought in the region."

Naz paused for breath before continuing.

"The problem of the underground water supply becoming

exhausted is one thing. But I think what's more desperate is that the water extracted by industry becomes polluted with substances harmful to human health and the environment, and is then pumped back underground. Take the leather industry, for example. There are two types of tanning processes: vegetable tanning and chromium tanning. With vegetable tanning, it takes about four months for the leather to become usable, but with chromium it only takes a week. Chromium is a mineral that is very dangerous to human health: it can cause ulcers and lung cancer. But of course the leather industry prefers chromium because it saves time. And it's not only chromium. Chemicals like sodium sulphate, hydrosulphide and dimethylamine are also used in tanning processes. These substances are then rinsed out of the leather with water drawn from the underground reservoir. Do you understand what I'm saying?"

Naz had been talking fast and furiously, but her explanation was clear.

"Yes," I said. "I understand. Do you, Fofo?"

Fofo nodded. He had been listening intently.

"The water that is now polluted with various chemicals, the worst of which is chromium, is then pumped back underground," said Naz. "Our underground water reserves are being irrevocably contaminated."

"Oh my God! But why? Why pump poisonous water underground?" cried Fofo.

"Because it's illegal to release the water into the river. Checks aren't made very often, but if they're caught, the factories have to pay a fine. So they avoid the risk by pumping the water back underground. As I'm sure you know, there used to be leather workshops in Istanbul and Kazlıçeşme."

"Fofo wasn't in Istanbul at that time, but I remember. They moved out all the workshops," I said.

"They moved the workshops at Kazlıçeşme to an industrial district in Tuzla, where they all had to have purification plants. But the industrialists made a huge fuss. Do you know why?"

"Why?"

"Because their electricity bills shot up as a result of using purification plants and, since there was no underground water at Tuzla, they also had to pay for the water they used. The Tuzla industrialists quite rightly asked how they could compete with industrialists in Thrace, where it was possible to process leather so much more cheaply. They had a point. In Thrace, the attitude is 'take the water and to hell with the consequences'."

"That's incredible," said Fofo, his face as white as a sheet. "Abominable!"

"Abominable indeed. But that's just the leather industry. Thrace has many other industries: glass, textiles, pharmaceuticals and so on. They all pollute the environment in one way or another. Unchecked industrialization started here twenty years ago, and I've been fighting against it for ten. We see what's happening, but are powerless to do anything about it. However, a certain amount of good has come of it."

"What might that be?"

"Well, our popular support has grown over the last few years. We started the campaign ten years ago as five youngsters, three from Lüleburgaz and two from Çorlu, drawing on family and friends for support. They didn't object to the industrialization, just the lack of regulation, which was understandable because the factories were bringing financial benefits to a lot of families in Thrace. But my mother says now that her eyes have been opened. So we're getting there, but it hasn't been easy."

"I guess yours is the most organized of all the villages."

"That's thanks to my parents. They've been completely won over. This process hasn't only made people more environmentally sensitive, it's also changed their views on life. They've started questioning themselves and taking a more critical approach to what's been going on. Of all the villages around Lüleburgaz, Kayacık is the only one that allows Romany workers to set up their tents. I see that as an achievement. Did you see the tents when you drove into the village?"

"We couldn't miss them."

"As I said, we're mainly targeting the factories, yet we know they can cut us down at any time. Meanwhile, we try to appreciate the little things, because we haven't managed to achieve anything significant so far. A law is about to be passed, but we can't enforce it. Anyway, we've nothing against the erection of a few tents, if they're necessary."

"It's not much of an achievement if Romany labourers work for lower wages. If everyone was paid at the same rate, then you'd have achieved something worthwhile," I commented.

"Have you been researching the wages paid out here?" asked Naz in surprise. "What made you think of that?"

"I was involved in anti-discrimination protests in Germany in the 1980s, so I know a bit about this sort of thing," I said.

"Ah, you have experience in these matters. When we started, our greatest weakness was that we didn't have any. We lost a lot of time learning through trial and error how to get results. I now understand there are certain things that villagers can never be made to accept. For instance, they won't even speak to you if you propose anything that involves putting their hands in their pockets!"

"It's not only villagers, I can assure you. City dwellers are just the same," I said.

"Pay for Romany workers is one of those issues," said Naz, with a rueful smile. "I hope we'll be able to change it. This year, for the first time, my father agreed to pay his Romany workers the same as the Bulgarians. Next year, maybe a few others will—"

"Excuse me," I said, rising from the table because my mobile was ringing. It was Pelin. I moved away so that I could speak more easily. She said that Batuhan had come to the shop and wanted to know if he should wait for me.

"You didn't tell him I was in Lüleburgaz, did you?" I said to Pelin.

"No," she said.

"Did you tell him where I'd gone?"

"Are you still at Lale's place?"

"Don't say anything to Batuhan."

"Okay," said Pelin.

"Pass the phone to him."

I told Batuhan that I wouldn't be back in Kuledibi until late and he shouldn't wait for me, but we could meet the following day if he liked.

"Tomorrow's impossible, but we can meet on Friday," said Batuhan.

We agreed to meet at the shop early on Friday evening.

When I returned to the table, Naz and Fofo were deep in conversation. Fofo was saying how much he loved Istanbul and how he could never leave it.

"Do you ever visit Istanbul?" I asked Naz.

"Of course. I spent my student days in Istanbul and have lots of friends there. I'm even thinking I might stay in the city for a while. I came back to Lüleburgaz to recover after the funeral. I also need to get the forensic report, and there are a few people I want to see."

"Will they hand the report over to the family?"

"They should do. In any case, the people who write the forensic reports are friends of mine. I'm sure they'll give it to me."

"If you get the report, might we see it?"

"You're not allowed to have a copy of it without official status, are you? My father told me that you're not the police. You don't look anything like the police, anyway."

What a smart father and daughter! I was beginning to like this family.

"Actually, it would be great if we could go to Sani's house," I said, taking courage from her comment.

"The police have sealed it off, which I presume is just routine while they conduct a forensic search," said Naz.

"They might have sealed it off, but they won't have thought of changing the locks," I said.

"Sani's keys should be at my parents' house. I'll get them tomorrow, and we can go together."

"Apparently there was a laptop," I said. "Her secretary Sevim said that Sani never let it out of her sight."

"She certainly didn't," said Naz. "Sani hung on to that laptop as if it were physically attached to her. What's happened to it?"

"It's disappeared, apparently," I said.

"Disappeared? How could it disappear?" said Naz, frowning.

"It wasn't in her apartment or her office. Have the police said anything to you about it?"

"No, they haven't. My mother was taken ill at the funeral and we had to rush back to Lüleburgaz. They might be trying to contact us."

It seemed to me that Batuhan was failing in this investigation. He hadn't even seen the victim's family yet! Still, I suppose I'm always hypercritical of the Turkish police.

"Might she have left her laptop in her car?" I asked.

"Sani didn't have a car," said Naz. "She sold it recently because she wanted to buy a newer model. What you said about her laptop is very strange. I suppose it must have been stolen. I wonder if anyone was in her apartment when she died?"

"Or maybe a burglar entered the apartment after she died that day and omitted to tell anyone. I know it's unlikely, but not impossible. Things will be clearer when we get the forensic report," I said.

It was past six o'clock.

"We must go," I said. "We're going to get caught in the evening traffic, and we should at least try to get home before midnight."

"It takes less time driving from Lüleburgaz to Istanbul than it does getting home after reaching the city," remarked Fofo.

"It can't be that bad. You're exaggerating," said Naz.

"It is that bad," I said. "And it gets worse by the day. Throughout the month of Ramadan, there's complete gridlock during the hours before the evening meal."

"I don't know if I can get things sorted for tomorrow, but I'll definitely be coming to Istanbul the following day," said Naz, walking alongside us.

"In that case, come and see us," I said.

I described where the shop was, gave her my phone numbers and said that I'd be at the shop until noon on Friday.

On the way back to Istanbul, Fofo and I quarrelled four times, because he kept criticizing my driving. Perhaps I was going a little fast, but old habits die hard. And anyway, it wasn't my fault that German motorways had no speed restrictions.

We arrived home feeling disgruntled with each other and with Istanbul's endless rush-hour traffic. I spent a long time under the shower.

After setting the alarms of both my clock and my mobile, with the intention of waking early the next morning to get some work done, I drifted off thinking how the best thing about a tiring day was being able to get a good night's sleep.

As soon as I entered the shop the next morning, I went online to look up the group Sniff and its lead singer Sinan. Various websites showed that they were appearing at the Kara Bar in Beyoğlu on Friday night. Thinking I might be able to have a few words with Sinan after their performance, I decided to go there and take Fofo with me.

I looked on Skyrat, but there was nothing new of any interest. Then, to fill in time, I googled the Ankaralıgil family, Aylin Aköz and her husband, the contamination at Ergene Basin, the GreTur website, and the Mercedes bought by the industrialists for the Kocaeli governor. Once I'd started, it was difficult to stop. To give myself a break, I phoned Lale, who was about to go into a meeting and had no time to talk. We agreed to meet at the weekend.

Fofo finally showed up at the shop.

"I've only just woken up. How did you get here so early?" he said, his eyes still puffy with sleep. "Hasan phoned. He wants the car back so that he can take his mother to the airport, and you've still got the keys."

"Well, don't be too long. I might need to go out," I said.

Fofo paid no heed to what I said, as usual, and was gone for over two hours. The moment he returned, I left the shop and went home.

The next day, Naz turned up just before noon.

"What a lovely shop," she said on entering. "So you specialize in crime fiction?"

She sat down in my rocking chair, something I normally don't allow anyone else to do. However, I let it pass.

"Would you like some tea?" I asked.

"Please. And would it be possible to order something to eat as well? I came out without having breakfast, so as not to be late."

"Cheese or pepperoni toasted sandwich, doner kebab sandwich or borlotti beans," I said, listing the snacks that were on offer in Kuledibi.

"Pepperoni toasted sandwich, please."

Recai, our tea boy, had retired the previous year and been replaced by his idle son Muslum, who spent the whole day sitting next to the stove betting on horses and making no attempt to sell teas. It irritated me that I had to press a buzzer several times to place my order, instead of being greeted by Recai, tray in hand, the moment I set foot in his teashop. Occasionally, Muslum was given a stern warning by his father and things would improve for a few days, but he soon reverted to his old ways. At least two days must have passed since the last warning, because Muslum was still nowhere to be seen when the sandwiches arrived from Petek Snack Bar. I gave up and went over to the stove to pour out the teas myself.

While I was busying myself putting the sandwiches on a plate and pouring teas, a text arrived on my mobile, saying "R u alone?"

The message was from Fofo, who was obviously wondering if Naz had turned up. I felt no need to satisfy his curiosity, and didn't reply.

Naz brushed the crumbs off her skirt and also asked if we were alone. Did she think someone was hiding behind the curtain in the kitchenette?

"We're alone," I said. "Why do you ask?"

She went over to the shop window and stood gazing into the street, like a KGB agent in a Cold War film worrying about being followed.

"I need to talk to you about something. But it must remain between us."

What did she mean? That I shouldn't tell Fofo?

I was ruffled by this. There were of course certain things I might choose to keep from Fofo. I might criticize Fofo and fall out with him, but I didn't let anyone else treat him that way. If someone told me a secret, I didn't expect to make it a condition that I couldn't tell him. Surely my darling Fofo was to be trusted. Anyway, I certainly wasn't going to let a stranger dictate such matters.

"I can't promise not to tell anyone at all. Fofo and I work together, as you know," I said, looking annoyed.

"Oh, I didn't mean Fofo," said Naz. "It's just that I don't want this information getting out. The safety of someone I care about might be in jeopardy."

Oh dear!

"If I told anyone, it'd be Fofo," I said, thinking that perhaps she knew about Sani's relationship with Sinan.

If that was the big secret, I thought, what could it have to do with the safety of someone Naz cared about? In my mind, I concocted a scenario in which this person was Sinan and she was afraid that Cem Ankaralıgil might have him bumped off too, as an honour killing, if the relationship were exposed.

Everything seemed to be falling into place. Yet I had doubts about Cem Ankaralıgil being the type to commission an honour killing. In my experience, it was only primeval idiots who took such action. Normal Turks, like most people, waited for their spouse to return, and if he or she didn't, then they got divorced.

"You don't need to worry about your secret getting out," I said, wanting to reassure Naz, whether or not she'd been referring to Sinan and Sani's secret love affair. "I can guarantee that."

"That's what I wanted to hear," said Naz, but she still looked uneasy.

"You don't seem comfortable here. We can go to my place to talk if you like. It's not far away," I suggested.

"Yes, I'd like that. It's very nice here, but it is a shop, after all. Someone could walk in at any moment."

"I'll phone Fofo and ask him to come over. He's at home at the moment, but can be here in no time."

"Good," said Naz. "And I suggest we start using the familiar 'you' from now on."

"Good idea," I said, as I dialled Fofo's number.

I went to make coffee as soon as we entered my apartment. Naz followed me into the kitchen.

"My father wants to pay you and Fofo – or at least take care of your expenses."

"No way! What are you thinking?"

"But you must be out of pocket with all this."

"Yes, and you've been spending your money fighting the industrialists," I said. "I thought your father and I had a tacit agreement over this. If Sani was murdered, then the perpetrator is of interest to me too, and to Fofo."

Fofo hadn't actually spent a cent of his own money so far, but I wasn't going to mention that.

"It all started because of my curiosity, but now—" I added.

"Yes, and now?" interrupted Naz.

"Now that I've met you and your father, and seen what you're doing—"

79

"You haven't really seen anything, because we haven't been able to achieve anything," said Naz sadly.

"But you're trying to, which is worth a lot. You could also say that I knew Sani. We used to run into her several times a week at lunchtime."

"At that little restaurant downstairs in the business centre?"

"Do you know it?"

"Of course. Sani used to take me there when I came to Istanbul."

"What's more, I like what I've heard about Sani – the way she went to stay with her uncle after finishing primary school so that she could go to middle school. Was there no middle school in your village back then?"

"No. We had to go to Lüleburgaz. It's not very far, as you know. A minibus used to go round all the villages collecting the kids to take them there. My uncle and aunt offered to take care of my sister's education because they didn't have children of their own, and my parents accepted. But then a few years after Sani went to stay with them, my uncle and aunt had a child of their own, so she brought them luck."

"Did you go to middle school in Lüleburgaz?"

"I was in Istanbul, as a boarder at Galatasary Lycée."

I poured out two cups of coffee and said, "Let's go back into the sitting room."

"Can I smoke in here?" asked Naz.

"Why not? I've only just given up. There's an ashtray up there on the shelf."

"I wish I could give up too. I don't actually smoke very much."

We sat down at either end of my large red sofa, facing each other with the tray of coffee between us.

"So, what's this secret?" I asked.

"I don't know if you remember an armed organization called the KLA, the Kosovo Liberation Army, which sprang up during the Kosovo War."

I nodded. I might claim not to read newspapers, but I'm not completely ignorant.

"The organization continued to be active until 1999, but when the war came to an end, so did the KLA. A few of its members were put on trial, and it's claimed that some took up official posts in Kosovo while others were taken into the American army. Meanwhile, the KLA, which in 1997 had been branded by the Americans as a bunch of terrorists, was taken off the list of terrorist organizations in early 1998. Later, it transpired that not only had the KLA been trained by the CIA, it had also received support from Germany in return for protecting German interests in the Balkans."

"Interesting, but what does all this have to do with us?"

"Be patient. I'm explaining. There isn't a direct link, of course. Despite many disclaimers, certain myths grew up around the KLA. For instance, it was said that the KLA obtained arms from Bin Laden, that they killed any Albanians who objected to violence, that they organized narcotics cartels throughout the Balkans and ran the Albanian mafia. But all that still didn't prevent them being perceived as heroes."

"The army and government apparatus was in the hands of the Serbs," I said, "and the Albanians were an oppressed minority, so it was only natural for people to feel sympathetic towards the KLA."

"Very true," nodded Naz. "They aroused a lot of sympathy."

"So?"

"As I said yesterday, my family is Albanian."

"Yes, you did," I said, realizing that all this was linked to the comments about ethnicity she'd made the previous day, when I hadn't understood the connection.

"A lot of people from Albania live in Turkey. Not only Albanians, of course. There are Bosnians and Pomaks too. You find them living near the northern Aegean in places like Izmir, Manisa and Istanbul, but mainly in Thrace. It's impossible to say how many. They've mostly been assimilated and forgotten their mother tongue, since they're second-, third- or even fourth-generation immigrants. The wave of migrants that arrived to escape death during the Balkan Wars came at a time when the Balkans were much more developed than Anatolia and, more importantly, their people were better educated. Consequently, many of them were appointed to good positions in the newly formed Turkish Republic, which is why, in my view, there have been few ethnic or cultural issues until now."

Naz's last sentence startled me. What did she mean by "until now"? And what issues was she referring to? The jigsaw pieces seemed to be gradually falling into place.

"Are you saying that an organization like the KLA has been formed in Thrace?"

"It's called the TLF," said Naz, taking a sip of coffee.

"TLF?"

"Yes, it stands for Thrace Liberation Force."

Feeling unsure how to respond, I turned and rearranged the cushions behind me.

"What does the KLA have to do with this?" I asked.

"It's seen as a model. I don't think there's any other connection. I'm told the TLF is 100 per cent local."

"But why have we heard nothing about this organization?" I asked.

"Because they're not active yet, that's why. That is, unless it was one of them who killed my sister."

"Hang on," I said. "Do you really think the TLF could be behind Sani's death?"

"It was rumoured that the KLA killed any Albanians who didn't support them. Since the TLF is an offshoot of the KLA, this might have been their first initiative."

"Did Sani oppose the TLF?"

"I don't know if she opposed them exactly, but I can say that she wasn't prepared to adopt their methods. The TLF is an armed organization – in short, they're prepared to use violence, something which Sani and I always opposed. We share the TLF's aim of having industries that don't damage the environment or human health, and we believe in controlled migration. We want all that, but if violence was involved, who knows what the outcome would be? There's no guarantee that the organization wouldn't turn into a bunch of separatists. When actions become radicalized, thoughts become radicalized too. We'd never had anything like that in mind."

"But how would the TLF know that you didn't support them?" I asked.

"Are you asking if the TLF contacted us?" asked Naz, showing that she hadn't understood what I was getting at.

"Yes."

"They contacted me six months ago, and my sister later on. As far as I know, the organization was formed about a year ago, and they've been all over Thrace finding out who's prepared to support them and who might be persuaded. They speak to anyone known to be concerned about the environment or unhappy with the current state of affairs, so we weren't targeted especially. They might have put more pressure on us than others, but a number of people—"

"They used pressure? What kind of pressure?"

"Oh, they've been making phone calls and leaving propaganda for me at the hospital."

"I'm going to get some water. Do you want some?" I said suddenly, rising from my chair.

I needed a few moments on my own to digest what I'd heard. When I returned to the sitting room, I was convinced that I'd been listening to the ramblings of someone on the edge of sanity.

"Propaganda, telephone calls, pressure..." I muttered.

"Are you wondering what the propaganda was about? What is it you want to know?" said Naz.

My mind was so befuddled that I'd lost the ability to construct a proper question. In fact, I didn't really know what I wanted to ask, anyway.

"Just a minute. Let me summarize what I've understood so far," I said. "An armed organization called the TLF has been formed in Thrace, and its members want to establish an independent state. Is that right?"

"No," said Naz emphatically. "They're not seeking independence, at least not at the moment. They want to put an end to illegal industrialization, move some of the factories out of Thrace, impose restrictions on migrant workers and strengthen the local administration. Of course, the last point could develop into a demand for federalization."

"And then independence?"

"They don't use the word 'independence'. At least, they've said nothing to me about it. They're demanding cultural rights for people whose mother tongue isn't Turkish, but that's secondary, I think. Their list of demands is long, and I don't remember them all. They refer to themselves as a 'regional body'."

"And do they have a support base for this?"

"Well, they're trying to build one. There's been a lot of dissatisfaction about developments in Thrace over the last twenty years, and it's created a serious security issue for the major political parties. Many people take the view that Thrace is being plundered and, having lost their land once during the Balkan

Wars, when they were lucky to escape with their lives, they now feel under threat again from migrants."

"Do you think they're likely to support such an organization?"

"They might. Yet everyone's so afraid that I'm not sure if they'd go through with it."

"It's natural for people to get scared when they're about to lose something," I said, concentrating on biting my nails.

"The thing is that governments come and go without resolving our problems, and the situation gets worse by the day. Thracians are very aware of what's happening, unlike people in the rest of Turkey. Their level of education is higher, the region is more developed, the villages have roads and schools—"

"But could an armed organization win over these people?"

"In this country, businessmen – the very men who cause the most environmental pollution – get awards for their contribution to the economy. Just imagine if one of those men were killed on his way home with the trophy in his arms. Do you think anyone whose father had died of cancer caused by pollution from his factory would mourn him? Would anyone regard it as tragic if a factory that had been pumping poisonous water underground went up in smoke? The people have had enough. Of course such actions would have an impact."

"Yes, of course," I said, pressing my fingers to my temples in an attempt to avert a crushing migraine.

"Thrace could be economically self-sufficient without all these industries. It has the Maritsa, Tunca and Ergene rivers, flood-plains and basins. A new natural gas field is discovered almost every day. The university's good. Everything would be rosy without the environmental problem and ever-increasing migration. Standards in Thrace are much like those in central Europe. It's the only region in Turkey to have developed sufficiently for EU membership, a fact that's much exploited."

"Are you trying to persuade me to accept the idea of a Thrace Republic?"

"No, I'm not. I'm pointing out the arguments being used to win over people living in Thrace."

"Back at the shop, you said that the life of someone you care about is in danger."

"I suspect that a former boyfriend of mine is mixed up in all this."

"And you still think the TLF might have killed Sani?"

"I don't know how they make their decisions, and I don't know what role my ex has in the organization. He may know nothing about this."

"I expect you realize," I said, "that there are weaknesses in both my theory about the industrialists and your TLF theory."

"Why's that?"

"Why would Sani have let them into her home? The police said the door wasn't forced. So if Sani was murdered, she must have opened the door to the murderer. In other words, she knew the person well enough to let him or her in." I paused for a moment before adding, "Living in Istanbul makes you lose your trust in people, doesn't it? You never open the door to anyone."

"Let's say you become more cautious. It's a big city, and you have to be on guard all the time," said Naz, turning to gaze out of the window.

In the autumn sunshine, I noticed lines around her eyes and on her forehead that I hadn't seen before. Her face suddenly looked full of sorrow, etched with life's struggles, gains, losses, missed opportunities and dreams.

"I'm losing my faith," she said, closing her eyes for a moment. "Each day since my sister's death, I find I've lost it a bit more. I don't believe in myself, my ability to cure patients, to save Ergene, to be happy... I no longer believe in anything. For the first time in my life, I feel completely spent."

"Why now? Yesterday you were fine and seemed to be coping with your grief."

"Really? I don't think so," said Naz. "I suppose everyone mourns differently. It's as if I've been drained of all emotion and I'm left completely empty. And it's worse when I see the state my parents are in. What's going to happen now? What on earth can happen after this?"

"We'll make a plan," I said, knowing that this was probably not what she meant, but I'd learned from Fofo that scenes of high emotion were best kept short. "You're going to go to the forensic pathologist, and I'll talk to the police officer in charge of the investigation this evening and find out what they know. How about that?"

"Good," said Naz.

"Would you like some green tea? Or something else?"

"It's still early, isn't it?" replied Naz, looking at her watch.

"Yes it is, so let's go and eat. It'd do you good to get out for a bit."

"Can we go a bit later?"

"Of course. We'll go whenever you like," I said, opening the window to fill the room with fresh air and sunshine.

Everything will sort itself out, I thought. My left eye was aching as if it had been punched. A migraine.

5

"Where's Fofo disappeared to this time?" I asked Pelin as I entered the shop.

It was almost five o'clock. After Naz had left to go to the forensic pathologist, I'd watched a bit of daytime television until I could bear it no longer and then sought refuge in a novel I'd left half-read for days.

"He was meeting a friend and going out for dinner. He said he'd see you at home tonight," said Pelin.

"But we were going to a gig this evening," I said.

"Who's playing?"

"A group called Sniff. Have you heard of them?"

"Yes, they're good. Where's the gig?"

"At Kara Bar."

"That's an awful place. If Sniff are playing there, it'll be horribly crowded. Unbearable, in fact."

Unbearable or not, I was going. I called Fofo and arranged to meet him later.

"I'm exhausted. While you're running around all over the place, I get landed with all the work," complained Pelin.

"In that case, why don't you go home now?"

"The thing is, it's Friday and I'm meeting friends in Beyoğlu this evening, so what would I do if I left now? It takes two hours to go home and get back," said Pelin, obviously hoping I'd suggest she went to my apartment.

"Why don't you go to my place? You can relax there for a bit before going out this evening," I said.

"You're a star!" said Pelin, springing to her feet, snatching up my keys and disappearing.

I began going over the weekly accounts, but couldn't concentrate at all. I kept glancing at the door and at people in the street. Waiting around for Batuhan wasn't easy. Deciding to leave the accounts for another day, I started looking at the online press, but it was the same old boring news about who'd said what to whom. Then, unexpectedly, I had three customers and, without any effort on my part, sold five books within thirty seconds.

I went back to my desk and started drawing spirals, obsessively making sure they were all exactly the same size. When I ran out of space, I took another piece of paper and started drawing daisies with Pelin's pink mother-of-pearl biro, but that wasn't as much fun as spirals. An elderly shoeshine man who occupies the doorway of a derelict apartment building overlooking the square knocked on the window to say goodnight as he passed the shop at the end of his shift. I found myself looking at the clock every seven minutes or so. The new tea boy, Muslum, looked in, obviously having had a scolding from his father, and asked, "Miss Kati, do you want anything before I close up?"

"No thanks, Muslum. Say hello to your dad," I said.

I started a game of patience on the computer but, not having the patience to play it, I soon stopped. At one point, Dursun, one of my most valued customers, popped in. Dursun used to sell pirate DVDs from a tiny shop in Galip Dede Street, but he was hounded by the police and set himself up in the basement of the chandelier shop opposite the synagogue. After his goods were confiscated there, he started selling DVDs from the doorway of an apartment building in Çeşmeli Passage. He copied all his films on to disk, so I just had to email him if I wanted anything and it was delivered to me the next day.

"Things aren't going well, Miss Kati. The police never leave me alone. Bastards! They just won't give me a break," said Dursun, adding that the previous week they'd seized over two hundred films and taken him into custody for a night.

"I need large orders if I'm to keep up a home delivery service," he continued. "It's no good having the odd DVD order here and there. If things don't get any better, I'm thinking of going into fruit juices."

Dursun went on to explain at length how sales of fruit juice had shot through the roof during the previous autumn and winter. I must say that I was particularly partial to pomegranate juice, and also a mixture of orange and grapefruit juice.

"My uncle's selling slices of coconut and pineapple from his handcart in Galip Dede. He says that business is booming," said Dursun. "I've found a little shop and, providing I can sort everything out, I'm going into the tropical juice business. I'll be expecting you, miss."

After he left, I went to the toilet, making sure the shop door was locked so that no one would enter in my absence. By the time I came out, Batuhan was waiting outside.

"Another minute or so and I'd have left," I said.

"We've been very busy. Two of my staff left early for a birthday party, so I had to do their work. Life would be much easier if we could take you on as an adviser," said Batuhan with a laugh.

"Oh yes! You know how much I like the Turkish police."

"The Turkish police like you too. But I sense a certain chill in the air," he said, laughing again.

"There haven't been any murders in Istanbul for a while. What can I do? That's not my fault."

"No murders? There's actually been an increase in the number of murders, but nothing seems to have aroused your interest. Still, I suppose you stick to incidents in and around Beyoğlu."

"Well, this time it's Paşabahçe. I guess I'm prepared to go as far as the Black Sea."

"You're expanding." More laughter.

"Have you come here to criticize me, Batuhan?" I said, deciding that his mockery was becoming irritating.

"Is that how it seems from where you're sitting? In that case, let's swap seats," said Batuhan. More laughter, but this time I joined in.

"Very witty!" I remarked sardonically.

We both fell silent, me in my rocking chair and he in the armchair opposite.

"Would you like some tea?" I asked.

"No thanks, I've had too much today."

"Something else?"

"No thanks. So tell me, is business good at the moment?"

"Is that what you concluded when I offered you tea?"

"Come on, you have two people working here now. That girl, and the guy I saw the other day. What's his name?"

"Fofo," I said.

"What kind of name is that? Sounds like the name of a poodle to me," laughed Batuhan.

What a boorish man he was, I thought.

"It's a Spanish name," I said, ignoring the mocking tone in his voice. "Business isn't too bad. We get by."

"Readers of crime fiction are obviously on the increase. Actually, I'm thinking of writing my memoirs when I retire. The title will be *Thirty Years in the Homicide Squad*. What do you think?"

"Too long."

"Maybe *Thirty Years of Homicide*, then."

"Yes, that might do. Would you include the Sani Ankaralıgil case in it?"

"No, but I'm thinking of including you in it. I was thinking of a chapter called 'German sleuth hunts for clues in the streets of Beyoğlu'."

"It sounds a bit heavy-going to me," I said, thinking that such originality was a bit too much for a policeman. "I'm making green tea for myself. If you want one, say so."

"How can you drink that acidic stuff?"

"It might be acidic, but it's good for you. Do you want some?"

"Okay, I'll have one too."

While we were in the kitchen waiting for the water to boil, I heard the shop door open. It had to be a customer. What timing! You wait in an empty shop for hours on end, and then...

It turned out to be an Australian couple who wanted to tell me all about their adventures during their trip to Cappadocia, where they'd collected enough material to keep them talking until morning. I practically elbowed them out of the shop and locked the door. I know it wasn't right to turn away customers, but I really didn't want to try Batuhan's patience further.

I reheated the water and brought in the tea.

"Where were we?" he asked.

"We were talking about the book you're going to write when you retire. Is Sani going to be in the book?"

Batuhan rested his chin on his hand and stared hard at me. "That chapter could be called 'A Suspicious Death'."

"Not murder?"

"Are you trying to put words into my mouth?" he said, rolling his eyes.

"What makes you say that?" I asked, noting that Batuhan's powers of intuition had increased noticeably in the years since we last met.

"You go first," he said.

"I know nothing," I said. "I have my suspicions about some factory owners in Thrace who are trying to avoid being penalized."

"A criminal gang, huh?"

"Well, if they can organize the purchase of a Mercedes for the local governor, then hiring a killer—"

"Are you saying they could have had Sani murdered?" interrupted Batuhan.

"I only said it because you asked. We can just sit here making fun of each other if you prefer."

"The woman wasn't killed, she died," he said, more seriously now, though his face still showed traces of his previous idiotic expression.

"What do you mean by that? She died as the result of a fall, didn't she?" I asked.

"Exactly. What are you trying to say?"

"If she fell because someone pushed her, then she was murdered. If she slipped and fell, then she died. Do you know how she fell?" I said, and sipped my tea.

Green tea is so good for you. Its antioxidants definitely help the brain to work, even if they do nothing to improve the skin.

"Was there perhaps a closed-circuit camera in the house?" I asked.

"You're confusing me," said Batuhan, leaning back and crossing his legs. "You should be the one writing the book. You'd write great crime fiction with your overactive imagination. Did someone push the person who slipped and fell, or did they merely slip and fall? How can anyone know?"

I was mulling over what I'd learned from crime fiction writers about murders solved using advanced technology on samples taken from under fingernails, a strand of hair found clasped in a hand, DNA tests, a drop of blood, dog hairs and so on. Anything like that would be useful for proving that someone had killed Sani. Yet Batuhan was saying that the woman had simply died. How could he know without seeing CCTV footage that proved Sani was home alone at the time of her death?

Batuhan looked at me as if he'd got the better of me. If Fofo had been there, he'd have said, "Revenge is a dish best served cold", though his translation into Turkish would have sounded something like "revenge, like gazpacho, should never be eaten hot".

Batuhan suddenly rose to his feet.

"I was going to order you a kebab," I said.

"Another time. I have to get back to the station and do some more work. I'm up to my eyeballs."

"As you wish."

"I'll just give you one more thing to work on as part of your intellectual gymnastics: we know that Sani wasn't murdered, but there was someone else in her apartment."

"Now you tell me! Go on then, enlighten me!" I cried.

This time, Batuhan laughed as he used to in the old days. Was he beginning to soften a bit, perhaps?

"I really have to go, otherwise I'd have stayed for a kebab," he said.

"But if someone had been with her, surely they'd have saved her, wouldn't they?"

"Exactly! She could have been saved. Or at the very least that person could have called an ambulance. But they didn't."

"But it's not murder, you say?"

"It's not murder, but we have to find out who was with her in the house and why they didn't try to help her."

"Why are you so sure that someone else was in Sani's house?" I asked, immediately remembering her missing laptop. "Was her computer stolen from there? Is that it?"

"We Turkish police have our own methods," he said calmly, his face absolutely deadpan.

"And there I was thinking that torture was a thing of the past," I remarked, immediately regretting my words. It was a bad joke.

"Excuse me. I must be going," he said.

"So what are your methods?" I asked, wondering if my joke had made him uneasy.

"Ha ha! I've said too much already," he laughed.

I let it go, because I had no intention of upsetting Batuhan in the middle of a murder investigation. We left the shop together.

Pelin was sitting in front of the TV.

"I cooked some pilaf, because there was nothing else," she called out as I entered the sitting room.

"I'm not eating," I said, for once not feeling hungry. "What time are you going out?"

"If you have something to do, just say so and I'll leave straight away," said Pelin, sitting bolt upright.

"I only asked," I said, wondering why people had to be so touchy.

"We're meeting at eleven."

Oh great! She could have travelled to and from her place a dozen times before eleven o'clock. But I said nothing. Anyway, there hadn't been a squeak out of Naz. I wondered if she'd genuinely intended to come to see me the moment she got the report. After all, young people could be very unreliable.

If the mountain doesn't come to you, then you must go to the mountain, as they say. I decided to call Naz, but found the screen on my mobile was blank. The battery was empty and the wretched thing had shut down. Still, at least it was better than Naz being unreliable.

I started to search the apartment for the charger. Sharing anything with Fofo was always a terrible idea, because he'd leave my things in such obscure places that I could never find them. I checked the plugs, desk and under the bed in his room first, then the plugs in the sitting room, my bedroom, study and the guest room, which was empty apart from a bed, the plug above the fridge (I'd previously found it there on more than one occasion), and the plug for the hairdryer in the bathroom. Whenever I had to find something urgently, I wished that everything had a sound mechanism which responded instantly when its number was called, like a mobile phone.

For instance, if I'd mislaid a book and was tearing my hair out wondering how it ended, I'd simply say its name: "*Selige Witwen* by Ingrid Noll". No response? Then I'd repeat it louder! And, as if by magic, I'd find it under the bedside table, where it had been all the time.

Or, say I'd been hunting for the terracotta (red was definitely out) lipstick I also used on my cheeks and was running late for a date, I'd just call out, "Lippy, lippy!" No, actually; I'd have to be a bit more specific or every lipstick in the apartment would start replying and I wouldn't be able to hear a thing. But if I shouted, "*Chanel Sorcier*!" – hey presto – it would respond from a handbag I hadn't used since the previous winter.

Take Fatma. She only came one day a week, but she spent at least eight hours in the apartment, which she believed gave her more rights than the people actually living there. She craved a system that would give her total control, especially in the kitchen. Fatma could get very agitated if she thought even a bottle opener was in the wrong place. I couldn't understand why anyone would want to move something so trivial, but it was of the utmost importance to her. Thus, if I decided to have a soda while watching a film on TV, I'd find the soda, but it would be another thirty minutes before I could get back to the film because I couldn't find the opener. I'd look in all the drawers, on the floor, under the sink, behind the rubbish bin, inside the food cupboards, but to no avail.

In the old days, when we went camping, there were always a few guys in the group who could open a beer bottle by chipping away at it with a cigarette lighter. But I lived with Fofo now, so no one in my apartment had such skills. Finding the bottle opener was the only option. Eventually, I'd spot it, and guess where it would be? In a glass tumbler on the shelf. What on earth was my lovely little bottle opener doing there? If my signal system were invented, all I'd need to do was say "Opener, opener" and it would respond to me from inside the tumbler on the shelf, without me getting so worked up or missing crucial scenes in my film.

I called out, "Charger, charger" just in case, but of course there wasn't a squeak. If only I'd had the foresight to write down Naz's number, I could have called her from the landline. Something would certainly have to be done if we continued to live in black holes that swallowed everything up. Numbers should always be written down.

"Why are you yelling? And why are you hopping about like a chicken with burnt toes?" Pelin called out.

"The expression is 'a bitch with burnt toes', not a chicken," I said curtly.

"I don't like to refer to you as a bitch, so I said chicken."

"Well, instead of overdoing the politeness, why don't you help me look for the charger?" I grumbled.

"Oh! Are you looking for the charger? I borrowed it to charge my phone. It's plugged in behind the TV."

I felt like exploding. However, I managed to contain myself, with great difficulty, and finally succeeded in phoning Naz.

*

"I couldn't reach you because your phone was off," said Naz predictably.

"The battery went flat," I said. "Where are you?"

"I stayed to have a drink after work with a friend from forensics. I'm in Beyoğlu."

"Great. Can you come and see me? Did you get the report?"

"Yes. Did you speak to the police?"

"Yes," I said, remembering that although I'd spoken to Batuhan we didn't get very far.

"In that case, I'll come round," said Naz. "What number is it?"

"Number twenty-two. It's the first building after you turn the corner. Take care as you go down the slope. There are sometimes pickpockets waiting to ambush you."

"Will do."

Galip Dede Street was deserted at night because all the shops were closed. The previous year, a vagrant crouched in a supermarket doorway had tried to steal my Swiss friend Liz's handbag. He didn't succeed, but made the poor woman fall and fracture her hip. She was taken to hospital for an emergency operation and had only started walking again after months of rehabilitation in a Swiss clinic. I'd advised her to find somewhere else to spend her retirement, so she returned to her lovely house in the country as soon as her treatment ended.

When Naz arrived, I told Pelin to switch off the TV and go to my study.

"I won't make a sound if you let me stay in here," she protested.

I looked at Naz, thinking that she'd be uneasy about someone else hearing our conversation.

"Don't worry on my account," said Naz, shrugging her shoulders.

"All right, Pelin, but one word and you go to my study. Understood?" I said, realizing that my threat was utterly pointless, as it soon proved to be.

"What happened at forensics?" I asked.

"They can't get rid of Naz with the findings in the file."

What did she mean, for heaven's sake? Was it some sort of doctors' code language?

"What do you mean, 'they can't get rid of Naz'?"

Naz went to fetch her bag from the hall stand, took out some papers and handed them to me.

"Here. Read the last paragraph."

The report was as follows:

Chemical Analysis Specialist Department report number 8334 of 21 September 2006 states that the blood and urine samples contained no traces of alcohol, narcotic substances or any of the poisonous substances listed in the report attachment, that pathological examinations of samples of the brain, spinal cord, heart, kidneys, liver and lungs showed no lesions, and that there was evidence of autolysis in the pancreas.

Biological Specialist Department report number 6879 of 21 September 2006 states that sperm was found in samples 1 and 2 taken from the deceased's underwear.

An external examination of the body showed that the superficial abrasions found in the autopsy, including 1 x 1 cm on the right elbow, 0.5 x 1 cm on the left elbow and 1 x 2 cm on the right knee, the needle puncture marks on the left forearm near the fold of the elbow, and a bleed measuring 7 x 10 cm beneath the right parietal section of the scalp cannot be established as the cause of death. This report finds that, in order to establish the exact cause of death, this department must be provided with full medical records so that the deceased's state of health at the time of death can be determined.

"Apparently, she hit the right side of her head when she fell, but it wasn't enough to kill her," said Naz.

"And the needle marks?"

"Yes, there were needle marks on her arm, but no narcotics or poison in her blood."

"Do you think she used drugs?"

"I've no idea how those needle marks got there," said Naz.

We looked at each other anxiously.

"She was obviously with a man. But who was it?" I murmured, glancing over the first page of the report again. "I see there was some brown leather dye under her fingernails. What does that signify?"

"It could have been from her bag, her shoes or the armchair. Leather dye is everywhere. It might not mean anything."

"Or it might have huge significance and we haven't recognized it yet," I said, putting the report down on the coffee table.

Pelin snatched up the report, gave it a cursory glance and said, "She wasn't murdered."

"No, she wasn't murdered, and there's no clear cause of death," said Naz. "Her head wound wasn't fatal, she didn't have a heart attack, and nor was she strangled or poisoned – yet still she died."

I'd read thousands of crime mysteries, at least one a week since I was fifteen, but I'd never read about a death like this. No sign of drugs or poisoning, yet there were needle marks in her arm. It wasn't caused by the bang to her head. As far as I could recall, none of the books I'd read had featured a person dying of natural causes like this.

Why had no crime author made a victim's murder look as if it were due to natural causes? Why didn't any of the novels give me a clue? The answer, of course, was simple: people who die of natural causes aren't the stock-in-trade of the genre. Without a murder to solve, crime fiction wouldn't exist.

In the fictional world of crime, everything is rational and logical with no irrelevant details, no confusion and no misdirection. Everything happens with perfect timing, even if events are frequently dictated by the undesirable outcomes of fate, destiny and chance and characters display unconvincing inconsistencies, contradictions and complexes. However, in real life it's possible for an amateur sleuth and friend to pursue a mystery case.

"There was someone at her apartment when she died," I said.

"How do you know?" asked Naz. "Did the police tell you?"

"Yes. They're convinced someone was there."

"How can they be so sure?"

"That I don't know. But we need to find out who it was."

"If someone was there, they should have got help when Sani fell."

"Exactly. The fact that no call was made meant that someone didn't want his or her presence there to be known. Someone from your TLF, maybe?" I said.

"What's the TLF?" asked Pelin.

We ignored her.

"Or," I continued, "maybe someone hired by the industrialists came to the house to kill Sani, but decided to leave after she fell, thinking that she was going to die anyway."

"But why?" asked Pelin.

"If we can establish the reason, it'll be easy to work out who it was," I said.

"Have the police seen this autopsy report?" asked Pelin.

"Of course," said Naz. "The district attorney asked for an autopsy the same day. The police went to the autopsy room at four-thirty that afternoon and spoke to the pathologists without even waiting for the report."

"Why did the press report it as an accident? Was it just to confuse people?" asked Pelin.

"Apparently, when the district attorney visited the scene of the incident, he was accompanied by a general practitioner from the Paşabahçe health centre. And that doctor said something to the press, probably without thinking," said Naz.

"If they took a doctor with them, the district attorney must have had suspicions right from the start."

"My friend in forensics said that the death of a young woman in her own home is always regarded as suspicious. Even if the death is assumed to be an accident, it has to be proven. When the police hear about such an incident, they immediately inform the district attorney, whose permission is needed to start any preliminary investigations, and they take someone from forensics with them. That's normal procedure. Every district in Istanbul has a forensic pathologist, even Paşabahçe. But the day this happened, the local pathologist had been called away elsewhere, which is why the doctor from the health centre went along."

"I understand that the district attorney has to be accompanied by a forensic pathologist when someone dies unexpectedly at home, but do they always do an autopsy?" I asked.

"An autopsy is performed to establish the cause of death if no medication or treatment for a fatal illness is found on the premises and if there are no reliable witnesses. If the deceased is a member of a well-known family like the Ankaralıgils, then an autopsy is carried out anyway, whatever the person's age or medical history."

"If you remember, they did an autopsy on the author Aziz Nesin," said Pelin, "So it's not only the rich. Aziz Nesin was old and sick, and there were friends with him when he died. Nobody suspected that he'd been murdered, yet they still did an autopsy."

"Stop interrupting!" I cried. "You promised!"

"But she's right," said Naz. "Why are you so obsessed with the autopsy? There's nothing unusual about an autopsy being performed."

"I'm trying to fit the pieces together: accident, autopsy, death from natural causes, industrialists, TLF..." I said. "It's all very confusing, and I think the best thing I can do is make some green tea," I said, getting up to go to the kitchen.

When I returned, Naz and Pelin were watching TV.

"I needed to switch off for a while," said Naz.

We all settled down to watch a film about a robbery, even though we'd missed the beginning.

6

"Aren't we going out this evening?"

"You're late again, Fofo. Twenty-five minutes late," I retorted. "The gig's already started, and we're still here."

I'd never wanted him to develop Germanic punctuality, but I found it extremely irritating that he was always late for everything. You'd think he could be on time just once, even accidentally. But no.

"I couldn't get away any earlier. What time does the gig start?"

"It's already started. And I wanted to be there early," I said.

I wasn't interested in the music, but I'd hoped to have a few words with Sinan before the show.

"Do you know the group?" I asked.

"Well, the girls go mad for them. Their music's not bad, actually. Not bad at all," said Fofo.

"Come on, then," I said, getting to my feet just as Fofo sank into an armchair.

"I really need a drink," he moaned.

"You can have a drink there. Anyway, you've just had a meal, haven't you?"

"I was going to have some coffee."

"You can have coffee there. Come on, get up!"

"But it'll be horrible there," Fofo complained, getting reluctantly to his feet.

However, I wasn't in the mood to give in after being made to wait so long.

*

The Kara Bar was in a basement in Sıraselviler, and was one of those places with bouncers scrutinizing everyone going in or out of the building. I made Fofo pay the entrance fee. It was the least he could do.

Inside there wasn't room to breathe, let alone move. I retreated to a corner by the door. It was impossible to see the individual members of the group properly at that distance, which didn't matter to me. However, I was curious to see what sort of person Sinan was, and I hadn't thought of looking him up on Google Images.

Fofo was already lost in the music and making strange attempts at dance movements. I had to admire the boy's energy. Sniff played well, actually. I wouldn't have played their CDs at home, but it was good music.

At the interval, I tried to push my way through the crowd to the backstage area, which was impossible, of course. The solid mass of flesh in front of me and the smell of cigarette smoke combined with perfume and sweat made me feel quite nauseous.

"What are you doing?" Fofo shouted in my ear, as if it wasn't noisy enough in there.

"I'm going backstage," I said.

"Why?"

"I want to talk to the lead singer."

"That's all we need! Why do you have to be so adolescent? And why didn't you tell me this before?" said poor Fofo, obviously under the impression that I'd taken a liking to the singer.

"I didn't get the chance," I said, with as much innocence as was possible in a place where everyone is on top of each other.

"Let's go outside. Come on," said Fofo.

"I want to go backstage. Why go outside?"

"Come with me. Trust me," insisted Fofo.

The street was no less noisy than the nightclub. The sirens of ambulances trying to reach the local A & E department mingled with the horns of taxis touting for custom. Fofo told one of the bouncers that we wanted to speak to Ruhi.

"Ruhi Bey's busy," said the man, without even glancing at us.

I pulled Fofo to one side.

"Who's Ruhi?"

"He's the manager here, and the only person who can get us anywhere near the group," said Fofo. "He used to go to Alfonso for Spanish lessons."

I didn't need to ask who Alfonso was, of course. Alfonso was Fofo's former lover, with whom he'd run off and left me.

"Would you please tell Ruhi that Fofo's here? He's expecting us."

The bouncer still didn't bat an eyelid.

"Hey you! Can't you at least look us in the face?" I shouted at him, before venting to Fofo. "This is disgraceful! He won't even look at us!"

"It's hardly his fault," said Fofo. "Every night he has to deal with name-droppers hoping to get in without paying. He's not to know that we really do know Ruhi. He wouldn't even be allowed to let his own father in free. It's nothing personal, so don't get upset."

"Why not? It's because of you that we came outside."

"Don't worry, we can go back inside any time we want," said Fofo, pointing to the entry stamp on the back of my hand.

"But the interval's nearly over, and we'll have to wait until the end of the gig to see Sinan now."

Actually, I'd no wish whatsoever to go back into that airless place.

"Be patient. I have an idea. I'll call Alfonso and ask him for Ruhi's mobile number," said Fofo, then, seeing how pleased I looked, added, "but that doesn't mean you're off the hook."

"Why? What have I done?"

"You conned me into thinking we were coming here to listen to the music, when all the time you were bent on chatting up the lead singer," replied Fofo.

"But Fofo, darling, you didn't give me the chance to explain everything to you," I said, stroking his hair, or what was left of it. My dear friend's head was becoming very sparsely covered.

Fofo paced up and down the pavement, talking first to Alfonso and then Ruhi.

Finally, he turned to me and said, "The situation is this. Ruhi will see us immediately, but Sniff will be onstage again by now so we'll have to wait until later to see them."

"Okay, so we'll wait. What else can we do?" I said, reflecting that much of our work involved waiting.

The bouncer, who only a short while before wouldn't even glance at us, approached us holding some sort of radio device and said, "I'm to take you to Ruhi Bey's office."

We went through a narrow door into a long, dimly lit corridor. The bouncer knocked on one of the doors and we waited until a voice inside said, "Come in."

"*Querido*, Fofo," said Ruhi, embracing Fofo.

"You should have carried on with the Spanish. It was going really well," said Fofo.

"I'm so busy, you have no idea. We're opening two more clubs, and I can't do everything. I heard that you and Alfonso had split up."

"I feel as if I've been reborn," said Fofo.

Fofo had never intimated to me that he'd been having a hard time with Alfonso.

"My boyfriend and I split up last week too," said Ruhi.

"But you'll get back together again. You're always splitting up," said Fofo, in a tone of voice that told me he was really fishing to find out how serious the separation was, rather than expressing faith in their relationship.

Ruhi delivered immediately. "No, this time it's serious. He's gone," he laughed, though he was obviously deeply hurt. "There's a woman in his life. And what a strapping specimen she is. You should see her. When someone makes such a radical change, you expect it to be for someone really stunning."

"What do you mean by 'strapping'?" asked Fofo.

All the while they were talking, I was aware of unseen people hovering outside the still-open door.

"Oh, I don't know. Big, fat and ugly, I guess," said Ruhi.

"Ruhi goes in for interesting expressions," said Fofo, turning to me.

What was interesting about that? I thought.

"You haven't introduced us," said Ruhi.

"Kati, my boss, housemate, friend, my everything."

"Didn't you live in Cihangir once? We used to bump into each other at the café in Firuzağa sometimes," said Ruhi, turning to Fofo and adding, "I knew this lady before I even met you."

"I've moved to Kuledibi now," I said.

"Please, sit down. What can I get you? Whisky?"

"Yes please," I said, sinking into a leather armchair.

"Tell me, what brought you here?" asked Ruhi, as he filled some glasses from a bottle of Lagavulin.

"We'd like to meet tonight's lead singer," said Fofo.

"Everyone wants to meet him. But he's no use to us," said Ruhi, giving Fofo a wink.

"Ice in your whisky?"

Ice in Lagavulin? That would be a crime.

"No, thank you," I said.

"What business do you have with Sinan?"

"Kati's a great fan of his," said Fofo.

"That's right," I said.

"What's he like?" asked Fofo.

"He has class. Not the usual type you get in places like this. I don't know him well, but he certainly has plenty of charisma," said Ruhi.

"Can you really introduce us?" I asked.

Fofo and Ruhi laughed as if I'd said something stupid.

"Introductions aren't a problem," said Ruhi. "Just a minute, I need to see what's happening inside. Stay here and I'll be back. Best not to leave the staff unattended."

I hadn't been happy about lying to Fofo, so now we were alone I took the opportunity to explain my real reason for meeting Sinan.

"Sani was in a relationship with Sinan. That's why I wanted to meet him. I'm not really a fan of his at all."

"What kind of relationship?"

"A relationship. What kind of relationship do you think?"

"Is that why you dragged me here? Why didn't you tell me before? Why keep it from me?"

Fofo always repeated questions like this when he was annoyed.

"I didn't keep anything from you," I said, wondering how I was going to make amends.

"Then why didn't you say anything before?"

"I didn't get the chance," I said.

"Didn't get the chance? What do you mean, Kati? Who are you kidding?" he shouted, going red in the face.

"I mean, I didn't get the chance because I've only just found out about it," I said.

What else could I have said? If I'd confessed to knowing about Sinan for a few days, he'd have eaten me alive.

"We haven't been able to speak openly because there's always been someone else with us," I continued. "If you hadn't come back from your date twenty-five minutes late, I'd have told you before we came out."

"You could have told me on the way here."

"Fine. Should I have told you on İstiklal Street or in Taksim Square? Maybe, if you'd apologized for being late, I might've—"

"Oh God! Let's change the subject. Arguing with you is impossible. You're like olive oil – you always manage to come out on top," protested Fofo.

"That's odd. I was just thinking the same thing about you, Fofo," I shouted.

"I refuse to argue with you, Kati," he said, crossing his arms over his chest.

Then we kissed and made up, and sat waiting for Ruhi to return.

"Follow me," said Ruhi. "They're about to leave through the back door, but we'll catch Sinan before he gets away."

We gathered up our things and I tossed back the last mouthful of my whisky. I wasn't going to leave a single drop of that Lagavulin. Then we followed Ruhi down the corridor, where one of the doors opened and someone pushed us inside.

"Sinan, I have some friends here who want to meet you. They're big fans of yours," said Ruhi.

A tall man with short brown hair and sideburns down to his chin, wearing a T-shirt that clung to his body with perspiration, walked over to us. What a divine creature! Sani didn't have it bad at all, I thought.

Fofo and I told him our names, and he nodded in response.

"I wonder if you could give us a little of your time? We need to speak to you about a private matter," I said.

"I'd love to, but it's impossible. We're leaving straight away. However, I can give you a photo."

"What kind of photo?"

In all seriousness, I hadn't understood what he meant. It wasn't every day that I met a singer who had fans.

"A signed photograph."

"Actually, we wanted to talk to you about Sani," I whispered, realizing it was time to give up the pretence of being a fan.

Sinan's expression changed immediately. His rock star image of self-confidence and condescending arrogance was replaced by a blank and bewildered look. However, he was still an Adonis. No one could change that.

"Who are you?" asked Sinan.

"We're not the police," I said.

"I can see that. But who are you?"

"We can explain," said Fofo, taking a breath as if about to give Sinan his full life history.

"We need to talk. When can we meet?" I interrupted, finding Fofo's behaviour very inappropriate given that this man was a suspect in a possible murder case.

Sinan bit his lip and thought for a moment before saying, "Tomorrow's Friday. Come to my place in the afternoon. Is three o'clock all right?"

"Fine," I said in chorus with Fofo.

"I live at Rumelihisarı. When you get there, go to a café and give me a call. My brother will come and pick you up. See you tomorrow," said Sinan, and turned and left.

"You haven't given us your number," Fofo called out.

"Oh, haven't I? Sorry, I forgot. It's been a busy week."

The talk about his brother collecting us and his attempt to leave without giving his phone number convinced me that Sinan was going to stand us up.

"I bet you anything that his mobile will be turned off when we call his number tomorrow," I said to Fofo as we left the room.

"Do you think so?"

"I certainly do. Otherwise, why not give us his address like any normal person?"

Fofo was still spellbound by Sinan and in no fit state to think properly. I prodded him in an attempt to bring him back to his senses.

"So what should we do?" he asked, as if emerging from a dream.

"Let's get his address from Ruhi," I said. "Does Ruhi have it?"

"If he doesn't, he can get it."

And he did.

On Friday, I remembered that I'd arranged to meet Lale at noon.

"Fofo and I are going for a walk along the Bosphorus today before heading out this evening. I'd completely forgotten that I'd arranged to meet you," I confessed.

"How are you going to find a new man if you keep going out with Fofo and his gay friends?" commented Lale.

"But it'd make no difference if I was out with you," I said.

"One of Erol's friends is having a barbecue in his garden tonight," she said.

"Are you telling me that sitting around eating barbecued *köfte* with a group of fashionistas and their kids and dogs is a better option?" I said, finding it incomprehensible that women still clung to middle-class fantasies of finding a lover, even when those women were my best friends!

"It's not a good alternative, I admit, but it's a potentially productive alternative."

"What's the definition of a productive Friday night? Because I can tell you that eating *köfte* in Kemerburgaz isn't on my list," I said.

"I didn't say the house was in Kemerburgaz," said Lale.

"When you said it was in someone's garden, the first place that came to mind was Kemerburgaz. So where is it?"

"It's in Paşabahçe," said Lale. "Never mind. Perhaps we can meet during the week one evening when I'm in Kuledibi."

"Hang on. Where in Paşabahçe?"

"How should I know? Is the idea of eating *köfte* with fashionistas more appealing if it's in Paşabahçe?"

Paşabahçe used to be a small place situated in a wooded area on the Asian side of the Bosphorus. In the past, the majority of its residents had been workers at local factories making *rakı* and glassware. Then the area was "discovered", and subjected to substantial building development. Now the coastline of what had once been one of the ancient Bosphorus fishing villages was covered with countless new villas, and my intuition told me that there would be people at this *köfte* party who would love nothing more than to discuss the gossip on Skyrat. It was an opportunity not to be missed.

"Actually, it might be nice," I said. "I've had enough of Beyoğlu nightlife. I think a change would... Could Fofo come with me, perhaps?"

"What are you up to, Kati?" asked Lale darkly.

I can't bear having friends who know me too well. A person's entitled to a few secrets in life, aren't they?

"I'll explain later," I said.

"We can pick you up from somewhere. How would you get there otherwise?"

"Bus, *dolmuş* and taxi—"

"That'll take for ever! We'll collect you from the ferry at Üsküdar."

We left early in the afternoon to go to Sinan's place and, since the weather was fine, we decided to get out of the taxi at Arnavutköy and walk the rest of the way. At exactly three o'clock, we seated ourselves on a bench overlooking the Bosphorus and I called the number Sinan had given us.

"It's ringing," I cried in amazement, wondering if I should start trusting people more.

"See! We should have believed in him," said Fofo.

The phone rang for a long time before cutting off automatically.

"It rang, but he's not picking up," I said.

"Try again. He might not have got to it in time."

I tried a few more times, but there was no response.

"We weren't wrong about him," I said. "Let's get a taxi and go home."

"Do you think it's all right to simply not turn up?"

"We took the trouble to come all this way, and for what, Fofo? Anyway, have you ever come across a detective with good manners? I'd love to know if any detective has ever prearranged a meeting with a suspect like we did."

"But we don't work on conventional principles. We don't invade people's privacy, even if they're suspects, which is why we're liked."

"Liked?"

"Well, we could be. We could make a name for ourselves that way."

"Never mind being liked. We don't have a chance of solving this case, the way things are going. If Sinan is the murderer, of course he's going to avoid meeting us. And he'll get away with it if we behave like polite wimps and leave him alone on the grounds that he might be a little unwell," I said, thinking I sounded perfectly reasonable.

"Fine, then, let's go home. But at least call him one more time," said Fofo.

I tried the number again. It rang for a long time, and then cut off.

"That's it. We're leaving."

While I was trying to explain the meaning of "polite wimp" to Fofo in the taxi, my mobile rang and showed "private number".

"You called me," said a drowsy voice.

"Sinan Bey, is that you?"

"It is."

"We spoke last night and arranged to meet today."

"I've just woken up. I didn't hear the phone."

People with a greater capacity for sleep than me always amaze me.

"We're in a taxi on our way to see you."

"Did I give you the address?"

"No, you didn't, but we've got it anyway," I said.

"Can you come in half an hour to give me time for a shower?" he said, showing no sign of annoyance that we'd managed to get hold of his address.

"Of course," I said. What else was I supposed to say?

We told the taxi driver to turn round and go back to Rumelihisarı, where we sat in a tea garden and gazed at the sea in silence. Not only was I cross that there would be no time to go home and change before meeting Lale and Erol, I felt disinclined to pander to the whims of a celebrity, however handsome he was.

Eventually, we took another taxi. This time, the driver didn't know the area at all and we had difficulty finding the house. After stopping at a corner shop and then a butcher's to ask the way, we finally got out of the taxi at the entrance to a cul-de-sac.

"Sinan was right. It isn't easy to find," I said to Fofo.

"Istanbul taxi drivers even have difficulty finding Taksim Square," commented Fofo.

"Oh, don't start complaining about taxi drivers again, please."

"But I'm right, aren't I?" he said, and rang the doorbell without waiting for me to reply.

The door was opened by a young man who looked a few years younger than Sinan. He was at least as handsome, and wore nothing but a towel around his waist. Fofo was clearly spellbound, so I forced myself to speak.

"We have an appointment with Sinan," I said, my voice sounding a little hoarse.

"Come in. I'm Sinan's brother, Alkan."

"Pleased to meet you," I said with genuine sincerity. After all, I don't encounter such fine specimens every day.

Alkan led us up to the first floor of the narrow-fronted detached house.

"Sit down here, and I'll be back in a moment. I was making coffee," he said, and disappeared downstairs, his towel flapping as he went.

We were in a room containing a sofa and two armchairs squashed between shelves of CDs that lined the walls. Before long, Alkan returned, still with the towel around his waist, carrying two large cups of coffee in his hands.

"I'll just get the milk and sugar."

"Not for me," I said.

"I'd like some," said Fofo.

As Alkan went downstairs again, Fofo bent over and whispered in my ear, "What if his towel were to fall off?"

I gave him a reproachful look. Why do some people become such sex maniacs when they're without a lover?

Alkan returned, this time with sugar in one hand and milk in the other.

"I'll just go and see what Sinan is doing," he said, and disappeared again.

"We've been hanging around here since three o'clock," I said to Fofo, who was happily sipping his coffee without a care in the world.

By the time Sinan appeared, I was ready to lose my temper. It seemed to me that he'd been hoping that we'd simply get up and leave if he made us wait long enough.

"Sorry to have kept you waiting," he said.

"No problem. It doesn't matter at all," said Fofo, still totally enraptured.

To avoid creating unnecessary tension, I refrained from blurting out the words that were on the tip of my tongue.

"Shall we get straight to the point?" said Sinan. "Last night you said you wanted to talk about Sani."

"And you asked us who we were," I said, thinking it was essential to get this out of the way first. "We're working for Sani's family."

My words were not totally untrue. After all, her father had offered to pay us.

"So you're private detectives. But no crime has been committed. I don't understand why the family has hired a private detective."

"Actually, I have a bookshop in Kuledibi," I said, as if I hadn't heard his last sentence, because it seemed wise to wait a little before broaching the matter of murder.

"Kuledibi? Don't tell me you specialize in crime fiction!"

"Are you one of our customers?" said Fofo in disbelief, wondering how such a man could have escaped his attention.

"Not me, but my mother is. She reads a lot of crime fiction, and is probably one of your best customers." Then, raising his voice, he called out, "Alka-an! They own the bookshop that Mama likes."

"Tell me, what does your mother look like?" I asked.

"She's in her fifties, and has blonde hair which she wears in a ponytail. She always wears sunglasses, even when there's no sun," said Sinan.

An image was forming in my mind.

"Does she prefer to read in English?" I asked.

"She generally reads in English because she says most of the crime fiction translated into Turkish is pretty awful."

"Don't tell me your mother is Perihan Hanım!" I said, reflecting that it'd never have occurred to me that, attractive as she was, she could produce two such gorgeous sons.

"That's right. Well done!"

"Perihan Hanım is one of our best customers," I said.

Fofo had still not worked out who she was.

"What's up?" asked Alkan, who had now replaced the towel with a pair of ripped jeans but was still naked above the waist.

"They know Mama. They have the crime fiction bookshop in Kuledibi," said Sinan.

"Kati's the owner. I just work there," said Fofo modestly.

Was he trying to play for sympathy, I wondered?

"Sorry, I've forgotten your name," said Sinan.

"Fofo."

"You have a slight accent. What is it?"

A smart way of asking a person where they come from, I thought.

"I'm Spanish. I came to Istanbul six years ago," said Fofo.

"You've learned to speak wonderful Turkish in six years. That's a real achievement for such a short time."

At this, Fofo puffed up like a turkey and turned to me as if to say, "Hear that?"

"Your relationship with Sani—" I interrupted, not wanting to waste time with small talk after waiting so long.

"I'm curious to know how you found out I was seeing Sani," said Sinan.

"I promised not to reveal the identity of the person who gave me that information."

"I understand," he said with apparent sincerity. "Did that person also say that we'd split up? You can at least tell me that."

"Had you split up?" I asked, instantly realizing this would mean he wasn't the person who'd been with Sani just before she died. Either that, or he was lying.

"We split up on 19 June."

How strange to remember the specific date on which they'd split up. Still, some people are obsessive about such things.

"19 June is my birthday," said Sinan.

I breathed a sigh of relief. After all, no one wants to get involved with an obsessive.

"We'd met at my place that evening. Sani was worried about her husband finding out about us and wouldn't meet anywhere in public, so we always met here. After we'd eaten, she said it was all over, and that was the last time I saw her. I phoned her a few times, but she was very distant with me and I stopped calling."

Unless he was a good actor, he was obviously still angry, or at least offended about being ditched.

"You didn't go to the funeral?" I asked.

"How could I? The media were going to be there and people would have asked what I was doing there. Why would I attend the funeral of a married woman? Sani had never wanted to go public about our relationship. The age difference between us was a bit of an issue for her, but the real problem was that she was married."

"What was the age difference?" I asked, merely out of curiosity because it had no bearing on the investigation.

"Eight years."

That meant he was twenty-five. A man in his prime!

"Sani was always scared. Scared that her husband was having her followed, scared that photos of us together would get out, scared that we'd get caught – scared of everything. She was convinced that her husband would do whatever it took to get out of paying alimony. But actually, she had no need of alimony.

She was so well educated and multitalented that she could have found a job anywhere, any time. But I couldn't persuade her of that. For some reason, she felt very inadequate."

Sinan's portrayal of Sani didn't conform at all to the image I had of her. I'd imagined someone with initiative, who was prepared to fight for her beliefs to the bitter end.

"I was really surprised when I got to know her properly," continued Sinan. "Do you know what I think? I believe everyone's born with a certain amount of fighting spirit, but that if someone is forced to struggle at a young age it can get used up too early. It's as if Sani had lost her ability to fight. She'd grown accustomed to the material benefits provided by her husband and could no longer imagine any other life."

"Yet she didn't want to live with her husband," I said.

"I've no idea what went on in that relationship. She didn't tell me, and I didn't want to know, because I don't like discussing previous relationships. I could tell that Sani had been hurt, but she always kept her lips tightly shut, which was why I was surprised that you'd heard about us. Did she tell her sister?"

I remained silent.

"The secretary at her office saw us together. Maybe she told you."

Again, I remained silent.

"Aren't you going to say anything?"

"I gave my word that I'd say nothing," I said.

There was an uncomfortable silence, which only became worse as I tried to think how we could make our excuses and leave.

"Do you know anyone who might want to kill Sani?" I finally asked.

Sinan leaned back in his armchair and laughed. Alkan looked at his brother and also laughed. Those brothers seemed to know how to enjoy themselves.

"You sound just like someone who reads crime fiction," said Sinan. "Mother is the same. Whoever it is and however a person dies, she always assumes that it's murder. When her aunt of eighty-seven died, Mother was convinced that she'd been poisoned by the man from the corner shop. Even reading about a traffic accident sets her off looking for a sinister motive behind it. And she wonders why we don't read crime fiction!"

"It doesn't seem to occur to her that thoughts like that can actually make you paranoid," said Alkan. "Supposing the husband killed Sani, supposing he was trying to avoid paying alimony, supposing this, supposing that—"

Sinan stared hard at his brother and then turned to us, asking, "Do you suspect her husband?"

"It's common procedure to suspect those closest to a murder victim," I said, sounding like a typical reader of crime fiction. "If you asked your mother, she'd say the same."

"If all the husbands who don't want to pay alimony started killing their wives... Oh no! I don't think Cem Ankaralıgil is the type to commit murder in order to avoid paying out a bit of alimony. However, if Sani took up with someone else after me, and he found out about it... Well, I don't know. Jealousy would at least be a rational explanation."

"Money, jealousy, revenge, broken heart, hurt pride..." I said. "Any of those could be a reason for a person who's been rejected."

"In that case, I must also be on the list of suspects," said Sinan, narrowing his eyes. "I told you myself that Sani had left me."

"I'm not saying that you're on a list of suspects. We're merely talking," I said, thinking that it was hardly polite to accuse a person of murder when you're sitting in his house drinking his coffee.

"Sani upset me, if you really want to know," said Sinan. "I was very unhappy when she left me and I tried to persuade her to give it another go. But killing her or wanting her dead—"

"Yes?" said Fofo expectantly.

"I wasn't that smitten. Not enough to kill her," said Sinan as he paced round the room, his eyes filling with tears.

He seemed very convincing, though I couldn't quite put my finger on why. It certainly wasn't because of his tears, nor his eloquence, which was unusual in a man of twenty-five.

"We should go," I said. "You can call me if anything else occurs to you."

"Sani and I were only together for three months," said Sinan. "When we met, she was about to leave her husband. Everything happened so quickly... and then it was all over."

"How did you meet?" asked Fofo.

Good question, I thought.

"She was working for the same organization as my aunt Aylin. We were asked to do a performance for their organization, which was when we met. Do you know Aylin?"

"We want to talk to her, but apparently she's been abroad. Do you know if she's due back yet?" I said.

"I didn't even know she was away," said Sinan.

Since it was unlikely that we'd learn any more from Sinan or that he knew anything else that could help us, I signalled to Fofo that we should go. However, he appeared to have no inclination to move, and would probably have been quite happy to spend another few days gazing at the two brothers.

"Come on, Fofo, we're invited to a party. We mustn't be late," I said.

"I'm saving your number in my mobile," said Sinan. "I'll call you."

"If you come to the shop, we'll definitely give you a reduction," said Fofo, finally rising to his feet.

At the time, I honestly didn't think there was the slightest probability that Sinan would either phone or call in at the shop.

*

"Well, we didn't learn much, but those two brothers are quite superb. There are few people with looks as good as theirs – including Hollywood stars," said Fofo as we left the house and made our way towards the seafront.

"You're not serious."

"Why not? To me, Brad Pitt looks like an oaf compared to Alkan."

"That's not what I meant," I said. "You said we didn't learn much."

"So what did we learn?"

"If it's true that the husband was having Sani followed, then whoever was following her must know if she was alone when she died. Why didn't Cem say anything to the police?"

"Oh darling, it didn't take long for you to abandon your theory about Ergene industrialists, did it?"

"You know very well that we're still in the process of creating theories. This is just a new one."

"So did you really take that business seriously about her being followed? It's just a cheap trick used by cougars who fall for younger men," said Fofo, shaking his head as if he despaired of me.

"What do you mean? What trick?"

"Our little Sani invented that story to get Sinan excited. She was saying, 'See? Everyone's after me, but I'm giving myself completely to you.' It's a cheap whore's trick, so learn, baby! He was just an infatuated toy boy who thought, 'Wow, what a woman! With a husband like Cem Ankaralıgil still chasing her, she actually chooses me.' Think how exciting it must have been for young Sinan!"

"Fofo, you're terrible!" I cried, laughing out loud.

"Me? I'm terrible? Me?"

"What on earth makes you think up things like that?"

"Sani wasn't so different from me. I know exactly how she'd have gone about ensnaring a man like Sinan," said Fofo. "This hair of mine hasn't turned grey from running after crusty old lawyers like you do."

Fofo disliked my lovers as much as I disliked his, but he had a particular distaste for Selim, whom I'd left the previous year. The barb about "crusty old lawyers" was obviously intended for him.

"All right, all right. Next time, I'll ask for your approval to make sure I fall for someone better than Selim," I said. "Now, listen to my theory."

"I can't concentrate at the moment. The fact that you didn't understand Sani's cheap trick has really thrown me. I need a bit of time to build up my respect for you again."

"Oh, stop being silly!"

"Believe me, I'm serious."

"Fofo, listen!" I shouted in his ear, as he so often did to me.

"Okay, okay. Carry on!"

"If we suppose the husband really was having Sani followed, who else might know about it? Aylin? Naz?"

"Sani probably told her sister. But never mind all that. I told you, the business about her being followed was a lie."

The *köfte* party was in the garden of a house in a complex of nine villas. As expected, the male guests were all accompanied by their wives, children and, in some cases, dogs. Fair enough. After spending a few hours with Sinan and Alkan, the only things I noticed about the men at the barbecue were their expanding waistlines, squeezed into carefully laundered jeans, and their sausage-like fingers.

Also as expected, once the *köfte* were eaten and the children asleep, the women sat around the table discussing Sani, while the men were at the bottom of the garden talking politics and making salacious comments. Fofo stayed inside watching television.

"Did you know Sani Ankaralıgil?" I asked a dark-complexioned woman with an enormous mouth and hair that stood up like a parachute.

"I didn't know her, but Simin told me that that she'd moved here. Her husband knew Sani from Istanbul Technical University."

"I used to say hello to her when I went out jogging in the mornings," said a woman with stylishly cropped hair sitting next to me, the only person there worth looking at, other than Lale and myself, of course. "There's not much opportunity for sports in Paşabahçe, so we all go jogging."

I considered mentioning how Beyoğlu, where I lived, was a mecca for sport lovers. You could indulge in long jump, skating, obstacle courses, steal and run, chase the hooligan... It was all there, whatever your heart desired. However, I didn't want to digress, so I remained silent.

"This isn't a very desirable area. It's too far from the city centre. However, we can get to Levent in twenty minutes via the second bridge."

"But shopping is very difficult, especially with small children," said another woman, leaning over to Parachute Hair and whispering loud enough for everyone to hear, "I heard that Simin's husband used to be Sani Ankaralıgil's lover. Do you think it's true?"

"Really? I've never heard that before," said Parachute Hair. "Have you seen the winter roses in Simin's garden? They're imported. Isn't the way they open out divine?"

Was she intentionally changing the subject?

"Simin's garden is truly magical. I wish she could pass on some of her knowledge to us."

"She's out there every day, planting seeds and cuttings. There's no gardener – she does everything herself," said Parachute.

The subject had changed radically, and I felt a panic come over me.

"Did Sani Ankaralıgil really have a relationship with Simin's husband?" I asked, not caring what anyone else thought.

"Of course she did, darling. They were the talk of the university in those days. It was everyone's idea of 'true love'," said someone else with a short bob which she'd had blow-dried into a most unfashionable style.

"She was a truly beautiful woman," said the woman with cropped hair.

"She'd had too much cosmetic work done for my taste," said Parachute.

"Everyone gets work done these days. Even Demi Moore's had her knees lifted," said someone else.

The ladies glanced surreptitiously at each other's knees. I was glad that there'd been no time to change out of my cargo pants. Life was full of surprises! Who'd have thought that I'd be pleased by something like that?

"My stomach was quite deformed after the second birth. It was a Caesarean." said the hostess.

"Darling! You call that deformed?" said a size twenty blonde sitting to the right of Parachute.

"Stomach operations are very risky," said Lale, who of course knows everything.

"Operations don't carry risks if the surgeon's good," said Parachute.

"The main thing is to be at peace with oneself," said Size Twenty and, thinking she'd been ignored, added, "Fat is beautiful."

"Who is Simin?" I asked in a low voice so that only the woman with the cropped hair sitting next to me could hear.

"Simin and Orhan Soner are a couple. Don't you know them? Orhan Soner is one of our best-known architects. He built the blue skyscraper in Levent, the Venus Hotel in Bodrum and the Zeugma Museum building in Antep. They live around here," she said, indicating the roof of a nearby house. "Why do you ask?"

"Her name came up and I just wondered."

"Everyone watches everyone here. It's like a village."

"Is Sani Ankaralıgil's house here too?"

"You can't see it from here," said Cropped Hair, sitting up and looking towards the Soners' house. "But Sani lived opposite Simin and Orhan. Most of the houses on that side are vacant. Apparently, there was a construction problem and they didn't sell, so a number of them are rented out. Sani lived in one of those."

"It seems odd that, of all the places in Istanbul, she should move to a house opposite that of a former lover," I commented.

"Do you think so?"

"Don't you find it strange?"

"The past is the past. They had an affair and it was over. I'm on friendly terms with some of my previous lovers. Why hate someone you've been so close to?"

I didn't ask whether Cropped Hair's husband was on friendly terms with her previous lovers, because it was irrelevant. Instead, I merely said, "If the affair is over for both parties then what you say is true, but it isn't always like that."

"I wonder if Orhan was still in love with Sani. Or she with him? We'll never know now," said Cropped Hair.

We didn't know, but I could always find out.

7

"What do you know about your sister's love life?" I asked, as our latte macchiatos arrived.

Naz and I had taken refuge in a café to escape the crowds of men who made a habit of strutting around on Sundays. Every day was crowded in Beyoğlu, but the sight of these Sunday males was scary enough to make the cranes, trucks and diggers that wrought havoc on other days in İstiklal Street seem quite welcome. For one thing, the men never operated alone. Taking courage from each other like ancient warriors, they'd set out on the prowl in groups of at least three, pestering any single women they encountered, no matter what their age. They'd come to Karaköy by bus from outlying neighbourhoods, visit the brothels in our area and then go to wash in the hammam at the end of the street. Then they'd set out in high spirits, pushing and shoving each other, to ogle, assault and terrorize the women in İstiklal Street.

These men took no interest in the beautiful old architecture, the hidden courtyards and alleys, or the sea views that could be glimpsed between tall buildings. They were like strangers who stuck to main roads and never strayed into side streets for fear of getting lost. Whenever they encountered a woman unaccompanied by a man – for them a joke in itself – they'd stop shoving each other and focus their interest on the woman, making lewd comments, supposedly among themselves but loud enough for her to hear. By dark, they'd be on the bus home, where they held themselves responsible for the honour of their mothers, sisters and wives.

"Why do you want to know about my sister's love life?" asked Naz.

"I'm trying to find out everything there is to know in the hope of finding a clue that will lead us to a solution, however unlikely it may be," I said.

That's what happens in crime fiction, isn't it? In fiction, you never find a murderer tearfully owning up to a crime as soon as it's been committed.

"Do you know Orhan Soner?" I asked.

"Sure," she said, avoiding eye contact with me.

Why did she shrink from talking about her sister's ex-lover, if it was all in the past? And, even if she found the subject difficult, why was she unable to hide her discomfort from me? I was only a curious amateur detective. I felt sure that if only I could have fired my questions at her through a haze of cigarette smoke, I'd have got answers more quickly. However, nicotine withdrawal meant that my head wasn't as clear as it once was. Not a permanent effect, hopefully.

"Orhan was the love of her life. No one thought they would ever split up," said Naz.

"Why did they?"

"After Sani graduated, she was offered a scholarship in America. Orhan wanted to stay in Istanbul because he'd found a job with a good firm of architects, but he followed her over there. Sani's scholarship wasn't enough for two people to live on, so Orhan spent a long time looking for work and finally took a job as a petrol-pump attendant, which he hated. He couldn't stand it for long and came back after six months, on the assumption that Sani would be returning soon afterwards, but she didn't. Orhan was in a bad way at that time," said Naz, still not looking directly at me. "That's why they separated."

"So that's the great love story."

"If Sani had given up everything to be with Orhan, it would have been a betrayal of all that she'd worked for," said Naz.

I didn't like to ask what Naz would have done, because I had the impression that had she been in that situation she'd have sacrificed everything, and women like that frightened me. Weren't we all impotent in the face of women prepared to give up everything for love? Or was I just turning into an old romantic?

"Did you know that her house in Paşabahçe was directly opposite Orhan Soner's?"

"Is that so?" said Naz.

Did I imagine it, or did her voice tremble? I found it strange that she knew so little about her sister, but of course not all siblings are close friends.

"Do you think it's possible that she and Orhan had rekindled their affair?"

"Don't ask me," said Naz. "Sani could be very unpredictable."

"Even when it came to love affairs?"

"She was like that about everything. Some people are consistent, but Sani wasn't. She insisted on doing her PhD in America, even though it meant leaving Orhan, whom she claimed to love so much. Then, a few years later, she gave everything up to be with Cem and decided to become a housewife. Why she decided to divorce Cem, I've no idea. It was all very sudden. I couldn't keep up with her love life, or the decisions she took."

I remembered what Sinan had said about her the previous day. It seemed that he was right when he said that once Sani had finished her doctorate her fighting spirit came to an end too. She no longer wanted to work, struggle and wear herself out.

"Do you know someone called Sinan?" I asked.

"No. Who's Sinan?" said Naz.

"Sani was with him for a while. It started when she was about to leave Cem."

"Are you suggesting that she decided to divorce Cem because of Sinan? How did you find that out?"

"It's my job to find out everything."

"Sani didn't talk about Sinan to me. She wouldn't—" said Naz, as if talking to herself.

"Her closest friend was Aylin, yes? Perhaps she discussed these kinds of things with her."

"I very much doubt it. I don't think she spoke to anyone. You didn't know Sani."

"But she must have told someone. Everybody confides their secrets to someone."

"Well, if she did, I don't know who it would have been," said Naz. "Aylin was a friend of Cem's too, so Sani would have been crazy to confide in her. Anyway, Sani was a closed book when it came to relationships. She never discussed them or gave a hint as to what was going on. You could spend twenty-four hours a day with her and still know nothing about her personal life. It was the same when she was little. She never gave anything away, just used to write everything down in a diary."

"A diary? Why didn't you say so before?" I said excitedly. "Maybe she was still writing it."

"That's something you do as a child," said Naz, pursing her lips. "Why would a grown woman waste time keeping a diary?"

"Have you ever kept a diary?"

"I started a few times, but always got bored after a day. It's not for me."

"I've never kept one either. But it can become a real compulsion, and I don't mean just for children. It can go on for a lifetime," I said, thinking of Patricia Highsmith's famous diaries, which were supposed to have measured thirty metres when all the volumes were placed side by side.

"You mean it becomes a habit?"

"Habit or compulsion. One or the other. But some people keep a diary all their lives."

"Actually, I've just thought of something," said Naz, tilting her head up and looking at the ceiling. "She might indeed have been keeping a diary."

"What makes you think that?"

"After Orhan came back from America and before Sani met Cem, she was very lonely for a while. She didn't really know anyone in America, or at least didn't warm to those she did know. We used to write to each other at the time. In one of her emails, she said something like 'I've nothing to put in my diary. Every day is spent either working in the library or asleep at home.' When I read that, I remember being amazed that she still kept a diary."

"Which year was that?"

"Six or seven years ago. It wasn't recent."

"Nevertheless, it seems she was still keeping a diary as an adult. Do you have her door key with you?"

"Are you asking if we can go to Sani's house?"

"I'm not asking. We're going there."

We went by metro as far as Levent and from there by taxi to Paşabahçe. By the time we reached the housing complex, Naz was obviously feeling badly on edge.

"Perhaps we should find the nightwatchman first," she said.

"Once we have the nightwatchman on to us, we'll never get away from him. Let's find the house first."

The housing complex was on top of a hill. It consisted of seven villas situated around a large swimming pool. Signs of life were visible in only three of the villas; the others looked very empty, which confirmed what I'd heard the previous night.

"This is the one," said Naz, stopping in front of the villa nearest to the main road.

An official notice with a red seal was wedged between the door and door frame, stating that breaking the seal and entering would incur a penalty. I'd secretly entered sealed-off places before, as my dear readers will know. However, this door was visible to any passer-by, and also to the Soners opposite. It was a greater risk than I was prepared to take.

"What should we do? Find the nightwatchman?" asked Naz.

Why did she keep going on about the nightwatchman?

"He's not likely to let us in, and it's better if we don't linger here staring at the door," I said, heading towards the side of the house. "Is there only one way into this enormous house? Isn't there a back door?"

"I don't know. I only came here once before, when my parents stayed with Sani for a few days and I came to collect them," said Naz. "Anyway, if there's another door it'll be sealed off too."

"Let's look round the back," I said.

We both smiled upon seeing that the back door wasn't sealed. Batuhan, bless him, had clearly been doing wonders with this investigation!

"Let's just hope that Sani gave my father a key to this door."

While Naz tried each of the keys she was holding, I looked to see if we'd been noticed, but everything was as silent as before – no twitching curtains, no opened windows and no neighbours' voices. One of the keys finally fitted the lock, and we breathed a sigh of relief.

We went through a hallway into a completely vacant sitting room that overlooked the street and the sea.

"She lived upstairs," said Naz. "Downstairs was always empty."

Naz clutched my arm, as if my presence gave her strength, as we went up the stairs to the first floor. In a sitting room, we saw the outline of how Sani's body had been positioned on the wooden floor. Remains of the black dust used to take fingerprints were sprinkled over the furniture. A heavy smell pervaded the airless room. Was it the smell of death? It was certainly unbearable.

One part of the spacious sitting room was raised slightly to give a better view of the Bosphorus. The position in which the corpse had been found suggested that Sani had hit her head on the steps leading to this raised area.

"Ouch," I winced, as Naz tightened her fingers on my arm like a vice.

"Sorry, sorry," she repeated a few times and drew her hand away, immediately swaying as if unable to remain upright without my assistance.

"Do you want some water?" I said, taking her arm.

"No, I'm all right."

"You go and sit down. Remember, we mustn't touch anything."

"I'm fine," said Naz, making her way towards the desk, where the drawers had been opened and their contents neatly lined up, obviously to be photographed. Scattered across the desk were other items, presumably from Sani's handbag, which included a lipstick, hand mirror, cigarettes, lighter, black fountain pen and a half-full bottle of perfume. The police must have removed the handbag and any other items that might be evidence, so even if she'd kept a diary, it was long gone.

"What did the diary look like?" I asked.

"When Sani was little, she wrote in a little pink notebook. An uncle in Istanbul bought it for her. But I've no idea what she would have been using recently."

"Didn't you tell me that she never wrote anything by hand and claimed to have difficulty even signing her name? Was that you?"

"What do you mean?" asked Naz, shaking her head from side to side absent-mindedly.

"I'm asking if you're quite sure that she kept a handwritten diary."

"Are you suggesting that she wrote it on her laptop?" said Naz, still staring at the desk.

"Well, why not?" I asked.

Naz swayed again, and I caught her hand as she reached out to grab the desk.

"We mustn't touch anything," I said. "Might there be any rubber gloves in the kitchen?"

Naz didn't reply, so I took her arm and led her into the kitchen, which was immaculate and showed no sign of ever having being used to cook a meal. A toaster, an espresso machine and two small cups stood on the worktop. We stood motionless in the middle of the kitchen, our arms still linked, while I summoned up the courage to ask my next question.

"Let's get out of here," said Naz, disengaging her arm and turning towards the stairs.

"No!" I said. "Take a look at this."

"What is it?" said Naz, stopping at the top of the stairs.

"Do you know how this espresso machine works?"

"Are you saying you want an espresso?" asked Naz, as if it was the most unimaginable request for anyone to make. Perhaps at that moment, in the house of a dead person whose effects we were examining, she was right.

"Do you think Sani put those cups out to make coffee for two?" I asked, pointing to the cups standing next to the coffee machine.

"Hmm, I wonder why there are two out," replied Naz, who seemed to have recovered slightly.

"Look and see if she put enough coffee into the machine for two. But first we need to find some gloves."

"It has nothing to do with how much coffee you put in the machine. You just put another capsule in for each cup."

"How do you mean? I don't understand."

"Each cup is made separately. You put a capsule in and turn the machine on, then discard the empty capsule, put another in and press the button again."

"Hmm. But there are two cups. Is there no way of finding out if Sani was going to make two cups of coffee?"

Naz shook her head.

"Where did she keep the capsules?" I asked.

"I don't know," said Naz.

"How do you know how this machine works?"

"I have the same model."

Why didn't I know anything about these espresso machines, when everyone else seemed to be using them?

"Let's just check the other rooms before we go," I said.

"I need to sit down for a bit. You go and look," said Naz.

"All right, but don't touch anything. The police might come back to look for more fingerprints."

I looked in the bedroom, bathroom and the empty rooms on the top floor. If anything had escaped the attention of the police, I couldn't find it. When I returned to the sitting room, Naz was sitting cross-legged on the floor.

"Did you find anything?" she asked.

I shook my head and asked, "Why are you sitting like that?"

Naz handed me a tiny yellow metal item shaped like a narrow-brimmed bowler hat. The top of a bottle, perhaps?

"Where did you find this?" I asked, examining the item closely.

"It was stuck between one of the desk legs and the wall. I saw it when I sat down."

"It's probably the top of a bottle."

"It's a very elegant bottle top," said Naz.

I held the item to my nose, as I did with everything I picked up. It smelled of perfume, a mixture of spices and flowers.

"It must be the top of a perfume bottle," I said. "Sani obviously liked heavy perfumes."

It smelled very similar to the Guerlain Samsara perfume that was on the desk.

"Let's go now," I said, holding out my hand to Naz to help her up.

"While we're here, why don't we call in on the neighbours?" I suggested, while checking that the door was properly shut.

"Which neighbours?" said Naz.

"Orhan and Simin Soner. Their house is just opposite, so it's possible that they saw—" I said hesitantly.

"No," interrupted Naz. "I don't want to call on them."

"But their house is just here. A couple of paces away."

"No!"

Naz clearly didn't want me to pursue the matter, but why? Was she still angry with Orhan for coming back to Turkey and leaving her sister in America? That was all very well, but, having come all the way to Paşabahçe, I'd really hoped to see more than a couple of espresso cups.

"We were going to speak to the nightwatchman," I said.

"Okay," said Naz. "Let's talk to him."

"Do you know which his house is?"

"It can't be far."

"The person in the corner shop will know," I said.

We entered a rather sleazy shop where a young woman was sitting in front of an array of alcoholic beverages, which I found surprising. It was certainly not a scene you'd find in the slum districts of Istanbul.

"A corner shop selling alcohol! Even Kuledibi only has one of those," I remarked, as we followed the woman's directions to the nightwatchman's hut.

"It's like that in the hills above Paşabahçe," said Naz. "Can you smell it in the air?"

It was impossible to miss. The air was filled with the scent of aniseed from a nearby *rakı* factory that had recently closed. I yearned for a glass of ice-cold *rakı*.

"Islamists don't like living right next to a *rakı* factory, so this area is mostly inhabited by liberal types," said Naz.

"You're joking!"

"It's no joke. Anyway, that's what I was told. And it makes sense. If it's a sin to drink alcohol, why should inhaling it be any different?"

"Do you know this man?" I whispered, as Naz went to knock on the door of the shack that we'd been directed to by the woman in the shop.

"No. Why would I? As I said, I only visited Sani's once before, when I came to pick up my parents."

A woman who was presumably the nightwatchman's wife opened the door. She appeared to be in her mid-fifties. However, the daily grind of living took its toll on women like her, who were usually a good ten years younger than they looked. I guessed she was about forty-five.

The woman stared at us, and tucked in the ends of her headscarf.

"I'm Sani Ankaralıgil's sister," said Naz.

"I knew you looked like someone, but couldn't work it out. Don't you look like her? Come in, don't stand there on the doorstep."

We removed our shoes and placed them on a piece of newspaper laid on the floor next to the front door.

"It's nearly Ramadan, so we're all in a rush. Sorry," said the woman.

"We should be apologizing for turning up at your door out of the blue."

"Not at all. Sincere condolences, my dear."

We entered a largish room with a stove in the centre around which a few cushions had been neatly placed. The enormous wall-mounted plasma TV screen – at least one hundred centimetres wide – was probably the most expensive thing in the house. Actually, if I'd owned one, it would have been the most costly item in my apartment too. But that's another matter.

"Shall I light the stove?" asked the woman.

"It's not cold," I said.

"I'll make some tea. Our youngest daughter-in-law is usually here to do it, but she went to visit an uncle today."

"Please don't bother yourself on our account," said Naz.

I was dying for some tea, but I said nothing.

"You must let me serve you some tea," said the woman, ignoring Naz.

"My condolences," said the woman again when she returned a few minutes later. "Sani Hanım was so young and pretty. They say she fell and hit her head or something."

"I understand that it was your husband who found her?"

"That's right, he did. I wasn't here. I go and clean for an old lady in Kandilli on Thursdays. Been going there for years. She won't let anyone else touch her things."

"Did your husband go into Sani's house alone, then?"

"Aylin Hanım phoned him and told him to go and take a look. I keep a set of Sani Hanım's keys, but I never leave anything lying around. My children and grandchildren always come to me if they lose something. Their keys went missing last year and my eldest son bought me a mobile so they can phone me whenever they lose something. Anyway, when my hubby went into Sani Hanım's house, he saw her lying on the floor and ran straight out without touching a thing. The police told him he did the right thing not to touch anything. He's a wise old thing, my hubby. Had no education, but always knows what to do. Nobody believes he's just a nightwatchman. People ask him who got him that job, but nobody got it for him. We don't know people who can get anyone a job. It's just that he's good at everything he does."

"Which days did you go to clean at Sani's?"

"Tuesdays and Fridays were Sani Hanım's days. Mondays and Wednesdays I go to Sibel Hanım, and then over to Kandilli on Thursdays. The rest of the time, I take care of my grand-children."

This meant she'd been cleaning at Sani's on the day of her death.

"Had you been on that Tuesday?"

"Of course. Just the same as always. I even kept going when I had toothache for weeks."

"Did you see Sani that day?"

"Sani Hanım said she didn't want me hanging around, so I never got there too early. But it was a lot of work for one, and I'd be there till evening."

"What time did you leave that Tuesday?"

"I left at dusk."

What did she mean by dusk?

"Did you see Sani before you left?"

"No, she was never back that early."

"When would she normally come back?"

"Never before evening prayers, but sometimes in time for night prayers."

The woman obviously measured her days by the calls to prayer. But how was I supposed to know what time they were?

"What time are evening prayers said?" I whispered to Naz.

"About half past six at the moment, I think," replied Naz.

"Yes, that's it. About half past six," said the woman. "Near enough, anyway."

The days were of course getting slightly shorter every day, so when Sani died, evening prayers were probably recited a little after seven.

"So you didn't speak to Sani that Tuesday, but did you see her come home that night?"

"I saw her light on."

"Was that after evening prayers?"

"Yes. It was late and I saw the light on my way home. That Tuesday, we'd called in on my eldest daughter-in-law, who'd just come back from her mother's village. On our way home, I saw Sani Hanım's light on. When I got up for morning prayers, I saw the light was still on. I went to my husband and..."

"Yes?" I said, encouragingly.

"It was the same on Wednesday night. And the light was still on when I got up in the morning."

"But you don't know if she was alone or not," I said. "Did Sani have a friend with her when she returned on Tuesday evening?"

"Good gracious, no!" said the woman, looking as offended as if I'd cast a slur on Sani's honour. "We've never seen her with any sort of 'friend'. She was pure as they come. But a single woman is an easy target for gossip, even after death. I swear by almighty God, I never saw her with a friend, or with anyone else."

"But you can't possibly see everything," said Naz.

"Indeed I do, as God is my witness," said the woman.

"Okay, but when you saw the light was still on on Thursday morning, why didn't you do anything?" I asked, paying little attention to her claim, which I assumed to be mere words.

"Of course we did something. My hubby phoned Cem Bey."

"Your husband called Cem Bey?" I asked with surprise, since it was the first I'd heard of this.

"That's right, he called Cem Bey."

"Did you know anything about this?" I asked Naz, who was looking as surprised as I was.

"And while I was at work," continued the woman, "Aylin Hanım phoned my hubby and told him to go and take a look."

"But you phoned Cem first, yes?"

"That's right. We phoned him. That is, my hubby did."

"But how did you know Cem's phone number?"

"He gave it to us."

So Cem had given his phone number to his soon-to-be-divorced wife's nightwatchman. That didn't seem like normal behaviour to me, but it had certainly proved to be useful.

"When did he give it to you?" I asked.

"He came here, just like you did today, and had some tea," said the woman. "He gave us his phone number, which my hubby said was a mobile number. He says Cem Bey's a very powerful man who could get a job for our youngest boy, if he felt inclined. Our boy works in a button factory, but his wages aren't good enough."

"Why did Cem give you his number?" I asked.

"Well, you see, I stand at the window when I'm cooking. I'd never impose on my daughter-in-law. I tell her she'll have plenty of time to cook when she's got a place of her own. Anyway, I don't like other people's cooking. Everyone has their own ideas when it comes to how much salt or oil to use."

I felt my stomach contract.

"Can you see Sani's door from your kitchen?" I asked.

"When I look out of the kitchen window, her door is right opposite. Cem Bey told me to keep an eye on everyone who goes in and out. You know how women who live alone always have people chasing after them, especially if they're young and pretty like her."

"So you're saying that Cem Bey gave you his number so that you could phone him if you saw anyone going in or coming out of Sani's house. Is that right, or have I got it wrong?"

"Yes, that's right."

"Can I take a look out of your kitchen window?" I asked.

"Come," said the woman, placing a hand on her knee to support herself as she rose from her cushion.

It was true. Sani's door was certainly visible, and from a very good angle. While the woman was busy making tea, I went back to Naz and asked, "Why do you think Cem made a pact with these people to keep an eye on Sani?"

Naz's eyes were filling up.

"Only the front door is visible from the kitchen, so she wouldn't have seen anyone going in through the back door that we used," I said.

"Maybe he hired someone else to monitor the back door. Do you think she was paid to do this?" asked Naz.

"Not her, perhaps, but I bet that capable husband of hers was," I remarked.

"Are you going to talk to her husband?"

"The police have already spoken to him. Anyway, we've learned all we need to know."

"In that case, let's go," said Naz.

The woman returned with a plate in her hand.

"I made some pastries for our pre-dawn breakfast. Stay and have some while the tea's brewing," she said.

"We have to go," said Naz.

"But you can't. The tea's not ready yet."

"Sorry, we can't stay for tea," said Naz, rushing to put on her shoes and hurling herself out into the street as if being chased by wild horses.

We returned to the back door of Sani's house. From here, all that could be seen was an empty building opposite and a villa that stood to one side, with net curtains at the windows.

"Let's go and ask the people living in that house," I said.

"Do you think they might be Cem's agents?"

I wasn't thinking about Cem's agents. I wanted to find out if anyone had been seen entering or leaving the house between Tuesday evening and Thursday noon. An eyewitness would make our work much easier.

An elderly but fit-looking lady with an elfin haircut opened the door.

"Hello, I'm Sani Ankaralıgil's sister, Naz Kaya."

"God rest her soul. My sincere condolences," said the lady.

"Thank you."

"If you have time, we'd like to ask you a few questions," I said.

"A police officer came here the day after it happened, and I told him everything I know," said the lady.

"We won't take up much of your time, if you wouldn't mind—"

"Not at all, of course. I didn't mean... Oh, please come in."

The layout of the house was the same as Sani's. We went towards the raised area of the sitting room, which was furnished with some rugs, a sofa and a couple of armchairs.

"Leyla Kantar," said the woman, holding out her hand.

We introduced ourselves.

"Can I offer you anything?" she asked.

"We won't be staying long," I said, thinking I didn't want to have to abandon any more freshly brewed tea.

"My husband's in his workshop. Excuse me, I'll just call him," she said. "He'll be more help to you than I will."

"I doubt if these people are Cem's agents," said Naz, when Leyla left the room.

"But they might have seen something," I said.

Leyla soon returned, carrying a tray with four glasses and a bottle of wine.

"I didn't ask if you preferred red or white, but they say a few glasses of red each day are good for you. We've made it a habit to round off the day with some red wine while we enjoy this beautiful view. Only since we've been retired, of course. It was never possible while we were working."

"So you're retired," I said, wanting to ask about her former employment yet aware that middle-class Turks didn't care for such curiosity.

"I retired two years ago," she said.

"And I run a bookshop," I said, hoping that she would reciprocate by telling us what her former job was.

"What a lovely occupation. If you ever need any staff, you know where I am," said Leyla.

We all laughed at the idea of this lady serving behind the counter in a bookshop.

"I never had the opportunity to read before retirement, but now I constantly have my nose in a book. I've always loved reading, but when you're working so hard—"

"Where did you work?" I asked, unable to resist any longer.

"I'm a paediatrician, and my husband's a surgeon."

Why was there constant talk about doctors being brought in from abroad when the country seemed to be teeming with them?

"I'm a cardiologist. I graduated from Cerrahpaşa," said Naz.

"We studied at Çapa. Of course, it's a long time since we graduated," said Leyla.

"Are you telling them about our past adventures?" said a tall thin man who had just entered.

"Gani Kantar," he said, shaking our hands so vigorously that our arms almost fell off. "My wife tells me you're Sani's sister. We were extremely sad to hear what happened."

"Thank you," said Naz.

"I expect you think we might have seen something, but—"

"Did you?" I blurted out, unable to stop myself interrupting these well-mannered people because I had more important things on my mind than observing the rules of etiquette.

"Well, we didn't say anything to the police because we didn't think it right to rake over the poor lady's life if there was no suspicion of murder," said Gani.

"It's true that the police don't suspect murder. However, it might well be treated as a suspicious death," I said.

"Really?" said Gani, turning towards his wife with a thoughtful look.

Was he worried because he hadn't told the police whatever it was they knew?

Gani turned back to Naz and said, "If she was your sister, you must have received a copy of the autopsy report from the district attorney's office."

It hadn't even occurred to us that this was normal procedure.

"Yes, I have a copy of the autopsy report," said Naz.

"The press kept saying it was an accident, but we... What was the actual cause of death?" asked Gani.

"They say her death was the result of a pre-existing illness," said Naz.

Gani raised his eyebrows, lit a cigarette and said, "What they mean is that they found nothing in the autopsy."

"How do you think she might have died?" I asked, pleased to finally have the chance to speak to an experienced doctor.

What a stroke of luck, when we'd only come to ask if they'd seen anything!

"It could have been anything. She could even have died of a heart attack that didn't show up in the pathological analysis," said Gani, adding politely, "Of course, Naz Hanım would know about that better than I do."

146

I wished he'd addressed me, because Naz didn't seem to know anything.

"There was a needle mark on her arm," said Naz. "But no poisons or narcotics were found in her blood or urine."

"That doesn't mean anything. In my time, they used to look for up to forty different poisonous substances at the Forensic Medicine Institute. That number must have increased to about forty-five by now. They look for the most commonly used poisons. However, a poison that hadn't been used in Turkey, or at least not used in the last fifty years, would be impossible to identify in a routine forensic investigation. For example, the Institute's routine investigations wouldn't cover a poison obtained from the root of a plant grown in Africa. In such a case, the report would state that the person died from a pre-existing illness. That way, they'd be covered, even if the cause of death was an unidentified poison."

Marvellous, I thought, as I'm sure you did too.

"Are you saying that she could have been poisoned?" I asked.

"No. All I'm saying is that, as the lady said, a needle mark on the arm always looks suspicious," said Gani.

Naz hadn't said any such thing, but Gani was trying to be polite.

"None of this had occurred to me," said Naz, looking down at the floor.

"That's perfectly normal," said Leyla. "You're in shock because you've lost someone very dear to you. It's impossible to see details clearly when you're still experiencing the pain of bereavement. Even someone familiar with the system is incapable of absorbing all the facts when they're grieving."

Leyla's little speech was as comforting to me as it was to Naz. After all, if my colleague was so out of touch with the way things worked, then it was better to be able to attribute her failings to grief.

"But the report said nothing about—" muttered Naz.

"That's what forensic reports are like if they're not backed up by a police investigation. There's nothing abnormal about it. You can't eliminate any possibilities with that report," said Gani.

So we were back where we started. If we couldn't eliminate any possibilities, how were we supposed to reach a conclusion?

"If a murder has been committed." Gani paused and turned to his wife with a mischievous look. "Leyla will tell you that it's no simple matter solving a murder."

"I read a lot of crime fiction. That's why he said that," said Leyla.

"I love crime fiction too," I said. "Gani, you were about to say that you saw something suspicious, I believe."

"I don't know if it was suspicious, but when you said it wasn't an accident that killed Sani, I wished I'd said something to the police," he said.

"Why don't you tell us?" I said.

"It may have nothing to do with Sani Hanım's death," said Gani.

"Quite possibly," I said. "But tell us all the same."

"Well, we're old and don't sleep like we used to. I usually get up early and go straight down to my workshop. I used to see Sani go out jogging several times a week. On the Sunday before she died, I saw her coming back from her run. I didn't know her well, but we'd exchange greetings if we saw each other. That morning, she didn't see me—"

"But you saw her return from her run," I said.

"Yes. Earlier, I'd noticed a Mercedes A-Class parked on the pavement. I'm interested in cars, and they've only recently started importing that model," said Gani. "Anyway, I was taking a good look at it, from a distance, of course, and saw someone sitting at the wheel."

"All this makes it sound as if we're constantly engaged in idle snooping," said Leyla.

"It was nothing like that, my dear. It was just something I happened to see," said Gani calmly.

"Then what happened? Sani returned from her run... There was someone sitting at the wheel of the car—" I said, my impatience rising.

"The person got out of the car when he saw Sani return. He appeared to be young," said Gani. "Sani looked annoyed to see him. They talked for a while, but I couldn't hear what was said because our windows were closed. However, I could tell from Sani's face that she was upset. Then a quarrel broke out, or rather Sani pushed the young man away. He didn't respond, but I felt a need to intervene at this point. By the time I got outside, though, Sani Hanım was going back into her house and the Mercedes had disappeared."

"Do you think it was her husband?"

"I've seen pictures of her husband in the papers and I don't think it was him. Even though the young man had his back to me most of the time, I saw his face as he got out of the car."

"We don't want to lay suspicion on anyone," intervened Leyla.

"I think Cem Bey is about thirty-five," said Naz.

"Yes," I confirmed.

"This was someone younger," said Gani. "You could tell from the way he dressed. He was wearing trousers a bit like yours."

"Was he tall, with a light complexion?"

"I couldn't say. He was quite a long way away."

"Can you tell us exactly where he was parked?" I asked, wondering why the nightwatchman's wife knew nothing about this.

"There's a better view of the street from my workshop downstairs, but come over here," said Gani, leading me to the floor-to-ceiling picture window. "Do you see that fig tree? He was parked just behind it. I couldn't say if the Mercedes was there before I went down to my workshop, but I know it was parked there for at least twenty minutes."

"Do you have an Internet connection here?" I asked.

"Unfortunately we don't have ADSL yet. We do get the Internet, but it's a bit slow," said Gani.

"I want to show you some photos," I said.

"Please, sit down. I'll open up the computer," said Gani.

Five minutes later, we were looking at the photos I'd found on Google Images.

"Mmm, he resembled that young man. I couldn't swear to it, but—" said Gani, adjusting his spectacles.

"You couldn't swear to it, but what?"

"I think it was him."

"Thank you," I said. "You've been very helpful."

And indeed he had. If nothing else, he'd exposed a lie. He was a good man, who had no reason to lie about something so insignificant. Maybe our little encounter was less insignificant than I'd expected.

8

I opened up the shop on Monday, as usual. After half an hour of drinking tea and browsing the Internet, I began to feel imprisoned inside my lovely little shop. It was still too early for customers, who after all were not likely to have dreamt about buying books. It was also the first day of Ramadan.

Undoubtedly everyone at some time or other has found the walls of their comfortable home or office begin to cave in on them. I noticed that the barber next door was sitting in the street outside his shop. It wasn't something I'd ever done before, but that day I decided to follow his example.

"*Selamünaleyküm*," said two swarthy moustached men as they passed by.

Each of the men carried an enormous *davul* drum and wore an ugly, faded beige jacket that looked as if it had been pulled out of a sack and a tie that resembled a halter.

"And to you," I said, not feeling in the mood to respond with "*aleykümselam*".

"We're Ramadan drummers," said one of the men, pressing a flyer into my hand. "If anyone else comes round to collect tips, don't give them anything, miss."

No drummer who woke me up first thing in the morning would get a penny out of me, even if he were my own brother. However, it wasn't a fact I felt the need to broadcast. The men moved on and I glanced at their flyer, which showed photocopied headshots of the two of them.

It read:

"Dear residents of Bereketzade, we are the same Ramadan *davul* players you see every year. But please pay attention. In recent years, imposters with no knowledge of how to play the *davul* have been coming here, using our name and the flyers you have in your hands. They have falsely claimed to be our relatives and members of a group with our name, and have pocketed the money so kindly donated by your good selves. We are a duo, as you see in the photo on this flyer. Please do not hand over money to anyone other than us when we come to you with our *davul*s. You can ask the district mayor, governor or police for authentication. Thank you for your attention. God bless you during Ramadan."

Noticing me smile as I read the flyer, a girl from a nearby gift shop approached me, presumably having taken sitting outside as a sign that I wanted company.

"Isn't it forbidden to play the *davul* in Beyoğlu?" she asked.

"I've no idea," I said, because I didn't keep track of changes to regulations about drumming during Ramadan.

"Does anyone still rely on the *davul* to wake up in the morning?"

"I've no idea," I said again.

The truth was that I avoided getting involved in discussions about Turkish traditions. If you were a foreigner, or even a member of a minority, it was best to know where to toe the line and keep quiet when it came to sensitive topics, like cultural or religious traditions. What would happen if Turks in Germany criticized the shopping hysteria that began so many months before Christmas, or bemoaned the impossibility of finding a café or bar open on Christmas Eve?

"Anyone who wants to get up for their pre-dawn breakfast during Ramadan should just set their alarm," complained the shop girl. "There's no need to wake those who aren't fasting, is there?"

"Well, Ramadan does give the unemployed an opportunity to do a bit of paid work," I said, still determined to say nothing against the Ramadan *davul* and its players. "The *davul* players are either Romanians or unemployed people who come into the city from outlying regions during Ramadan. Is it such a bad thing if they manage to fill a few bellies?"

I could see that my populist stance was offending the young shop girl.

"It's just noise pollution. Since when has banging a drum with a mallet been called playing the *davul*? I've heard that in some districts players have to audition to get a licence. That'd make them improve."

It was the first time I'd heard this.

"You mean they get marked on their *davul* playing?" I asked.

"I'm just telling you what I've read in the papers. But if it's true, it'd put an end to these mallet-wielding *davul* players."

I remained silent. The girl hovered around a bit longer but then left, realizing I wasn't in a sociable mood that day.

Naz phoned at about noon.

"Haven't you left for Lüleburgaz yet?" I asked.

"Aylin got back on Thursday. I'm meeting her at four. Have you got time to come too?"

"Where?" I asked immediately. Of course I had time!

"At the Nişantaşı Brasserie."

If your brain has been tainted by prejudicial ideas about Turks, I'd recommend spending a few hours at the Nişantaşı Brasserie if you find yourself in Istanbul. You have to go properly dressed, of course. I'd certainly have to change out of my uniform of cargo pants and trainers if I didn't want a doorman to grab me by the scruff of the neck and throw me out like a drowned kitten.

Fofo had come in after I'd gone to bed the previous night. I phoned the apartment, but he was still asleep. Great! The person who'd brought this whole business down on my head was loafing about in bed.

"Where are you, Fofo? You're supposed to be at the shop by ten o'clock on Mondays! And where were you last night?"

"Had a bit too much to drink last night. I'm on my way," he mumbled.

I shouted at him a bit more, and within fifteen minutes he was in the shop, obviously having rushed out without even washing his face.

"What do you mean by turning up at this hour?" I said, pointing at my wristwatch.

"Okay, okay, I'll open up tomorrow. All right?" said Fofo.

"No, it's not all right," I said, remembering that the next day was Tuesday, Fatma's cleaning day, and I didn't want to spend it at home because she'd work me too hard. "Why were you so late in last night?"

"I met someone new," said Fofo.

"Oh great! So while I'm working my socks off, you're out enjoying yourself!" I yelled.

I eventually calmed down, stopped glaring at him and looked at him with a mixture of curiosity and concern.

"So-o? Are you in love?" I asked.

"No, sweetie," said Fofo. "He's a wham-bam-thank-you-ma'am kind of guy. Love had nothing to do with it."

"What do you mean?" I said, though I was pretty sure I knew exactly what he meant.

"What do you think I meant? I think they say 'light the fuse and it's over in a flash' here!"

"That's one way of putting it," I said, laughing.

"Shall I make you some green tea?" said Fofo.

"I'm off to meet Aylin at the Nişantaşı Brasserie."

"Well, I'd say that's great, if you were dressed in Stella McCartney shoes and Gucci trousers, but you won't get within two hundred metres of the place dressed like that," said Fofo, striking a pose.

"That's why I'm going home now."

"Wear the black trousers you bought in the sale last year with a white shirt and your red stilettos. You'll look great in those."

"Are you mad? I can't even walk far enough to hail a cab in those shoes."

"You could call Pera Taxis to come and pick you up," suggested Fofo.

He always managed to find simple solutions to complex problems. Do you see why I love him so much?

"Don't you think the cab driver might be annoyed if I'm only going as far as Nişantaşı? And it's Ramadan. All the drivers will be fasting," I said.

"Ah yes, I completely forgot that Ramadan started today. Never mind, you can give the driver a generous tip. They're all really polite at that taxi rank."

"Fine, that's what I'll do," I said.

It wasn't my habit to tip taxi drivers in Istanbul. Giving a tip for possibly the worst service in the world was against all my principles.

Fofo's advice had eased the stress I'd been feeling about having to get dressed up and walk through Kuledibi to get to Nişantaşı.

"I'm off. See you at home," I said. "You're coming home this evening, aren't you?"

"Do you think I'm getting old or something?" asked Fofo.

"What's the matter now?" I asked, somewhat exasperated that he wanted to discuss his existential issues with me.

"Actually, my favourite nights have been spent at home with you," said Fofo unexpectedly.

This strange pronouncement was obviously a translation from Spanish. As I walked home, I considered what he might have meant:

I like being at home most when I'm with you.

It's more enjoyable staying at home with you than going out.

You're fun to be with, and an evening spent with you is always worthwhile.

You're magnificent, fun to be with and beautiful.

As I opened the door to my apartment, my mobile started ringing. When I finally found it after rummaging in my enormous bag, I saw that Fofo's name was flashing on the screen.

"What's up?"

"You know that long silver chain you have? Wear that," said Fofo.

Good God! Anyone would think I was attending a fashion show instead of going to interrogate someone!

"Fine," I said.

As soon as the cab turned into Abdi İpekçi Street, we were hemmed in by traffic. And what traffic! It was at a complete standstill and people were yelling at each other. A man in a Land Rover the width of a truck tried to edge out of his parking spot and caught the bumper of a posh grey Porsche sitting in the queue. The female driver ahead of us slammed her hand down on the horn and a furious war of words commenced.

"We've hit the early evening traffic, miss," said the driver. "Those who've been fasting are desperate to get home for their evening meal."

"I'll get out here," I said, jumping out of the cab. "You can leave this road a bit further along."

It might not have been Berlin, but at least there were pavements in Nişantaşı, unlike some areas of Istanbul. I made my way towards the brasserie, a haze of strong perfume wafting over me from two women walking ahead. Once inside the restaurant, I headed for an empty table in the far right-hand corner. The windows were mirrored glass on the inside, which meant I could observe everyone sitting in the brasserie as well as those coming in or out. Since the purpose of being there was to see and be seen, I wanted to sit in a prime position.

The brasserie's clientele mainly consisted of Nişantaşı ladies, with only the occasional male. The ladies, whether fifteen or seventy, looked amazingly similar, with noses fashioned by the same cosmetic surgeon, swollen pouting lips and identical facelifts. They wore the same fashion labels and bore the signs of Botox injections, subcutaneous vitamin cocktails and several tanning sessions a week. I enjoyed observing these women, though personally I was repelled by skin burned orange on a sunbed.

I was early, so I decided to order a latte, despite a twinge of guilt about overdoing the coffee. It wouldn't count if it was decaffeinated.

"A decaf latte, please. And a glass of water," I said to the waitress.

The waitress replied in English. Was that because she'd noticed I wasn't Turkish?

"Why are you speaking English? I speak Turkish," I said.

"Sorry, I don't speak Turkish. I'll call my colleague," she said, summoning one of the waiters working behind the bar.

I had nothing against foreigners, but was it normal for a waitress working in Istanbul to speak no Turkish?

Naz and Aylin arrived a few minutes later. I was surprised to see that Aylin was a real Nişantaşı type. She was about thirty-four, with long, sleek, highlighted hair and a pert upturned nose.

She was dressed in blue denim hipsters and heels so high even I wouldn't have dared wear them, and she exuded an overpoweringly sweet perfume that I couldn't identify.

We didn't take to each other. Although, to be honest, I couldn't tell whether she liked me or not, because Nişantaşı ladies had the habit of looking down their noses at everyone. For instance, if one of them bumped into you in the street, they'd give you the evil eye rather than apologize. And it wasn't just ordinary people like me who they treated that way. They did it to each other. The worst offenders were always the richest, so there must have been an unwritten code of behaviour for such situations.

Serving these ladies had to be the worst job in the world. Perhaps that was why the brasserie employed waiters who didn't speak Turkish. My waitress was undoubtedly much happier than her Turkish colleagues, who understood what was being said around them. Someone like Sevim, Sani's secretary, wouldn't have stood a chance there. Having met Aylin, I now understood why Sevim had been so flustered when we saw her.

I wondered whether Sani had been like these Nişantaşı ladies. If so, there must surely have been a dozen people prepared, and even happy, to stand by and watch her die.

"I hear that you and your husband Remzi were among the first people to enter Sani's house," I said. "I understand that Cem Bey phoned you."

"That's right. Cem said that Sani hadn't been seen for a few days and wasn't answering her phone," drawled Aylin, rolling her r's and stifling a yawn. "I called the office, but she hadn't been there. Remzi told me to call the police, which I did. When we arrived at Sani's house, the police were already there."

"I presume Naz has told you—"

"Nobody's told me anything," said Aylin, with the same offhand drawl.

Naz explained briefly how Sani had died.

"Thugs!" said Aylin. "How could they leave Sani lying on the floor like that? What's the world coming to?"

I studied her face for any trace of anguish – and found it.

Aylin ordered, in English, of course, a herbal tea for herself and an espresso for Naz.

"Remzi's the person to talk to about this," said Aylin. "You have his phone number, don't you?"

"But you were Sani's friend, so you might know things that could be useful to us," I said.

"Like what?" asked Aylin.

"I understand Sani and Cem had made a prenuptial agreement. Did you know that?"

"Remzi could tell you more about it. He was handling the divorce case."

"Was there any tension between them when they started discussing their divorce?"

"Tension?" asked Aylin with a smile, as if it were a joke. "What do you mean by tension? Cem naturally didn't want to part with a single penny, and was prepared to do whatever it took to ensure that."

"But it wouldn't have included watching her die, presumably," I said.

"It might. Even if he didn't kill her personally, he might have watched her die, and even enjoyed it."

What? I looked at Naz in amazement. Wasn't this woman supposed to be Cem's friend? Everyone else had described Cem as some kind of angel. What was going on?

Aylin tossed back her hair and looked around at the other people in the restaurant.

For once in my life, I was lost for words.

"Men are capable of anything," said Aylin, turning back to us.

"Has something happened, Aylin?" asked Naz, who was just as startled as me. "Are you angry with someone?"

"Someone?" said Aylin, leaning her head on her hand. "Yes, I'm furious with someone."

"What happened?"

As if she'd been waiting for this question, Aylin started to explain.

"I went with Remzi to Paşabahçe on the day Sani died. It was six o'clock when we got back to this side of the Bosphorus. Remzi wanted to drop in at the office to pick up some papers, and I went in with him because I didn't want to be left alone. When we got there, the secretary was very flustered. She kept rushing about, doing anything she could to keep me seated in reception. And Remzi was clearly in a state. I suspected something when he suddenly announced that we had to leave. They were obviously trying to stop me going into Remzi's office, but I pushed them away and went in. A woman, the spitting image of Kylie Minogue, was in there. Remzi introduced her to me as a client called Şelale Hanım, but even her name seemed like a bad omen."

"Are you going to divorce Remzi Bey?" I asked.

"Some people would just take this in their stride and shrug it off, but I'm not one of those people. Of course I'm going to divorce him. I've engaged a lawyer."

"So you're getting divorced," said Naz.

"It's impossible for the marriage to continue. I was speaking to my lawyer just before coming here. From now on, I'm an impoverished woman who is about to get divorced. Apparently, Remzi told my lawyer that his assets amount to a four-by-four and a house, of which I'm welcome to half. He was even about to make demands for money from me! How is that possible? Apart from being a successful lawyer, he also has a construction company. I need to prove exactly what he does and doesn't own. But how am I supposed to know how much money he has and where he keeps it? I have to find proof that he's telling lies in order to get damages from him, but how do you prove that someone's lying?"

"What are you going to do?" asked Naz.

"I've no idea. He's obviously hoping to stop me from divorcing him. He told my lawyer to instruct me to make it up with him because any alimony I receive won't even cover my monthly hairdresser tips. The bastard!"

"Do you think you'll get back together?"

"No way. I'd do better to hire a private detective to prove that he's been lying to me."

Naz gave me a meaningful look, as if she was about to say that I was a private detective.

"I don't do that kind of work," I said hastily.

If Naz thought I'd said that in the hope of raising my fee, she said nothing.

"You might find it incredible," said Aylin, "but I never thought that the Sani and Cem situation would happen to us, that Remzi would cheat on me or lie about money. What a fool I was! It's been really tough discovering that there's a totally different side to him."

Poor Aylin! After years of living a fairy-tale life, she was reduced to this. Emerging from her cocoon of luxury and facing reality would be tough, of course, but Aylin's newly discovered theories about the fickleness of life were of no interest to me.

"What sort of person is Cem," I asked, "since you said he could even have been the killer?"

"I don't know if he could be the killer, but he used to openly threaten Sani," said Aylin. "Maybe that's what men do when they're getting divorced. Women swear, and men make threats. Cem said that if Sani divorced him, she'd have nowhere to go other than the village she came from."

"Did Sani tell you that?"

"No, Cem said it to Remzi. He might have said it to Sani too, but she wouldn't say anything. She couldn't."

"Why not?"

"Sani was very reserved. Extremely reserved," said Aylin. "Was it because she didn't trust anyone, or because of problems when she was younger? What do you think, Naz?"

Naz just nodded.

"Just when I thought Sani might be considering having a child, Remzi told me that she'd decided to get divorced. Yet she hadn't said a word about her relationship with Cem going sour. Did she say anything to you, Naz?"

This time, Naz shook her head to indicate no.

"She was getting advice from my husband because he's a lawyer, yet she didn't even tell me that she'd decided to get divorced. That's the kind of person she was. Maybe I was at fault. Maybe, because we're from different backgrounds, I made her feel—"

"Inferior?" I asked.

"Not exactly, but our pasts certainly had nothing in common," said Aylin.

"And you thought this created an imbalance that worked in your favour," I said.

"You put it very well," said Aylin.

I certainly had put it well. I keep telling you how good my Turkish is.

"But what's happening now, apart from the fact that you've decided to divorce your husband?" I asked out of curiosity.

"We all live the same life," said Aylin. "Whatever our financial status or background, the moment we deliver our fate into the hands of another, we live the same dreadful life. Remzi told me to go back to where I came from, which in my case was my father's apartment in Şişli. Can you imagine? Should I be ashamed because my poor father, who'd been an ambassador, only ever managed to save enough to buy one apartment in Şişli?"

It did seem strange for an ambassador to be so poor, but perhaps he'd spent his money in casinos. However, that was of no importance to me.

"Did Sani keep a diary?" I asked.

"A diary? I don't know. Did she?" replied Aylin.

"She used to," said Naz.

"You do know there was a burglary at GreTur, don't you?"

"A burglary? No, I didn't know that," said Aylin. "It must have been while I was abroad after Sani's funeral. I'd had two shocks in one day and needed to get away for a bit. But what was worth stealing from GreTur?"

"They took the computers. Do you know if there was anything on them that might have a bearing on Sani's death?" I asked.

"There were files on environmental matters and there were business files, but nothing personal. All the personal stuff was on her laptop, which she didn't leave lying around."

"The laptop's disappeared too."

"Was the laptop at the office as well?"

"We think they took it from her house."

"How interesting. I wonder if she was using her laptop to write her diary," mused Aylin.

Not bad. I certainly hadn't expected that from her. Perhaps I'd judged the Nişantaşı ladies too hastily.

"What makes you think that?" I asked.

"Sani used to say that she'd forgotten how to hold a pen," said Aylin. "She always carried a fountain pen, but complained whenever she had to use it. You wouldn't expect her to have such a horror of pens if she was keeping a diary, would you? Presumably it wasn't a handwritten diary."

"That was the conclusion we came to," I said. "And it seems that we weren't the only ones to think that, because all the computers have gone."

"In that case, it must have been someone who knew Sani at least as well as us," commented Aylin.

"That is, of course, if such a diary exists on any of the computers. Might someone involved with environmental work—"

"What's the environment got to do with anything?" asked Aylin.

"We thought the owners of the factories that are polluting the environment in Thrace might have had a hand in this," I said. "Would any of the computers contain anything that might upset them?"

"If so, it's news to me," said Aylin. "Remzi might be able to help you more on that score. He's been combing through the regulations looking for discrepancies, and there are plenty that might be of use in a court case."

"Tell me about the secretary who works at GreTur," I said.

"She's just an ordinary woman," said Aylin. "I think she has a brother with learning difficulties, either that or an illness that needs a lot of attention. She's always asking for time off to take him to the doctor's, which is quite disruptive to business. If it had been up to me, I wouldn't have kept her on, but Sani was too soft. Apart from that, I know nothing about her."

"How long have you known Cem Bey?"

"We met in America. My father's last posting was in DC, Washington DC. There was a very dynamic Turkish students' association there, which was where Cem and I met. In fact, I was the one who introduced Cem to Sani."

"Do you know Cem's family?" I asked.

"I've met them a few times. His parents aren't really social animals. They very rarely accept invitations. His mother's an elegant lady from a family with a distinguished pedigree and his father's a highly successful businessman. But I've no idea what sort of people they are."

"Does Cem have any siblings?"

"As far as I know, he has an older sister living in Bodrum. She's a painter. Her pictures are... Well, I don't like to put anyone down, so let's just say her work isn't really my type of thing. She's one of those artists who keeps producing work on the same subject."

"And what subject is that?"

"Harlequins. All kinds of harlequins – laughing ones, happy ones and sad ones. I heard that she was living with a singer much older than her. He sang in the bars at Bodrum. Why do you ask?"

"That must have caused their mother a great deal of grief. I'm told she didn't even approve of Cem's marriage to Sani."

"His mother? You mean Tamaşa Hanım?"

"Yes," I said, wondering what was so surprising about that.

"Cem's sister isn't Tamaşa Hanım's daughter. She's the daughter of Bahri Bey's first wife."

"Aha!"

As you might imagine, I was more than happy to hear this new piece of gossip about Cem's wayward half-sister.

"You didn't mention her name," I said.

Aylin frowned and thought before saying, "I can't remember it. Do you know what it is, Naz?"

"This is the first time I've heard of Cem even having a sister," said Naz.

"I'll find out and let you know," said Aylin. "I'm going to order a salad. Do you two want anything?"

"I'll just have a tea. Do you know anything about the contents of the prenuptial agreement signed by Sani and Cem?" I said, feeling that my questions were going round in circles.

"As I said, you should talk to Remzi," said Aylin, leaning her chin on her hand and pausing for thought before adding, "As far as I can tell, these agreements are all basically the same. They state that in the case of divorce, each party takes whatever was in their name before the marriage and makes no claims on the other's assets. If there's no prenuptial, all assets have to be shared equally, so husbands use these agreements as a loophole to protect themselves."

"And to ensure that their wives return to where they came from," I said.

"But even if an agreement is signed, it's still possible to do something," said Aylin. "Take my situation. If I can prove that Remzi's been cheating on me, I can get compensation. It was more difficult for Sani because Cem wasn't the guilty party, nor was he seeking the divorce. Under our system, compensation is only payable if you can prove the other party is guilty, whereas in Europe, so my lawyer told me today, the court either awards the wife generous alimony or a large lump sum. Do you know how much Luciano Pavarotti paid out to his wife when they divorced?"

"How should I know?" I said.

"He paid out €100,000,000."

"You mean Pavarotti the tenor?"

"That's the one. And guess how much Paul McCartney's wife asked for as a divorce settlement?"

We couldn't guess.

"€300,000,000. Paul McCartney supposedly had €1.2 billion to his name, and his wife demanded a quarter of it."

"I wonder how much money Cem has," I said.

"Well, there's the enormous Ankaralı Holdings," said Aylin. "Who knows how much that's worth? It's certainly one of the top ten companies. If you ask me, I don't think Cem really meant those threats about throwing Sani out with nothing."

"Can I just say something?" said Naz. "You keep talking as if all women do is try to fleece their husbands."

"Mmm, like getting hairs out of a pig," I commented.

"Well, I find that attitude very upsetting," said Naz.

"What do you mean?" asked Aylin.

"Well, when Sani returned to Turkey, her situation was excellent," said Naz. "She was in a position to find work with a good company. Alternatively, she could have stayed and worked in America, where she'd been offered several jobs."

"Yes, that's true," said Aylin.

"But what happened?" said Naz. "Cem wouldn't stop grumbling and quizzing her about where she was going to work and why. In the end, Sani couldn't take any more and decided to find a way of amusing herself rather than actually working."

"That's right," said Aylin.

"And the same goes for you, doesn't it?" said Naz. "Before you were married, you had a good job as a simultaneous interpreter. Why did you give it up?"

"I couldn't have kept it up after I got married. It would have been too much, with all those trips abroad and spending several days a week in Ankara."

"You were earning well, doing a job you liked," persisted Naz, "yet now you tell us you're trying to bleed Remzi for a few pennies."

"The worst thing is that you lose all self-confidence," said Aylin.

"It happens so often to women who give up working after they get married," said Naz. "It's not easy picking up where you've left off if you take a break from work. A person's self-confidence becomes so damaged during marriage that—"

"...she can't bring herself to start all over again," said Aylin, completing Naz's sentence. "What do you advise?"

"Me? I'd try to get back into work, of course," said Naz.

"I doubt if I'll ever get as good a job as I had before, but I'll certainly have a go. Perhaps I can find a nice little niche for myself somewhere."

"Shall we go now?" I asked, thinking I had better things to do with my life than spend it advising women on how to go about getting a divorce.

"Aylin hasn't finished her salad yet," said Naz.

"Sani was always eating salad whenever I saw her at lunchtime," I commented, noticing that Aylin hadn't even touched hers.

"She was always on a diet. But it wasn't a healthy diet. I kept telling her that one plate of salad a day simply wasn't enough," said Naz.

"The only way to shed kilos is to stop eating," said Aylin.

"That's not true. But I'm sure you do what you think is best, so I'll keep quiet," said Naz.

"Actually, you're right," said Aylin. "Hunger affects the nerves. Sani was totally worn out, what with the divorce and her strict dieting."

"Oh, I almost forgot," Naz blurted out. "I meant to ask you if... I'd suggested that she got some help from a psychiatrist. Do you know if she went?"

"Yes, yes. She went to one at a clinic in Nişantaşı," said Aylin. "In fact, we met up here that day. It was the Friday before the terrible event. She went from here to go and see him."

"Can you remember which doctor she saw?" asked Naz.

"I didn't ask his name, but I could find out. I know who recommended him to her," said Aylin.

"Yes, please do," said Naz.

While Aylin was prodding her mobile with her French-manicured nails, I leaned towards Naz and said, "What are you going to ask the psychiatrist?"

"About the needle marks on her arm," said Naz. "I think he may have some ideas."

"But he'd never divulge a patient's secrets to us. It would be unethical," I said.

"I don't want him to tell me any secrets. I just want to get an idea from him," said Naz.

"She's going to send me the number of the clinic, and the doctor's name is Ethem Tuğlacı," said Aylin, and as she spoke her mobile started ringing.

"Tell me the number, and I'll write it down," said Naz.

"The clinic's in Rumeli Street," said Aylin, and then read out the phone number.

"Why don't you phone the clinic? We could go there now," I said to Naz.

"All right, but I'll go outside to make the call," said Naz.

"It's noisier outside than in here," I said.

"It doesn't matter. I can talk more comfortably outside."

Naz went outside and Aylin started playing with her salad before finally giving up and laying her fork down.

"You never met Sani, did you?" she asked.

"I used to see her at lunchtime sometimes," I said.

"But you didn't actually know her," said Aylin, adding suddenly, "I think Sani was very jealous of Naz."

I had absolutely no idea what to say.

"Well, you do sometimes get a bit of sibling rivalry," I said, as if I was talking about two children.

I actually knew nothing about sibling relationships, because my much older brother had left home when I was still an infant.

"I'm not talking about normal jealousy. Hers was almost pathological," said Aylin.

"What makes you think that?" I asked.

"For instance," said Aylin, "she'd imitate everything that Naz did. A month after Naz coloured her hair brown, Sani claimed there'd been an 'accident' at the hairdresser's and she came out with her platinum blonde hair turned brown."

People base their conclusions on such strange evidence!

"But it might have been a genuine accident," I said.

"Then why was Sani devastated, like it was the end of the world, when Naz went lighter again?" said Aylin.

"I really don't know," I said. What could I say?

"And that wasn't the only thing," continued Aylin. "A week after Naz signed a petition about animal cruelty, Sani led a protest against raising hens in battery farms. When Naz had the misfortune to have her handbag stolen, Sani magically retrieved it from the thieves a few days later. That was quite a coincidence, don't you think?"

"It certainly was," I said.

"Do you realize how much Sani resembled Naz?"

"Yes, of course, but they're sisters."

"Take a look at their childhood photos. Would you have known they were sisters then?"

"What are you suggesting?" I asked.

"I'm suggesting that Sani presented pictures of Naz to a cosmetic surgeon and said, 'I want to look like her'," said Aylin.

"It can't be that simple to look like someone else, even after endless operations, can it?"

"Not simple, but not impossible. After all, we all look pretty much alike here, don't we?" said Aylin, indicating the other women in the restaurant, who certainly all had a very similar look about them. "Apparently, Sani had her operations while she was at university, so it went back that far. Must have been some sort of mental illness."

Aylin was talking rubbish now.

"But she had no money when she was at university, and

cosmetic surgery is expensive, isn't it?" I said, wondering if I should start finding out about such things.

"Sani taught maths and chemistry at a high school while she was a university student," said Aylin. "So she obviously wasn't that hard up."

"How did you find that out?" I asked.

"This is a small place. Everyone knows everything. You aren't from Istanbul, are you?"

"No, I'm not," I said, realizing that Aylin hadn't really worked out where I was from. "Was there a lot of talk about Sani having surgery to make her look like Naz?"

"No, not that much, but some people certainly knew about it. They also say that Sani stole Naz's lover when she was at university."

"So Orhan had been Naz's lover first?" I asked, but received no reply because Naz had returned.

"If we leave now, we can see him in ten minutes," said Naz. "Sorry to rush you, Aylin. I'll pay for these."

"Never mind me. You carry on," said Aylin. "Can I take your number, Kati Hanım? I might need your help."

"As I said, I don't spy on people," I said.

"Give it to me all the same."

There seemed no option but to exchange phone numbers.

The psychiatric clinic was on the second floor of a beautiful art nouveau building with a stairway covered in claret-coloured carpet leading up from the entrance hall. A concierge dressed in a grey jacket and baggy jodhpur-like trousers sat at a desk on the landing at the top of the stairs. Was that the best they could do?

A blonde girl opened the door to the clinic. I couldn't help thinking that if I spent much more time in Nişantaşı, I'd start to think that Turkey was a nation of blondes.

"Ethem Bey is waiting for you," said the girl, leading us to a room with a glass door.

Ethem rose to his feet to greet us and directed us to some easy chairs opposite his desk while he seated himself on the sofa.

"You said you're a cardiologist at Lüleburgaz State Hospital. Is that right?" he asked.

Naz nodded and said, "My sister Sani Ankaralıgil was a patient of yours. She'd been having a hard time because of her divorce and I advised her to seek help."

"I read in the papers that she'd died. I'm so sorry for your loss," said Ethem.

He looked more like a greengrocer than a psychiatrist to me, but he must have been good at his job because becoming a society psychiatrist was no mean feat.

"The autopsy found a needle mark on her left arm, and I thought you might know something about it," said Naz.

"Her treatment hadn't even started, so I hadn't prescribed her any medication," he said. "I checked her file again before you came. She'd been under a lot of stress recently and complained of spells of dizziness and breaking out in a sweat. On one occasion, she had a particularly bad turn—"

"Bad turn?" interrupted Naz.

"...and she collapsed," said Ethem.

The three of us exchanged glances. Why would a person fall, unless they tripped up or slipped on something? Low blood pressure? A brain tumour? Those were the only possibilities I could think of.

"What could cause someone to collapse?" I asked.

"It could be for all sorts of reasons," he said.

This was what I hated most about doctors. Why couldn't they simply tell you which disease your symptoms point to?

"Did she have a brain tumour, perhaps?" I asked.

Ethem clearly found my intervention unwarranted because he fixed me with an icy glare and said, "That's one possibility. But this patient's history of anxiety, exhaustion, sweats, blackouts and dizzy spells suggested a hormonal imbalance which could have resulted in goitre, a disturbed menstrual cycle or diabetes. I advised Sani Hanım to speak to Hale Gürsel, the internal diseases specialist at the American Hospital, and to have all the recommended tests done."

"Her appointment with you was on the Friday. Do you think she went straight from here to the hospital?" asked Naz.

"By the time Sani Hanım left here, our polyclinic was closed, so I asked my secretary to make an appointment for her. I checked the notes and she was booked in for Monday at two o'clock. If she attended that appointment, then—"

"Thank you very much, Ethem Bey," said Naz, rising to her feet. "You've put my mind at ease."

That's exactly what a good psychiatrist is meant to do, of course.

"If the specialist asked for a blood sample," said Naz, as we descended the carpeted stairway, "that would explain the needle mark on Sani's arm. But we'll have to wait until tomorrow morning to find that out."

"The American Hospital is just here. Why don't we call in now?" I suggested.

"The doctor will have gone home. No one will be there at this time," said Naz.

"We don't need to speak to the doctor," I said. "If an analysis was done, we can get the result from the lab."

"They wouldn't give us the results."

"Why not? We don't have labels saying 'I'm not Sani' on our foreheads. No one's going to ask questions. We'll find an assistant or a nurse," I said.

"Do you think we'll get away with it?"

"Of course!"

And we did. It was raining when we left the hospital, and we rushed into a nearby pastry shop. In the time I'd known her, I'd never seen Naz look so pleased as she sat nodding her head and studying the results of the blood analyses.

"If she wasn't poisoned, which was what I'd thought," she said finally, "then the probable cause of death was hypoglycaemic shock."

"What's that?" I asked.

"It's caused by dangerously low sugar levels. Anyone with hypoglycaemia needs to avoid hunger, and Sani was always going around half-starved. What's more—"

"Yes?" I said.

"We've been assuming that someone was with her in the house... If she'd had an argument... Well, that could have triggered a sudden drop in her sugar level."

"So you're suggesting that she died of hunger?"

"Exactly."

Sani Ankaralıgil starved to death? Who'd have thought it?

9

I'd never known Ramadan to have so little impact on city life. Anyone who remembered the attacks at provincial universities on students who'd refused to fast, even up to the Nineties, would have said that life in Istanbul had become a bed of roses compared with the past. Despite the inevitable tension in the air, there had been no serious incidents so far.

I don't really know why it was different that year. Were fewer people fasting? Or had they become more tolerant? Was there a greater belief that people could live in harmony together? Even the *davul* players, despite handing out their leaflets, seemed to have disappeared. My only complaint concerned the traffic jams caused by hungry people rushing home for their evening feast.

I'd left a few messages for Batuhan during the day, but the time had come for a serious exchange of information. Batuhan called me back after I'd returned from lunch and just as pangs of hunger were starting up again in my stomach.

"Where are you?" I said. "We need to speak."

"There's no time to do our jobs with all the in-house training they make us do," complained Batuhan, who had just returned from three days of seminars at a police training centre in Bolu.

"Can we meet sometime today?" I asked.

"Come to the police station. I'm in Room 423."

"What time?"

"Whenever you like. I'm here until ten tonight."

It brought tears to my eyes to think of Turkish policemen sacrificing their lives to their work like that.

I'd said earlier that Ramadan had caused few changes to the pattern of city life that year. However, the Petek Snack Bar was closed so that the family, as always, could spend the month in their village. I wasn't concerned about trying to get into size eight clothes and had banished all thoughts of dieting since hearing the awful truth about how Sani had died, so I picked up a toasted cheese sandwich from the Minik Buffet and got into a cab.

The policeman on the door checked my ID thoroughly and phoned to let Batuhan know of my arrival before allowing me into the police station.

Dear Batuhan was waiting for me outside the lift on the fourth floor.

"What do you want to drink?" he asked as soon as we entered his office.

"Aren't you fasting?"

"I've got stomach trouble, so I can't fast."

I couldn't help wondering if it was the sort of trouble that only appeared during Ramadan. The cab driver had also spoken at length about his stomach problems and how he was unable to fast.

"I'll have a tea, if you're having one," I said.

"The tea isn't fresh at this time of day. Better to have something cold."

"In that case, I'll have a soda."

"What did you want to talk about?" asked Batuhan, sitting down in the armchair opposite me.

"We've found out how Sani died," I said.

"You've discovered the cause of death?" exclaimed Batuhan in disbelief.

Actually, I thought he should have been more surprised that

I'd actually volunteered this information than that I knew what had killed Sani.

"So how did she die?" asked Batuhan.

"It was hypoglycaemic shock," I said.

"And what does that mean?"

"It's also called 'the size eight disease'," I explained. "Starvation can make blood sugar levels fall, causing people to go into shock and fall into a coma. If they don't receive help within ten minutes – fifteen at the most – they don't regain consciousness."

"Whew! Never heard that before," said Batuhan.

"Size eight is all the rage in Turkey now," I continued. "You hear of young girls desperately dieting in the hope of becoming fashion models. Apparently in New York there are frequent delays on the metro caused by girls fainting. Who knows how many it happens to each day?"

"But not in Turkey," interrupted Batuhan. "Turkish men don't like their women scrawny. By the way, I see you've filled out a bit."

What did he mean by that? That I'd put on weight? I got up and looked down at my legs.

"It's these trousers," I said. "It's the way they're cut."

"Turn around. Let me look at your backside," said Batuhan.

Was this really happening in Room 423 of the police station?

"You should concentrate on yourself. You've got quite a paunch there," I remarked.

"I think it makes me look wealthy," said Batuhan, patting his stomach.

"Oh yes? A fine indication of wealth," I said, thinking that many of the richest people in the world choose to eat so little they almost starve to death.

"Yeah, I've put on a pound or two, but it suits me," said Batuhan.

"Aren't you going to ask me how we found out?" I asked, ignoring his absurd comments about weight.

"Found out what?"

"How Sani died."

"First I want to know who you mean by 'us'," said Batuhan.

"Sani's sister Naz and myself."

"Our guys have been looking for her," he said casually. "Tell her to come in to the station to make a statement."

"You don't seem very interested in our findings," I said.

"I'm more interested in you," he laughed.

I reached for my glass and took a sip of soda to give me time to collect myself.

"It's not a question of whether I'm interested or not, Kati," said Batuhan. "When you reach commander level, you get buried in so much admin that there's barely time to get out and conduct investigations. You wouldn't want to hear how I spend my time. I have to do the most boring work."

"I understand," I said, realizing this meant the end of those enjoyable days spent with Batuhan.

"So how did you find out that she'd died from shock, or whatever it was?" asked Batuhan.

"She had a blood test done at the hospital on Tuesday afternoon."

"Have you got the results of the test with you?"

Of course I had. "Here, keep it," I said.

"And what did you want from me?"

Finally, after all these years, Batuhan showed that he had an inkling of how my mind worked: an eye for an eye, a tooth for a tooth, you scratch my back and I'll scratch yours…

"Why were you so certain that Sani wasn't alone in the house when she died?" I asked.

Batuhan reached for one of the files lying on the table, took out a few pages and handed them to me.

"Read these. I'll be back in a moment," he said.

He rose to his feet and left the room. A moment later, I heard him shouting at some people out in the corridor.

The report from the police laboratory read as follows:

Ultraviolet photographs 1, 2 and 3 show that the nature of the scratches on the floor, and chemical analysis of the colour and type of dye found in these scratches, matches the colour and particulars of the size 38 black high-heeled woman's shoes found on the feet of the deceased person, as outlined in Doc. 2006/221. It is therefore feasible that the size 38 black shoes detailed therein made these scratches.

Ultraviolet photographs 4, 5 and 6 show marks made by size 40 flat-heeled shoes, as detailed in Doc. 2006/222.

So, whoever had watched Sani die in her house had been wearing size forty flats.

"Have you read it?" asked Batuhan when he returned.

"I have," I said. "It was obviously a woman in the house with her."

"Or a short man...Some men take a size forty shoe."

"Is that all you know?" I asked.

Batuhan leaned over my shoulder to look at the report I was still holding, and then handed me Document 2006/222, on which 'XOXO' had been scribbled underneath "size 40 flat-heeled shoe". Otherwise, there was no further information in this document. As far as I could remember, XOXO was the name of a sportswear chain.

"Could it have been the cleaner?" I suggested. "Or the night-watchman? They both went into the house. Why did you only find two sets of footprints in the sitting room?"

"Do you want to see photos of the watchman and cleaner's footprints?" said Batuhan. "I didn't show them to you because I didn't think they'd be of any use."

"I don't need to see them. I just wondered if they were there," I said. "I see the Turkish police have gone in for ultraviolet photography."

"Whatever technology they have in Europe and America, we have too," said Batuhan. "We lack for nothing here."

"I don't suppose it's possible to search for XOXO shoes in the houses of anyone related to this case who takes a size forty shoe, is it?"

Batuhan didn't laugh out loud, but he was clearly amused.

"If only, but our hands are tied by regulations," he said. "I need sound evidence before I can apply for a search warrant."

"Anyway, I suppose it would be pointless doing house searches for shoes that might have been disposed of days ago," I said.

"Even you were unaware that we use ultraviolet photography, so they might not have been," said Batuhan, then, suddenly looking serious, added, "You must promise not to say a word to anyone about these photos."

"Of course," I said, flicking a strand of hair away from my eyes. "You've interviewed Cem Ankaralıgil, haven't you?"

"Several times. Have you spoken to him?"

"I doubt if he'd talk to me, especially since I have no official capacity."

"It doesn't matter anyway. He has reliable witnesses," said Batuhan. "On the Tuesday evening, he attended a meeting at the Chamber of Shipping Transport and left at about nine o'clock. After that he went to a fish restaurant in Bebek, where he met up with some friends."

"And what did he do after leaving his friends?" I asked.

"He didn't leave them. They left the restaurant together and all went back to someone's house, where they carried on drinking. He returned home in the early hours of the morning. At nine-thirty on Wednesday morning he attended a meeting at his company headquarters, after which he went to a shipyard in Izmit. Then in the evening he attended a dinner at a sports club where he's on the executive committee. When the meal was over, his chauffeur took him to the family home, where he stayed until morning."

"He has a busier schedule than the Prime Minister," I remarked. "But is there any chance his friends might be lying? Maybe he didn't spend Tuesday night with them."

"They're in no position to lie," said Batuhan.

What did he mean by that? All the people I'd met connected with this case had lied.

"They're not the types to be bought off."

Over the previous few days I'd begun to think that no one was taking a handout!

"Who are these people?" I asked out of curiosity.

"Some of Turkey's most renowned businessmen, a foreign diplomat and a company director. Do you think they'd all lie?"

"Why not?" I replied, wondering if I'd lost all faith in humankind.

"For the simple reason that they wouldn't be willing to put themselves at risk because Cem had allowed his wife's blood sugar level to drop and watched her die, that's why. No one in their position would be stupid enough to go to prison for aiding and abetting," said Batuhan, and paused before adding, with an air of finality, "Anyway, Cem doesn't take a size forty shoe."

I have to admit that, in my humble opinion, this was a far stronger argument than any given in the witness statements. Nevertheless, the possibility still remained that Cem could have sent someone wearing size forty shoes to Sani's house.

"Tell me, why did you abandon your theory about a crime syndicate of industrialists in Thrace so quickly?" asked Batuhan.

"I haven't given it up. I've just been trying to look at the situation from other angles," I said. "Especially after learning that

Cem had an agreement with the nightwatchman and his wife to spy on Sani's house."

"Who told you that?" asked Batuhan.

"The watchman's wife."

"She confessed to that?"

"Well, not exactly," I said, thinking that it could hardly be called a confession, since the poor woman wouldn't even have known it was inappropriate to spy on another person.

"Cem's still a suspect, given that he stood to gain significant material advantages from Sani's death, but we haven't been able to find any evidence against him."

"Not only against Cem. There's no evidence against anyone, come to think of it," I said, and added triumphantly, "However, I think I know why Sani's laptop and office computer were stolen."

"And why's that?" asked Batuhan, his curiosity clearly aroused.

Since we were not really in competition with each other, I told him what I knew and what I'd guessed, with various embellishments. But only some of it, of course.

I went home, my mind brimming with fresh ideas. We needed to ask Murat at Skyrat how to contact Cem's sister in Bodrum. We also had to contact Remzi, the solicitor, to find out what was in Sani's prenuptial agreement.

"You phone Murat tomorrow, and I'll find a way of getting hold of Remzi," I said to Fofo. "Ask Murat if he's found out anything new. There might be some interesting gossip floating around."

"At your command, ma'am," replied Fofo, raising his arm in a salute.

*

I awoke at dawn the next morning and decided to go and open up the shop, even though it wasn't my turn, because I needed to do some Internet research on Orhan Soner.

The first thing that struck me was that he'd become a close friend of the architect Djevad Redzepovski, who three years previously had been made chairman of the Tirana municipality and had managed to transform the town on a very small budget. No one in the press, from left-wing British to conservative German, had a good word to say about this municipal chairman who, it was rumoured, had been put in post by the Tirana mafia. He and Orhan had drawn up a plan for the Tirana City Theatre that had received high praise in a respectable architectural journal. Having read this, I wasn't at all surprised to learn that Orhan had been appointed as the architect for a luxury hotel being built by a large construction company in Tirana.

Normally, I'd have been impressed by such a CV, but thinking about the TLF, Albania, Albanians, Tirana – and whether they were relevant or not – merely created a desperate urge in me to smoke. When Pelin came sauntering in later, she found me deep in thought in my rocking chair, pondering several questions.

Was Orhan the person Naz had referred to as one of her old friends in the TLF? If so, why had she been trying to protect someone who had abandoned her to be with her older sister? Yet what she'd actually done was to point the finger at Orhan. Had the love affair between Sani and Orhan been rekindled? Had that angered Naz?

When the telephone rang, my head was in such confusion that not even a cigarette could have remedied it.

"Hello, it's Sinan. We met on Saturday... Do you remember?"

Didn't he realize that no one was likely to forget him? Or was he trying to be modest?

"I remember," I said.

"I realize I said something to you that day which... Do you think we could meet?" he asked.

I didn't want to see anyone unless they took a size forty shoe – in fact size forty XOXO trainers – not even if that person was the most gorgeous man in the world.

"What about today?" I suggested.

"If that suits you," said Sinan.

"Fine," I said.

"In Bebek? At Lucca's?"

I knew from Fofo that Lucca's had recently become one of the most fashionable places in Bebek, though I didn't know exactly where it was.

"Fine. Is three good for you?" I asked.

"Can we make it four?" said Sinan.

It was only just coming up to eleven o'clock. What was I going to do for all those hours? Furthermore, I didn't want to get caught up in the evening traffic.

"I have another meeting this evening," I lied.

No meeting had yet been arranged, but I'd do whatever it took to ensure that it was.

"Very well," said Sinan. "Three o'clock at Lucca's."

I needed to make a phone call and wanted to be alone so that I could talk openly, so I sent Pelin out to the Minik Buffet to buy some freshly squeezed pomegranate juice. Why pomegranate juice? Because the antioxidants in pomegranates were supposed to have a rejuvenating effect by killing off floating free radicals.

"If the Minik Buffet doesn't have any, try the snack bars at Tünel, will you? I saw a sign in one of the windows there advertising pomegranate juice."

The moment Pelin left the shop, I was forced to deal with some customers who came in unexpectedly. It was just my luck that I'd sent her out on such a mammoth expedition and yet was unable to make my phone call before Pelin's return.

"I'm going home," I said, tipping up the plastic beaker of pomegranate juice and gulping it down in one.

When I reached my apartment, I made straight for the phone.

"What a coincidence! I was going to ring you today," said Aylin as soon as she picked up.

"Did you think of anything?" I asked.

"What sort of thing?" said Aylin.

"To do with Sani." What else did she think I meant?

"Remzi and I have sorted things out. I was going to let you know. He talked me round," she giggled.

Naturally, I didn't ask how he'd convinced her. I might be curious, but not that curious. What would I want with information that was of no benefit to me?

"So, I don't need you any more," said Aylin.

That was a bit much!

"I've already told you that I don't tail people," I said.

"Ah yes, so you did," said Aylin, as if my words were of no significance. Did this woman think that everyone could be talked round in the end?

"I called you to ask for your help," I said.

"Yes?"

"Didn't Sani have a single close friend," I said, and hesitated before adding, "apart from you, I mean?"

"Close friend? No, she didn't," said Aylin.

"But everyone has a close friend."

"Not Sani."

"You said that things between Sani and Naz weren't too good."

"She was just jealous of Naz."

"But it'd be more logical for Naz to be jealous of Sani, wouldn't it?"

"Jealousy is illogical," said Aylin. "Just take what happened to me recently. When I saw that woman in Remzi's office, it never occurred to me that she might actually be his client. Was that rational? Jealousy is irrational by its very nature."

What wisdom she had!

"That day at the brasserie, you said Sani took up with Naz's ex-lover while she was at university," I said.

"Orhan Soner," said Aylin, just as I expected. "He's a famous architect. You must've heard of him."

Of course I had.

"Do you think Sani and Orhan might have started up their relationship again while she was going through the divorce proceedings?" I asked.

"Oh, I've no idea. As far as I know, Orhan Soner's married, but... Well, why not? It's possible," said Aylin.

"But there wasn't any gossip about it going round."

"If Sani had been in a relationship before her divorce came through, she would definitely have done everything in her power to keep it quiet," insisted Aylin.

But I was far from certain about that. Moving into a house directly opposite that of a former lover was not the action of a cautious person.

"I don't think I've been much help to you," said Aylin.

"Actually, you could help me now that you've patched things up with your husband. Could you arrange for me to have a meeting with him?"

"Of course, darling. His secretary will phone you, all right?" said Aylin breezily.

"Today, late afternoon, if possible."

"Fine. I'll tell him now, and his secretary will get back to you."

"Thank you very much," I said.

Although Aylin looked like a Nişantaşı lady, she wasn't at all bad, nor was she stupid. Maybe all Nişantaşı ladies were like that, and I was just prejudiced.

Instead of getting lost in my own thoughts, I sat down with a cup of green tea and made a list of all the questions that still needed answers. I came up with seven.

Unfortunately, it was only after I'd put down the phone that I thought of asking Aylin if she'd found out the name of Cem's sister. In the meantime, with no word from Remzi's secretary or Fofo, I began to get stressed and decided to do some cleaning. There had to be something in the apartment that had escaped Fatma's eagle eye the previous day. There always was.

I started wiping the sitting room windows, which weren't really dirty, but I always find the room looks lighter when the glass is sparkling clean. Before I'd even half finished, I heard a key turning in the lock, and Fofo entered.

"I called in at the shop first," he said. "What are you doing home at this hour?"

"I'm cleaning the windows," I replied. "I can't think what else to do."

"I've found out something amazing. Stop what you're doing at once."

I went out of the room to discard the dirty wad of paper towels and to prolong the moment of delicious tension. My insides were burning in anticipation of whatever it was I was about to discover. The excitement I felt was like that of flirting with someone to whom you're attracted but know nothing about. Unfortunately, such dates tended to quickly become as hard to digest as a piece of tough steak. Far be it from me to belittle those who, despite knowing better, continue to chew

187

their way through tough steak for years on end. I never ate it, so I couldn't understand people who ordered it at a restaurant or bought huge chunks to cook at home. Why bother if fillet steak was on offer? Either they'd never tasted fillet, or they preferred meat that needed endless chewing.

"Are you coming?" called Fofo from the sitting room.

"Yes, I'm here," I said. "Tell me everything."

"Cem does have a sister," he said.

"Didn't I tell you?"

"She lives in Bodrum. It wasn't easy to find this out, of course. It took numerous phone calls, but eventually Murat managed to trace her."

"And?"

"She's a painter called Jasmin Gil, and she paints pictures of harlequins."

"Why doesn't she use her father's surname?"

"She discarded the Ankaralı part of the name, because she's one of a handful of heirs to the fortunes of the Ankaralıgil empire. Apparently, she's regarded as Bahri's problem child within their family circle. Anyway, her mother's German."

What did Fofo mean by "anyway"? Did he mean there might be a connection between Jasmin being a problem child and the fact her mother was German?

"Children who grow up straddling two cultures tend to be a bit strange, darling," said Fofo.

"You're entitled to your own opinion, Fofo, but I think it's a bonus for children to grow up in two different cultures. The ability to speak two languages and pick out the best of both cultures can produce highly creative people."

"I'm not going to argue about it," said Fofo. "Having a German mother may have nothing to do with it, but this painter woman is definitely strange."

"Why, what's she done?"

"What hasn't she done? They had to put her in a clinic when she was sixteen to get her off drugs. Then a few years later she attacked her father with a razor and cut his throat, but the wound wasn't deep and he survived. Of course, the press never found out. They merely said he'd cut himself while shaving."

"Hmm. What else?"

"There's a literary competition in Germany where the competitors go on stage to read out their work and are given points by the audience and adjudicators."

"I've heard of it. So, what happened?"

"Well, she entered it, but while reading her short story on stage, she started undressing until she was stark naked. Then she lay down on the table and started masturbating!"

"Someone told me about that," I said, "or else I read about it somewhere. It was a long time ago. Didn't she stand naked outside the venue for days on end afterwards as a protest?"

Fofo looked disappointed that I already knew this. I think he'd hoped to be the first person to tell me.

"So, that's your amazing bit of news!" I said, upsetting him even more.

"But you haven't yet heard the real bombshell," said Fofo.

"And what's that?"

"Well, it's like this—"

"Yes?"

"Her father went off with another woman, which made Jasmin hate her father and his new family. But it wasn't normal hatred. One evening, she attacked Tamaşa Hanım with nitric acid just as they were going out for dinner. If the bodyguards hadn't been quick off the mark, her face would have been completely ruined, as you can imagine."

I wondered what size shoes Jasmin wore.

"Did she hate Cem too?"

"What do you think? She hated him most of all. She stuck a photo of Cem on to the face of one of her harlequins that had blood gushing out of his stomach where a sword had been inserted. But she hates the whole family."

"So she probably detested Sani."

"Jasmin's pictures have been exhibited in several galleries in Turkey as a result of family pressure. However, the art critics ignore her, while she's hailed as a genius abroad. Apparently her paintings are very powerful."

I wasn't remotely interested in whether she was a genius or not, only in whether she could be the person we were looking for, that is whether she wore a size forty shoe. And it was looking more and more as if this woman might be the sort of person prepared to watch someone die.

"Did you manage to find out where we can find this Jasmin Gil?"

"As you said, she lives in Bodrum. Her partner's a hack musician who sings in bars. His mother still lives in Istanbul and they come here frequently. If we're lucky—"

"Did you get her mobile number?"

"Mobile number, email address...I have the lot."

"Bravo, Fofo!" I said, patting his knee.

"Worth my weight in gold, aren't I?" bragged Fofo.

The phone call I'd been waiting for finally came when I was in a taxi heading for Bebek.

"I'm calling from solicitor Remzi Aköz's office," said a girl. "Remzi Bey has an hour free between seven and eight this evening."

"Fine," I said, knowing there was no option but to accept this appointment. "But I don't have the office address."

Unfortunately, I had to admit to having no pen with me, which I found extremely embarrassing. A sleuth without pen and paper was like a rocket salad without lemon – not impossible, but pointless.

"I'll text the address to you," said the girl.

Thank goodness for practical people like her.

Fofo had told me to get out at the Bebek taxi rank, look across the road and Lucca's would be right there. I found it easily enough. In fact I was ten minutes early, so I popped into a stationer's to buy a pen.

Fofo of course had made a huge sacrifice by agreeing to take care of the shop instead of coming with me to meet Sinan. However, the universities had now reopened and Pelin had to attend an afternoon lecture, so there was no one else to run the shop.

I entered Lucca's exactly on time, intending to find a corner table away from prying eyes, but nobody came to a place like this for privacy. The tables were arranged in such a way that every customer was visible to people passing in the street as well as everyone else inside the restaurant. I chose a table and sat down. After fifteen minutes, I'd had enough. Being a little unpunctual was one thing, but this was inexcusable. He could at least have phoned! I called the waiter, paid for my tea and left.

Outside, I was trying to decide whether to get a cab home straight away or spend a little time at Gloria Jean's Café enjoying its wonderful view, when someone touched my arm. And what a touch! It was more like a caress. When I turned, I found myself face to face with Sinan.

"There was an accident and they'd closed off the road," he said.

I looked at my watch. Another fifteen minutes had now passed. What with asking for the bill, paying, and deciding whether to go home or to Gloria Jean's, it was nearly half past three.

"You're half an hour late," I said.

"It'll never happen again," said Sinan.

Again? Was he intending to make a habit of summoning me to random places to make a confession?

"Shall we go to Gloria Jean's Café? This place is a bit…" I said, searching for the right adjective. "It's more for young people like you."

All the nice street-level tables at Gloria Jean's were taken, so we went down to the lower ground floor, which had the appeal of being at sea level. I particularly liked it in springtime when it was warm enough to sit outside but not yet so hot that you fried if you sat in the sun. However, early October was too cold for that, so we sat inside.

"What were you going to tell me?" I asked.

"You don't waste time, do you? Are you trying to get everything out of the way quickly so that you can leave? I'd hoped we could have a bit of a chat," said Sinan, with a touch of reproach.

My goodness, was this boy coming on to me? I didn't know whether to be happy or sad. It certainly stroked my ego that such a handsome young man wanted to spend time with me. He seemed totally unaware that fit young men with a hint of grey at the temples could be extremely attractive. Thankfully, we were living in liberal times when it was not considered unreasonable for a middle-aged woman like me to be courted by a young man. It was no secret, moreover, that young men have always been attracted to "mature" women. I remembered how at high school, while the girls were going crazy for the boys in our own class, the boys were ogling Frau Fischer during Latin and Frau Koch in biology.

"Don't worry, if you don't have time. You said you have another appointment anyway," said Sinan, looking a little hurt.

"I'm not in that much of a rush," I said.

"Last night, I started reading a thriller by Elmore Leonard that I borrowed from my mother. It's good. I think I'll come to your shop and buy something else sometime. What do you recommend?"

Was he asking what I liked?

"I don't know what kind of novels you like," I said.

"Why don't we draw up a reading list together?" suggested Sinan.

I explained that I was opposed to reading lists and hated saying "you must read this"; that novels shouldn't be read as if preparing for an exam; that nothing equalled the pleasure of reading; that no one was forced to read novels but that I held readers to be better people than non-readers; and that my views were unimportant, anyway.

"They're important to me," said Sinan.

Then we spoke about music and he passed on his wisdom to me. His taste in music ranged from rock to classical. We talked about our favourite dishes and the towns we'd visited. I confided that if all the cigarettes I'd ever smoked were put end to end they'd encircle the world several times. We spoke of other things too: films we'd seen, faces we'd noticed, walks we'd taken.

"What time was your appointment?" asked Sinan.

"Seven o'clock," I said, looking at my watch and noticing that it was already six.

"You should go. Shall I drop you off? Where are you going?"

"To Nişantaşı. But I don't want to bother you, especially in the pre-dinner traffic."

"Don't worry. I'll call in on some friends. What time will you finish?"

"The appointment's from seven to eight."

"Why don't we meet afterwards and have dinner together?"

I didn't reply. Rushing into a relationship with a guy, whatever his age, always made me nervous.

"I had something to tell you," persisted Sinan.

"Were you going to tell me that you waited outside Sani's door on the Sunday before she died?"

"How did you find out?" said Sinan, looking startled.

"You aren't the only person I've spoken to," I said. "Why did you hide that from me at our first meeting?"

"Who knows?" said Sinan, looking down at his tightly clasped hands. "I suppose I didn't want you to know that I was still chasing Sani after so much time had passed."

Then he looked up at me and added, "Do you understand?"

"I understand," I said, fully aware that it would be a matter of pride for a young man of his age. "You don't need to come all the way to Nişantaşı. We'll meet up another time, all right?"

"As you wish," said Sinan dejectedly.

While he was getting out his wallet to pay the bill, I bent down and looked beneath the table at his shoes. As Lenin said: *Vertrauen ist gut, Kontrolle ist besser* – "to trust is good, but to check is better". Sinan's shoes must have been at least a forty-three. They were enormous, anyway. Of course, a person as tall as him would have had trouble remaining upright in size forty shoes.

Sinan insisted on walking me to the taxi rank.

"Will you call in at the shop tomorrow," I asked as he opened the taxi door for me, "to pick up the reading list?"

"I'll collect the list as soon as possible so I can get started on it," he said with a smile as he closed the door.

As you might expect, I thought of nothing but Sinan all the way to Nişantaşı. My head was spinning with excitement and crazy thoughts. But I'd never been a slave to madness. In fact, the moment I awoke the next morning, new suspicions were forming in my mind, which I'll explain to you in due course.

The taxi dropped me in front of the building that housed Remzi Aköz's office. I was only five minutes late, which could have been worse, given the traffic. I rang the bell and gave my name to a woman over the intercom.

"Go up to the third floor," she said, and pressed the buzzer to open the door.

"You made a big impact on my wife," said a man behind me.

Had I passed this person in the street, I'd have known immediately that he was a lawyer, having met so many of my ex-lover Selim's friends. He could have been nothing else. I couldn't help wondering if they were selected by type while at university or whether they grew to resemble each other during the articling phase.

"Let's go into my office. What would you like to drink?" he said.

"Nothing for me, thank you," I said.

"Whisky? Single malt?"

"Oh, in that case, I'll have a whisky," I replied, thinking it was one thing to refuse tea and coffee, but rejecting a whisky wasn't so easy.

I took a couple of sips and regretted for the umpteenth time that day that I'd given up smoking.

"So, what can I do for you?" said Remzi.

Naturally, I asked about the famous prenuptial agreement.

"It's not permissible for us to give out such information, as I'm sure you know. However, one might say it's in the public interest that the cause of Sani's death be explained."

Public interest? I hadn't mentioned anything about there being any public interest. However, if a lawyer said there was, who was I to argue?

195

"The agreement they signed stated that the separation of estates regime would remain valid as long as the marriage lasted. They were bound by a decision that neither party would request compensation or alimony from the other party during or after the divorce proceedings."

I didn't understand this at all. What did he mean by "as long as", "during" and "after"?

"Just a minute," I said. "Let me tell you what I've understood."

"Of course. Go ahead," said Remzi.

"Sani was going to divorce Cem without taking a penny."

"Correct," said Remzi. "That was in accordance with the agreement."

"She was to receive no alimony and no compensation. Nothing at all."

"Yes, that was the agreement. However, these agreements aren't always legally compliant, and theirs was definitely contestable."

"Could you have won?"

Remzi walked over to the window holding his whisky glass. It was like a scene out of a second-rate Turkish soap opera. All it needed was a peroxide blonde sitting in my place.

"I believe we would have won," said Remzi.

"On what grounds?" I said, with a blank look.

"There hasn't been a precedent in Turkish law, but..."

Remzi broke off, returned to his desk and attempted to give me a proper explanation.

"The civil law was changed at the end of 2001. Before that, the separation of estates regime was legally binding and anyone who got married was subject to it – unless an agreement stating otherwise had been made at the appropriate time."

"Separation of estates means that on divorce each party takes any assets registered in their name. Is that right?" I asked.

It was obvious that I didn't have a wealth of experience when it came to divorce.

"With immovable property and automobiles," said Remzi, "each person took anything that had been registered in their name. When it came to movables, what belonged to whom was negotiated on an ad hoc basis."

"Do you mean things like diamond rings and tie pins?" I asked.

"Yes, jewellery is a good example," said Remzi. "However, since the law was changed, the person in whose name the property is registered is now recognized as the legal owner. In other words, anyone who married after 2001 is subject to this law, unless they've made a prenuptial agreement stating otherwise."

"But Sani and Cem did make a prenuptial agreement stating otherwise," I said.

"Yes. However, it was up to the court whether or not to allow such an agreement," said Remzi.

"But," I said, "I still don't understand. Can't people make up their own agreements?"

"You understand the law a little, I believe."

"My father was a lawyer. A criminal lawyer, actually."

"I might know him. Did he practise in Istanbul?"

"His name was Abraham Hirschel," I said, feeling pretty sure that Remzi would know of him. My father had been one of the Jewish scholars who fled German fascism and was given refuge in Turkey.

"Ah!" cried Remzi, jumping to his feet. "It never even occurred to me. Of course – your surname is Hirschel too. So you're Abraham Hirschel's daughter. Your father was a great lawyer. He established the Institute of Criminology at Istanbul University."

"I don't suppose you studied under him," I said, thinking that Remzi was far too young for that.

"No, I didn't," he said. "But anyone who passes through

Istanbul University knows about him because its largest lecture hall carries his name. Your father's students were our tutors. Of course I know about your father. To be honest, I didn't realize that his daughter was in Turkey. Didn't he return to Germany?"

"Yes. In 1965," I said.

"Lots of people came to Turkey at the same time as your father," said Remzi, "but they didn't all have such an impact. Just think, all those thousands of students, not to mention their students... He was one of the last to leave Turkey, I believe."

"That's right," I said, recalling that had my mother not insisted my father would never have gone back.

"Did he teach at a university in Germany?" asked Remzi.

"Yes," I said, realizing that it was coming up to eight o'clock and we needed to stop discussing my father and get back to the reason for my being there. "But time's getting on and you have to leave soon, I believe."

"We'll leave together," said Remzi. "We'll collect Aylin and have dinner together. How about that? Or did you have other plans for this evening?"

"No, but I don't want to mess up your evening," I said.

"How can you say that? It would be an honour to have dinner with the daughter of Abraham Hirschel," said Remzi eagerly.

This was something I loved about Turks. Remzi Aköz was born in the year that my parents and I left Istanbul for Berlin, yet he showed such respect and gratitude for my father's memory. It was as if he personally had benefited from my father's role as the founder of the faculty that had educated so many lawyers in the years before Remzi's time. Throughout the meal, he delighted me with anecdotes about those days, and also told me some of the things I'd come to find out.

At the end of the evening, I felt very happy – and a little tipsy – as I said goodbye to Aylin and Remzi outside my front door.

10

Remzi explained to me that the text of a law meant little in itself. What really mattered was the way it was interpreted by judges and lawyers. In other words, no one yet knew how the new civil law would be applied, and the validity of Cem and Sani's agreement hadn't been tested in the courts. Remzi said he would have been creating a precedent as the first lawyer to contest such an agreement, which was why he'd agreed to take on the case despite never having practised family law before.

The law might have been new in Turkey, but similar laws had been in place in Germany and Switzerland for years. Remzi had observed how the laws were applied in these countries, and was pleased with his findings. For instance, the German Supreme Court considered an agreement to be invalid and contrary to the spirit of the law if a woman had no opportunity to apply for some kind of financial support or recompense during divorce proceedings. In this context, the term "spirit of the law" quite simply meant that it was intended for the protection of women; the legal system didn't accept a woman being denied the protective shield of the law if she was forced to sign a prenuptial agreement in order to marry the man she loved. Remzi was convinced that he would have won the case and that the agreement would have been judged invalid. He certainly managed to persuade me that Cem would have ended up losing the case and having to pay out to Sani. Nevertheless, I'd become uneasy that everything seemed to be pointing at Cem.

"What more is there to think about?" asked Fofo.

"I don't like the idea of Cem being the number one suspect," I said.

"You're the one who's always saying that spouses are the most likely people to have a motive for murder. So what's the problem?" said Fofo.

"Cem has a very strong alibi. Anyway, if the case were that easy to solve, we wouldn't have been running about to Lüleburgaz and Paşabahçe, would we?"

"Are you suggesting that we should have just stayed at home and assumed that Sani's killer was her husband? I don't understand you," said Fofo.

"I don't understand myself, either. But something is making me uneasy about this," I said.

"Your sixth sense, perhaps?" said Fofo, teasingly.

It was no secret that my sixth sense was not particularly strong, as you, dear reader, will be all too aware.

"And there's no tangible evidence against Cem," I said.

"That's for the police to find," said Fofo. "We know that Cem hired someone to watch Sani's house, and we know that he was going to have to pay out a lot of money to Sani. That's reason enough for him to watch Sani die without offering help, isn't it? We've done our bit now."

"Okay," I said, "so tell me, what do you have to say about Sinan taking an interest in me?"

"I'd say you're a very beautiful woman and, if I were straight, I'd chase after you too."

I was flattered by his words, but my mind was too preoccupied to dwell on them.

"I must be old enough to be his mother," I said.

"Oh Kati, what are you trying to say?" said Fofo. "I could list twenty guys with girlfriends young enough to be their daughters. Don't worry about it."

"Yes, but they all have wealth, class or fame. As for me? I'm just a bookseller who lives in a dilapidated apartment. What do I have to make a young, handsome man run after me? Nothing."

"A great deal. Beauty isn't something that disappears with age. You're an extremely attractive and entertaining woman. And there's plenty of evidence to suggest that you're good in bed."

"You're shameless, Fofo! What kind of evidence are you talking about? And how would you know?"

"I know about these things," said Fofo, nodding mysteriously. "You're not yet ready to analyse why men find you attractive. We'll talk about this again in ten years' time."

"You're sounding very upbeat today. Why's that, I wonder?" I asked.

"Possibly because I sense a holiday in the offing," said Fofo, tossing the phone to me. "Why don't you ring this Jasmin Gil? If she agrees to see us, we can go to Bodrum and have a bit of a holiday while we're there. I hear it's wonderful at this time of year. The tourists have gone home, the sun is shining—"

"We're not going all the way to Bodrum, so don't raise your hopes for nothing, Fofo," I said grumpily, thinking that I wouldn't be able to take advantage of the winter sales after spending so much on fuel and taxi fares recently. "I'll try and get Jasmin Gil on the phone."

"Kati, do you realize how much phone charges have gone up? It would be cheaper just to go there," persisted Fofo.

"Stop being silly," I said. "We're going nowhere."

We didn't go. Whether it was a twist of fate or merely luck, Jasmin Gil came to us. Or rather, when I called her she said that she was returning to Bodrum the following day, but that she would make time to see us that day if we went straight round. She felt certain there was something strange about Sani's death, but nobody had thought to contact her despite the fact that she was one of the family, and so on and so forth. Words rattled out of her like rounds from a machine gun.

"Did you say your name is Kati Hirschel?" asked Jasmin towards the end of our conversation, pronouncing my name with a perfect German accent.

"Yes," I said.

"Hirschel isn't a very common name," she commented. "*Sind Sie zufällig Deutsche?*"

"I was born and spent a lot of my childhood in Istanbul. I feel I belong here."

"But your family's German," said Jasmin.

"Yes," I said.

"*Ich wusste es,*" she said, happily.

Why was she so pleased with herself? It wasn't as if we were talking about little Liechtenstein with a population of thirty thousand. Anyone from Germany, the most populous country in Europe with its eighty million citizens, was bound to encounter a compatriot sooner or later – it was hardly something to get excited about.

"*Aber Hirschel ist trotzdem kein gewöhnlicher Name,*" said Jasmin.

Why did she insist on speaking to me in German? Perhaps she missed being able to speak in her mother tongue?

"My father's surname was Hirschel. He was a German Jew," I replied in Turkish.

I'd never felt obliged to show patriotism by speaking in my mother tongue to Germans living in Turkey. I spoke in whichever language felt most comfortable at the time. On the rare occasions that I missed conversing in the German language, I'd phone my mother rather than impose it on others. Over the last twenty-four hours, I'd had to explain my family history to everyone I met, and it was becoming tedious.

"I'm half German," said Jasmin, before putting the phone down.

She sounded happy to have found a topic that we had in common, other than her sister-in-law's murder.

Jasmin Gil had given me an address in Kurtuluş, but after everything Fofo had told me, I didn't even think about going there alone.

Kurtuluş had been an Armenian neighbourhood at one time. About sixty thousand of the previously large Armenian population now remained, and they were mostly elderly. It was a typical lower-middle-class neighbourhood, with rows of terraced buildings and small shops selling groceries, fruit and vegetables, pickles and meze. Despite its proximity to Taksim Square, the rents were quite low and Kurtuluş had become popular with singles, transvestites and gays.

Ergenekon Street was one-way, so we got out at Pangaltı and walked from there.

"Here we are," said Fofo, stopping in front of a handsome Fifties-style building.

We made our way up to the first floor, where we came face to face with a woman who looked very German in a way that I liked. She was slim and of medium height, with light brown shoulder-length straight hair that framed a face that had a sagging chin, bags beneath the eyes and a network of fine wrinkles. She wore flat shoes, which I estimated to be size forty, black trousers and a black V-necked sweater. Although probably in her fifties, her body looked younger than her face. Whenever I see women like her, I always wonder how they would have looked in their youth. But Jasmin Gil didn't look as if she'd ever been young. I don't know what I'd expected after hearing all the stories about her, but it certainly wasn't this woman.

The apartment was a big disappointment. The building had looked lovely from the outside, and even the stairway had a stylish air of the Fifties about it. However, the apartment had been subjected to atrocious modifications and was a real dump. The sight of its bumpy walls, lifting floor tiles and dreadful chipboard doors made me want to weep.

Jasmin showed us to a sofa and perched herself on a chair, looking as if she was about to get up and run away at any moment.

"*Es freut mich, dass Sie da sind,*" she said.

"Could we speak in Turkish? My friend doesn't speak German," I said.

"Are you Turkish?" asked Jasmin, turning to Fofo.

"I'm Spanish," he said.

"I lived in Barcelona for a few years," said Jasmin, "but that was a long time ago, just after Franco died. It was at a time when Spain was going through a big transformation."

"I'm from Granada," said Fofo.

Jasmin nodded as if she had nothing to say about Granada.

"Would you like some tea? Or coffee?" she asked.

"I'd like a glass of water, please," I said, not wanting her to disappear into the kitchen for too long because I needed to get back to the shop in case Sinan dropped by.

"Actually, I'd like some tea," said Fofo infuriatingly.

I glared at him with irritation. However, it wasn't long before Jasmin returned.

"I searched the kitchen, but couldn't find anything," she said. "This apartment belongs to my boyfriend's mother. She's in hospital for a minor operation, so we came up to be with her. But I have such bad memories of Istanbul that I can't bear to stay any longer, and I've decided to go back to Bodrum tomorrow. Now I feel guilty for leaving my boyfriend on his own here. Do you think I should stay a bit longer?"

"It might be better if you stayed, but if you don't want to..." I mumbled, not knowing how to advise someone I'd only just met about something so personal. Fofo said nothing.

"It's a difficult decision, isn't it?" said Jasmin. "I'll just go and look for the teapot."

"Don't worry about the tea. I'll just have a glass of water," said Fofo graciously.

"No, no, tea is on its way. I'll find the teapot in no time."

As we listened to her clattering about in the kitchen, my irritation at Fofo increased. We'd lost fifteen minutes of valuable time thanks to his craving for tea.

"I couldn't find the teapot," said Jasmin, finally returning with two glasses of water. "I guess Nefise Hanım doesn't drink tea. Either that, or she's hidden the teapot somewhere or other. She even hides the toilet paper before we come, claiming that I use too much of it. It's an age thing. But what can I do? Still, you came here to talk about Sani."

At last, we could get down to business.

"Did you know Sani?" I asked.

"No, we never met. I read in the press that she died as a result of an accident," said Jasmin. "But it seemed strange that—"

"Why did it seem strange?" I asked.

"Why? It's always strange for a young woman to die following an accident in her own home, that's why."

Bravo. Jasmin was making a pretty good first impression.

"So you never met," I said.

"Do you know anything about the situation between me and the family?" asked Jasmin.

"We've heard one or two things," said Fofo.

"They act as if I don't exist. *Als ob ich nicht existiere... Verstehen Sie mich?*"

"I believe your parents got divorced," I said.

"That's what people go on about, but they're hardly going to talk about Mother being killed, are they? Do you know, they had me certified insane so that whatever I said would be regarded as the ravings of a madwoman."

"Your mother was killed?" I said, knotting my brows.

"It's probably best if I tell you the story from the beginning," said Jasmin, noticing my interest. I could hardly help being interested if someone made a claim about a killing, could I?

"My father studied engineering in Turkey. When he graduated in the early 1960s, he went to Germany, learned German and found a good job. He studied mechanical engineering and specialized in shipbuilding at a time when Germany needed all kinds of skills. My mother was working as a multilingual secretary for a freight shipping company. Anyway, they met and got married. She was the daughter of a rich Hamburg family, and my father borrowed money from her father to set up his own business, starting with a small freight shipping company which he soon expanded. I was born in 1966."

I looked at Jasmin again. She looked very old for someone of her age.

"The Sixties were a time when Germans were very inward-looking. They didn't go abroad for holidays as they do now. There were few foreigners living in Germany, and Turks were viewed as figures straight out of a Karl May novel. Instead of struggling with these stupid prejudices, my father decided to return to Turkey. But my mother refused to set foot in a country of wild Turks, or 'Orientals and Muslims', as her family referred to them. In the end, they agreed on a compromise. My father returned to Turkey and my mother remained in Hamburg with me. The arrangement was that every two or three months either Father would go to Germany or Mother and I would come to Istanbul."

"Didn't your mother change her mind once she'd seen Istanbul?" asked Fofo.

It was a reasonable question. Given the chance, anyone who didn't want to live in my lovely Istanbul during the 1970s must have been an idiot, to my mind at any rate.

"All my mother's family and friends were in Hamburg. And of course you have to bear in mind that she didn't know any Turkish," said Jasmin. "However, despite all that, Mother eventually decided to settle in Istanbul because she realized their relationship wouldn't last the way they were living and my father was becoming increasingly distant."

"But by that time it was too late," commented Fofo, the relationship expert.

"It certainly was. My father was already completely caught up in Tamaşa Hanım's web and looking for a way to get rid of Mother. He was eventually able to divorce her without her consent, because they'd lived apart for so long."

Estranged wives, willing or otherwise, seemed to have become a regular feature of my life.

"You didn't explain how your mother was killed," I said.

"When they divorced, my mother was still in love with my father, so what do you think she did?"

It was by now perfectly clear how the sad tale ended.

"I don't know," I said. "She went into therapy and tried to find a way of getting on with her life without your father, perhaps?"

"It wasn't that simple. Not everyone is as strong-willed as you are."

Strong-willed? Me? Much as I would have loved to be, there was nothing strong-willed about me, unfortunately.

"Did your mother commit suicide?" I asked.

"Yes, it was horrible. I was the one who found her body," said Jasmin with a deep sigh, as though it had happened just before our arrival.

"Is that why you said your mother was killed?"

"That woman killed my mother. Now she enjoys the rewards of the company set up in my mother's memory. She lives on Mother's money as if nothing untoward had ever happened."

I decided that Jasmin was stupid rather than mad. It's never easy to accept it when a close friend or relative takes their own life, but she was only making herself more miserable by dedicating her life to the destruction of the person she held responsible for her mother's suicide. It wasn't smart thinking.

"You said you knew something about Sani's death," I said.

"She killed her too," said Jasmin, leaning forward in her chair and bringing her face close to ours. "Do you think I'm crazy?"

Even if I'd thought that (and I've already said I didn't), I was certainly in no position to say whether anyone else was crazy or not.

"Of course not," I said. "But do you really know something about Sani's death?"

"Indeed I do, and it's something they think no one knows about," whispered Jasmin, rising to her feet. "I'll go and make us some coffee."

Fofo and I were left alone in the sitting room.

"What do you think?" asked Fofo.

"I've no idea. I don't know what to say to her," I said.

Jasmin returned with a tray holding three large cups in which she'd mixed sachets of sweetened powdered milk and coffee with lukewarm water. If she drank that disgusting stuff every day, it wasn't surprising that she looked ten years older than her age. I took a few sips out of politeness, but left the rest.

"Aren't you curious to know more?" asked Jasmin.

"We're very curious," I said, though her games were beginning to bore me.

"*Der is schwul.*"

Ah!

"*Wer? Wer is schwul?*" I asked, wanting to be sure that I'd understood her properly.

"*Na, wer schon, Cem natürlich.*"

"What are you saying?" interrupted Fofo, bursting with curiosity.

"Jasmin Hanım says that Cem's gay," I said.

"He must be bi," said Fofo. "People who have relationships with men and women are called bisexuals." Dear Fofo couldn't bear any ambiguity when it came to matters of gender and sexuality. And there was nothing wrong in that. I wouldn't want anyone to refer to me as a man.

"I know very well what bisexual means. Cem was totally gay," said Jasmin.

"But he was married to Sani," said Fofo.

"They were married on paper. But nobody took the marriage seriously. Sani had been offered a deal whereby she was promised a life of luxury in return for living with Cem as his wife, and Sani accepted. It was his mother who organized everything."

Could it really be true? I certainly hadn't heard anyone say that Cem and Sani were deeply in love or even that they'd fallen in love at first sight, but was all that necessary in order to get married?

I'd have given anything for a cigarette right at that moment!

I was worldly enough to know that not every couple was madly in love when they got married. But their relationship could have been built on so many little things, insignificant in themselves, like how they made up after an argument, agonized when they were apart, wrote little notes to one another or looked at each other with affection. Yet no one had once mentioned anything like that about Sani and Cem. Why was that?

I began with one of the scores of questions whirling round in my head.

"We'd heard that Tamaşa Hanım didn't want Cem and Sani to marry."

"Don't believe everything you hear," said Jasmin, almost choking with laughter. "She couldn't let her friends think she'd given her approval to a marriage between her one and only darling son and someone as unsuitable as Sani, could she? But having made her statement to the press at the time, she decided to say no more about it."

Jasmin was right. We shouldn't have believed everything we'd heard.

"You're the first person to mention anything about Cem being gay," I said.

"It's a big secret. Hardly anyone knows," said Jasmin.

"In which case, it might be more accurate to say he's asexual rather than homosexual, don't you think?" chuckled Fofo.

Jasmin looked offended.

"I meant that very few people in his immediate circle know," she said sulkily.

"How do you know he's gay? And why is it such a big secret?" said Fofo.

"You live in Turkey, don't you? If something like that came out, it would be the end of Ankaralıgil Holdings. If nothing else, it would certainly have a detrimental effect on business. Have you ever heard of a gay businessman?"

"What a load of rubbish," said Fofo.

"It's not rubbish at all!" shouted Jasmin, clearly finding Fofo's attitude annoying.

"Anyway, it's not important whether businessmen are gay or

not," I said, trying to smooth things over. "How do you know that Cem's gay? That's the important question."

"I'm a member of the family too, you know," said Jasmin.

Never mind all the stories we'd heard, just hearing her talk in person convinced me that they were unlikely to have said anything to her about this if they'd kept it from everyone else.

"As soon as Cem finished high school, they bundled him off abroad and didn't let him come back for years, which was very suspicious."

"Let me get this straight. Is what you're saying based on suspicion or knowledge?" I asked.

"I know!" shouted Jasmin impatiently. "He had an affair with his high school PE teacher! It was covered up before a scandal broke out, and then Cem was sent away."

"Have you been to visit your father while you've been in Istanbul this time?"

"Why do you ask?" said Jasmin.

"I just thought it might have been while talking to your father that you got the idea that Tamaşa Hanım had a hand in Sani's death."

"My father hasn't spoken to me for six years. That woman won't let him."

"You mean Tamaşa Hanım?" I said.

Jasmin nodded.

"Is it true that you once tried to throw nitric acid in Tamaşa Hanım's face?" I asked.

"You have done your research, haven't you?" said Jasmin. "I thought that business was forgotten long ago."

"Was it after that incident that your father stopped speaking to you?" I persisted.

Jasmin didn't reply, but leaned towards the window and stared through the net curtains at the buildings outside.

"How does Tamaşa Hanım dress?" I asked.

"What do you mean by that?" asked Jasmin.

"Is her style classic or modern? Does she wear flat shoes, for instance?"

"My father's short. He calls himself a stunted Anatolian boy," said Jasmin. "But he always goes for tall women – at least, the two I know about. My mother was at least ten centimetres taller than he is, and so is his current wife."

"So does Tamaşa Hanım wear flat shoes?" I asked.

"I don't know if it's to please my father, but I've never seen her in heels," said Jasmin.

"You don't really know her well at all, do you? I take it you've never lived with them," I said.

"After my mother died, I went to a school near my grand-parents' house in Germany, but used to come to Istanbul in the holidays," said Jasmin. "How else do you think I learned Turkish? Of course I know her well, and a lot better then she thinks. She's so egocentric and self-absorbed that she has no idea just how well I know her."

"And you've known Cem since he was an infant," I said.

"Of course."

"But you don't speak to him."

"No, we're not on speaking terms," said Jasmin. "We haven't spoken for six years. After that incident, everyone cut me off."

Was the tremor in Jasmin's voice caused by regret? I wasn't sure.

"Do you have regrets?" I asked.

"Regrets?" she said, covering her face with her hands and taking a deep breath. "Yes, I have regrets. Deep regrets. I lost my father for the very stupid reason that I couldn't come to terms with him as he was, with all his shortcomings. It made me so angry to see how he trusted that woman."

I looked sadly at Jasmin's face and saw tears running down her cheeks.

"Tolerance doesn't come easily to us," she said. "I used to think Germans were more honest than most, but now I see that it's... *es ist eine Tugend*. What is *Tugend* in Turkish?"

"Virtue," I said.

"A virtue," she repeated. "There's no need to sanction every kind of human behaviour, but we should be tolerant of each other. It makes people happier. We don't choose our families, and we don't always share the same beliefs, but it's very important to try and get along with them."

The three of us sat in silence, staring into space. Perhaps each of us was thinking of people in our own families that we had issues with.

"You asked me how she dresses," said Jasmin, pulling herself together and wiping away the black streak of mascara that had run down her cheek.

"Yes," I said.

"She has a good figure and dresses well. She usually wears trouser suits during the day, and classic tailored dresses for evening."

That was not what I wanted to hear.

"Does she ever buy labels that young people are into?" I asked.

"Such as?"

"Sportswear?"

"I don't know. What kind of sportswear?" asked Jasmin.

I didn't want to mention the brand because it was confidential information.

"I don't know where she goes shopping these days. She hasn't always worn tailored suits and proper shoes. She used to go around in jeans and trainers, but they had to be the latest trainers, of course. Yes, she dressed well," said Jasmin, glancing down at her own shoes.

"What size shoe do you take?" I asked, realizing that my question was somewhat abrupt, but I had my reasons, as you know.

"Size forty," said Jasmin. "When I was young, Tamaşa Hanım used to get furious with me for wearing her shoes."

"Tamaşa Hanım takes size forty too?"

"My dress size is thirty-six and she's a thirty-eight, but we both take the same size in shoes, even though she's taller than me. I'm a mixture of both my parents – not as tall as Mother and not as short as Father."

"So you think Cem married Sani to hide the fact that he's gay," I said, struggling to find the logic in what Jasmin had been telling us.

"It was all planned by his mother," said Jasmin. "I know exactly how that woman's mind works. The only thing she thinks about is money. Money's the be-all and end-all of life as far as she's concerned. She just assumed that Sani, an ambitious little village girl, would be unable to refuse a marriage that would change her life. Most people would, I suppose."

"They might assume it, but to put a plan like that into action requires a little more than an assumption," I said.

"Well, whatever that 'little more' is, she had it," said Jasmin. "She was always very protective towards her darling son. When Cem was little, she used to wash him in bottled water, claiming that tap water was unclean and would give her baby germs. Bottled water used to be delivered to the house by the cartload. Yet they labelled me crazy without batting an eyelid!"

We fell silent again.

"Do you believe me?" asked Jasmin.

"Believing isn't enough. We need proof," I said.

"Have you spoken to her?"

I'd noticed that she avoided referring to Tamaşa by name, but now I wasn't sure who she meant.

"Spoken to whom?" I asked.

"That woman."

"We haven't spoken. So far there's been no good reason to contact her."

"Never mind finding a reason," said Jasmin. "You're private detectives. I'm sure she'd agree to see you immediately. She loves trying to outsmart and manipulate people. She'd give you an appointment, even if it was just to see if she could fob you off with a couple of lies. Yes, definitely. Trust me. Call her and you'll see that I'm right."

"Is Cem aware of any of this?" I asked.

"Any of what?" asked Jasmin, making me think that either her Turkish wasn't as good as I thought, or that her concentration came in waves.

"That his mother was involved in Sani's murder," I said.

Jasmin Gil looked shaken at hearing the word "murder", which was the reaction I'd hoped for. However, I knew that Sani hadn't been the victim of murder.

"Did you say 'murder'? Just a minute... How did Sani actually die?" gasped Jasmin. Finally, it had occurred to her to ask a question.

"The papers said nothing about murder. I assumed she'd committed suicide," she said.

It was now becoming clear. Jasmin believed that Tamaşa had "killed" Sani as she'd "killed" her mother. Finding common terms can be difficult, even when people speak the same language.

"It wasn't murder, actually," I said. "Someone was in the house with Sani when she died. That person – whoever it was – could have saved her, but did nothing."

"The monster!" cried Jasmin. "A young woman died before her very eyes and she didn't even call an ambulance! That's outright murder! What else would you call it?"

"Well, technically it isn't," I said.

"Technically?" she yelled. "What a vile woman. She simply got rid of Sani as soon as she'd served her purpose."

"Do you think Cem knows about this?" I asked.

"Cem? No, definitely not. Cem isn't the type to commit or commission a murder. You'd never believe that he's her son. He takes after his father. Very kind-hearted, even a bit naive."

Well, well! Someone else claiming that Cem was a good person. Which was all very well, but...

"I heard that you portrayed Cem as a harlequin with a sword stuck in his gut," I said.

"Have you actually seen the picture?" asked Jasmin.

I shook my head.

"It wasn't a sword stuck into his gut. It was his mother's fingernails. The poor boy was struggling to maintain a smile as he bled to death."

"And did you know that Cem had arranged for the nightwatchman to keep an eye on Sani's house?" I said, thinking that could hardly be called the behaviour of a naive person.

"The watchman?"

"Yes. He was paid to tell Cem about anyone who went in or out of Sani's house," I said.

"That must have been his mother's idea. Cem would never think of spying on anyone," said Jasmin dismissively, adding with a wistful smile, "He's like a child. An innocent child bathed in bottled water."

"We must go," I said, noticing that it was nearly six o'clock and wondering if Sinan had been to the shop. "Have you decided yet whether to leave tomorrow?"

"I don't think I can. It doesn't feel right. But you never know."

"You've obviously been here a while. When did you arrive in Istanbul?" I asked, as if it was of no significance. I'm capable of playing the part of a private detective, even if I'm not actually allowed to do the job.

"Two weeks ago. It's been six years since I spent such a long time in Istanbul."

"That's a long time," I said. "A very long time."

So, Jasmin Gil was in Istanbul when Sani died.

11

I was still trying to make up my mind as we jumped into a taxi to take us back to the shop. Should I stop off at the hairdresser's for a blow-dry? Or could I make do with a ponytail?

"What do you think, Fofo?" I asked, trying to see myself in the driver's rear mirror.

"I think that, if Cem is really gay, they couldn't possibly have kept it totally secret," said Fofo.

"I wasn't asking about that. I'm talking about my hair," I said.

"What about your hair?" he said, giving me a quick glance. "What's the matter with your hair? It looks very nice."

"You haven't even looked."

Fofo gazed at me blankly. "I'm looking now, and I see a pretty face with quite a cute ponytail."

The cute ponytail was the problem.

"Shall I go and get a blow-dry? Sort of Eighties style? What do you think?" I asked.

Fofo gave an exasperated sigh and said, "I'm not coming back to the shop. I'm going to Cihangir to see if I can pick up any gossip about Cem from the boys."

"But Sinan's coming," I said.

"So? What's it to me?"

"I thought you liked Sinan."

"Are you suggesting we should fight over him?"

"I just think it would be better if you didn't leave me on my own with him," I said.

"Am I supposed to hold your hand while the two of you flirt?"

"Oh, all right then, go to Cihangir," I said, thinking how irritating Fofo could be sometimes.

Before getting out of the taxi at Tarlabaşı, Fofo said, "Let me know if you don't want me to come back to the apartment tonight."

"I'm not that fast a mover," I said.

"I don't want to know," said Fofo, suggesting that he knew more about me than I realized.

As soon as I reached the shop, I sent Pelin home. It was past six o'clock and Sinan had neither been in yet nor had he phoned. Maybe our appointment had slipped his mind. This thought made me feel more at ease, if a little demoralized, because it meant I'd escaped a potentially sticky situation. I'd actually been feeling terrified, not just because of Sinan's age, but at the idea of a new relationship, a new person in my life.

Had I really been reduced to this since splitting up with Selim? Did I still miss him? Would it be betrayal if I started a new relationship? No, I was being stupid. Yet feelings could be stupid. It wasn't my fault if I didn't always think logically, was it? Obviously I intended to act like a mature person.

It was ages since we'd split up, and Selim probably had a new woman in his life by now. The problem was that we had no mutual friends to keep us in touch with each other. What was he up to? Was he living the dream with a new girlfriend, or still working every weekend and falling asleep on the sofa?

I'd forgotten the smell of his skin. However, I remembered how I used to lean my head on his shoulder and breathe in that smell. I'd kiss him in his favourite places while he was talking, which would annoy him because he'd think I wasn't listening to what he was saying. But instead of getting cross, he'd look happy. He was naive enough to think that I couldn't tell that he liked it. He'd sulk and go and sit in another chair, put on his glasses and pretend to read the paper as if he'd fallen out with me, not realizing that I knew he was putting on an act. Selim was so sweet.

For some reason my heart still raced whenever I thought of the happy moments we'd shared – in the mornings, evenings and at night.

When I was a child, if I cried because of a bad mark at junior school, or my classmates teased me for bragging or I missed my friend Behice back in Istanbul, Father used to say, "You'll have forgotten all this when you're grown up." He was right. Our minds are programmed in such a way that by the time we're adults we only retain good memories. My father was a good example. He'd managed to put all the bad things in his life behind him, including the painful knowledge that his aunt and two little cousins had died in a concentration camp. According to him, memory was a positive thing and it was contrary to human nature to remember negative things.

I now knew that to be true. In my mind, life with Selim was untainted by any trace of a single bad moment. It was as if a large broom had swept my heart clean of any unpleasant recollections, leaving only my love for him and other good memories.

"You look a million miles away," said a male voice.

I was so lost in my thoughts that I hadn't even noticed the door open. It was Batuhan. I looked at him, blinking away tears and wondering if I was dreaming or mistaken. He certainly wasn't the person I'd been waiting for.

"I had work to do around here, so I thought I'd look in on you," he said.

"I'm glad you did," I replied, not feeling the slightest bit glad, and fearing he might bump into Sinan. "Shall we go out? There's a nice café near here, and I haven't eaten anything since morning."

"Why don't we go to a kebab house? It's on me," said Batuhan.

"Let's wait for the rush-hour traffic to subside. How about a coffee first?" I said, grabbing my bag and closing the computer because I wanted to leave immediately.

"Where's this café?"

"At Tünel."

"In that case, I'll leave my car here."

"Might as well," I said, letting him help me lower the shutters on the shop window.

Deciding that İstiklal Street had too many potholes for us, we decided to turn off into Asmalımescit Street.

"This area's changed a lot over the last few years," said Batuhan.

"I love it. The taverns are great," I said. "Why don't we go to a fish restaurant instead of a kebab house? Bluefish is in season."

"You know I don't understand fish. I'm a meat man. Still, you decide."

"In that case, we'll eat fish for a change, but coffee first. Come on," I said positively, and led him into Şimdi Café.

"I have a favour to ask," he said as we sat down. "I'm going to ask you to do something, and then we won't talk shop again this evening."

"Go on," I said.

"After talking to you, I sent some of my lads to talk to Sani's neighbours, and I also did a bit of research myself. Apparently, Orhan Soner was the architect of Sani's house and he'd personally sorted out her lease. There'd been some sort of problem between Boğaziçi Construction and the estate freeholder, because the houses were intended for sale rather than the rental market. A court case ensued and the houses were being kept vacant until a verdict was reached. You must have noticed that most of the houses were empty."

"So Orhan Bey became an agent for his ex-girlfriend," I said.

"He did it to make sure that he had Sani well under control."

What an ugly thing to say. What was I doing having coffee with a policeman, anyway? Even if it was Batuhan.

"Or rather, that he could keep her close by," he said, realizing that I didn't like his choice of words.

Yes, that was better.

"Do you think they'd started seeing each other again?" I asked. My dear readers already know the way my mind was working.

"That's exactly what I'm thinking," said Batuhan. "Anyway, he was far too smooth-talking for my lads, who couldn't get anything out of him apart from a look at his passport, which contained stamps showing he'd been abroad on a ten-day business trip when Sani died. I obtained the flight lists from the airline company and they confirmed the dates he gave. However, as I said, he was playing games with my boys, and I think he knows a lot more than he's letting on."

"Do the Turkish police get foreign assistance?" I asked.

"Foreign assistance? We prefer any assistance we get to be local," said Batuhan, patting my arm and smiling.

"Now, now! It's time we went to the restaurant," I said, smiling. "Do you suspect Orhan Soner?"

"Not exactly, but... You know that sperm was found in Sani's underwear, don't you?"

"Which you can have DNA-tested," I said.

"Without any evidence against him, I have no grounds to ask for a DNA test. The attorney has to be persuaded. It can't just happen on my say-so."

"What if there was a witness?"

"But who? We know of two people who were previously in a relationship with her, but that was a long time ago," said Batuhan. "And Soner hasn't admitted that he was seeing Sani. Why's that?"

"Because he's married, of course, why else? He wouldn't have wanted everyone knowing about it, would he?" I said.

"Don't you think his wife has any idea? Surely she must have wondered what was going on when her husband's former lover suddenly moved into the house directly opposite."

"Maybe she didn't know about Sani," I said.

"Why don't you go and find out?" said Batuhan. "We'll discuss it later."

"Of course," I said.

"But no more talk about this tonight. My whole life seems to revolve around work at the moment."

"In that case, I shan't tell you what I've just learned," I said.

"Kati, please. My mind needs a rest this evening," said Batuhan wearily. "After all, murders don't disappear."

"Murders don't, but murderers do," I said.

Our suspect, if not a murderer, was certainly eluding us. Everyone I'd had suspicions about in this case had proved impossible to nail down: the Thrace industrialists, the TLF, Cem, Naz, Orhan Soner, Tamaşa, Jasmin Gil, Sinan. Potentially, they'd all had reasons to want Sani dead.

I woke up the next morning wondering who was stroking my hair. It was of course Fofo.

"What time did you get back last night? I didn't hear you come in," he said.

"It was late."

"How was your evening? Did you have a good time?" asked Fofo. Did we have a good time?

223

"Not bad. We ate fish and then went dancing," I said, burying my face in the pillow.

"Come on, get up," said Fofo, opening the curtains. "You can have a lie-in when the case is solved."

"No, I want to sleep now," I grumbled.

"That youngster obviously sapped all your energy. I thought it would have been the other way round."

"Which youngster?" Batuhan was younger than me, but hardly a youngster! No, Sinan was a youngster. Then I suddenly realized that Fofo thought I'd been out with Sinan.

"Sinan didn't turn up. He didn't even phone," I said.

"So who did you go out for dinner with?" asked Fofo.

"Batuhan called in at the shop and we went to eat in Asmalımescit Street," I said.

"I phoned you at about eleven to ask if I should spend the night somewhere else, but you didn't pick up."

"I didn't hear you call. It was very noisy."

"Maybe Sinan also called and you didn't hear," said Fofo.

"Are you trying to put Sinan back in my good books?"

He wasn't, of course. Darling Fofo was just trying to make me feel better about being stood up.

"I was just stating the facts," he said, as he shuffled away in his slippers. "Where's your bag?"

"In the sitting room, I expect. How should I know?"

He came back with it, saying, "Let's see how many unanswered calls you have on your mobile."

Noticing that my mobile was not in its usual place, I tipped everything out: notebook, two pens, lip balm, hand cream, purse and more.

"My mobile's not there," I said. "Do you think it's been stolen?"

"What's this?" asked Fofo, peering at a yellow metal thing he had in his hand.

What was it indeed?

"Where did that come from?" I asked.

"It fell out of your bag. Where else?"

"I've no idea how that got there," I said.

"It smells strongly of perfume," said Fofo.

Strong perfume?

"Now I remember where it came from," I said with a groan because my head was beginning to throb. "We found it at Sani's house. Or rather, Naz found it on the floor." In our rush to leave Sani's house that day, I must have thrown it into my bag.

"It looks like the lid of a bottle," said Fofo.

"That's what I thought. Where on earth is my mobile?"

"I'll call your number," said Fofo.

The call was answered immediately. After a brief conversation, Fofo turned to me and said, "You left your mobile at the shop yesterday. You have seven unanswered calls, but I didn't ask Pelin to look and see who they were from."

"Thanks, you did the right thing," I said. "Can you bring me an Alka-Seltzer?"

"What were you drinking last night?" asked Fofo.

"*Rakı. Rakı. Rakı. Rakı.* Whisky. Whisky. Tequila."

"Four *rakı*s, two whiskies and a tequila?"

"I think so."

"You'd better go and have a shower."

"I think I'd rather get some sleep."

"Come on, get up," ordered Fofo, throwing my arm over his shoulder and trying to drag me to my feet. If only I'd been light enough for him to pick me up in his arms – it would have meant I was a size eight. However, it would have lowered my chances with Turkish men who like their women more rounded, which, since I was still living in Istanbul, was an aspect that had to be considered.

"You're going to break my arm!" I cried.

"You've got to sober up. We have lots to talk about. My friends knew all about Cem being gay."

"Leave me alone," I said.

Fofo won. I went into the shower and, after drinking a thick black coffee, a grapefruit juice and an Alka-Seltzer, I curled up at one end of the sofa, my stomach churning as if I had an ocean inside me.

"You'd better eat something," said Fofo, standing over me with a plate in his hand.

"I'm not hungry."

"Maybe not, but you have to eat. We need to get the alcohol out of your bloodstream as quickly as possible."

Where does one learn something like how to get alcohol out of the bloodstream? I wondered if I should start reading the papers more.

"What's on the plate?" I asked.

"Bread and cheese."

"Bread and cheese," I repeated, which for some reason sounded ridiculous to me.

I started laughing. Fofo also laughed, not at what I'd said but at my predicament. I laughed so hard that I snorted some of the contents of my stomach out through my nose, which shut me up. I realized that my situation was bad and likely to end in tears. It had been a long time since I'd drunk so much. I had the occasional double whisky or a few glasses of red wine with a meal, but clearly my alcohol tolerance had dropped significantly. I felt bad, really bad.

"I'm going back to bed, Fofo," I said.

"In that case, I'll go to the shop. The best thing for you is to sleep it off," said Fofo, realizing that I was unable to function in my current state.

I dreamt that I was with Selim, eating fillet steak and chilli sauce. There was no cutlery on the table, so Selim called the waiter over, who turned out to be Sinan.

"What kind of restaurant is this?" complained Selim.

Sinan was wearing an apron with large pockets, from which he took handfuls of knives and forks and threw them on the table. He said that people in the Middle East used their hands to tear meat apart, which some might find repulsive but was not as barbaric as using knives at the table as Westerners did. I could hear a woman shouting "Barbarians, barbarians!" from a far table.

"This is sirloin. We asked for fillet," said Selim, as he tried, unsuccessfully, to cut up his meat.

"I can bring you a T-bone steak if you like, but not fillet," said Sinan, looking at me with a knowing smile. "We don't serve fillet steak to couples who've been together for more than three years."

Hearing these words made me sob. They were so close to my claim that long-term relationships lacked seasoning and spice and were comparable to tasteless, chewy steak. I then lied, saying that I used to have such thoughts until I met Selim, and felt enormously guilty for the horrible comparison.

I woke up feeling remorseful about everything. Remorse that I was no longer with Selim, that I'd met Sinan, even that I'd started trying to solve another crime. My limbs felt weak and my throat sore, possibly the result of catching a chill after cavorting around the previous evening, so I decided to ask Fofo to come back home. I went into the sitting room for my phone and found him there sitting on the sofa.

"So you're awake. How are you now?" he asked.

"I've got a fever," I said.

Even if I hadn't, I thought that he'd pay more attention to me if he thought I had. My only desire at that moment was to have his undivided care and attention.

"Lie down on the sofa. I'll get you a blanket," said Fofo.

I lay down and Fofo returned with a blue and navy patterned blanket that I detested.

"I want the yellow blanket," I said.

"I couldn't find the yellow one," he said.

"Fatma Hanım must have put it away. See if it's in the drawer with the sweaters."

Fofo came back still holding the same disgusting blanket. "I can't find it."

"I'm not putting that horrible thing over me!" I yelled, making my throat hurt, which made me feel so bad that I started to cry.

"What's the matter now?" asked Fofo, sitting next to me on the sofa and stroking my hair. "Sinan called you six times yesterday evening. See for yourself if you don't believe me."

"I don't care about Sinan," I cried. "I couldn't care less!"

I wanted Selim, but I couldn't tell Fofo that because he'd never liked him anyway.

"Let me take your temperature," said Fofo.

The thermometer felt icy cold on my skin.

"I'll go and look for another blanket," said Fofo and disappeared.

"The yellow blanket wasn't there. Shall I cover you up with this?" said Fofo, returning with my duvet.

"Yes, please."

"I've made you some chicken soup. You must eat something."

"I don't want to eat anything."

"You have to force yourself if you're going to get any better. Let me look at the thermometer."

Fofo turned the thermometer slightly to see the mercury level.

"It's not even thirty-seven, which is good. You'll be good as new tomorrow," he said.

"What a horrible day," I said, putting a spoonful of chicken soup into my mouth.

I then went back to sleep. It had indeed been a horrible day.

The next morning, I awoke hating life slightly less, at least until Fofo started pestering me to phone Sinan.

"I have better things to do," I said.

"He called you six times," insisted Fofo. "You have to phone him. Or at least tell him that you don't want to see him."

But I didn't want to tell Sinan that.

"I'll call him later," I said.

Fofo fetched my phone and put it next to my plate.

"Are you trying to make me ill again?" I asked.

"It won't make you ill. Just one short phone call," insisted Fofo.

"I don't want to."

"I'll dial the number, then!" said Fofo, ignoring all my objections.

"In that case, talk to him yourself. I'm not saying another word," I said, and fell silent.

It was like a scene out of a medical drama.

"You're just being stupid, Kati."

I said nothing.

"Come on, pull yourself together, Kati."

Still I said nothing.

"Tell him that you lost your phone and you've only just found it."

I looked away.

"You're not being fair on the boy."

I remained silent.

"It's not right to play with young people's feelings like that."

I carried on ignoring him.

"Don't you feel any responsibility towards the youth of today?"

Fofo was becoming ridiculous now and I was finding it hard not to laugh.

"Are you prepared to take personal responsibility if this kid hates all foreigners from now on?"

I stifled a laugh.

"I really thought you were someone with a sense of social responsibility."

"Oh, Fofo! All right then! Call him, and I'll speak to him!"

However, as always, Sinan didn't answer his phone. It would have been the crack of dawn for him, and he was probably sleeping.

Once the phone fiasco was over, Fofo asked what we were going to do that day.

"I'm going to look for a photo of Tamaşa Hanım to show to the neighbours. She might have been seen in the vicinity of the house," I said.

"Well, someone should go to Murat's office and pick up that magazine," said Fofo, as he went to the kitchen to make tea.

"Would you go?" I called out after him, realizing my throat still hurt when I spoke loudly.

"I'll go. But we don't want the one of her dressed in Valentino, surely. A photo that looks more like she is now would be better, don't you think? She's hardly going to be wandering around Paşabahçe in a Valentino gown and full evening make-up," said Fofo, as he came back and placed my glass of tea noisily on the table.

"Be careful, Fofo!"

"It slipped out of my hand."

I picked up a napkin to mop up the tea that had spilled over the plate of cheese.

"You're right. I expect she only goes around Paşabahçe wearing XOXO trainers," I laughed.

"By the way, you haven't yet told me what you and Batuhan talked about over dinner the other night."

I explained that by the time we reached the restaurant the bluefish had run out so we both ate tuna, which was pretty boring. The interesting part of the evening was when we started dancing, which of course was what my dear Fofo really wanted to hear about.

"Well, you have a birthday coming up. Perhaps your luck will change," he said, as I came to the end of my account.

Talk of my birthday reminded me of star signs, which in turn reminded me of the secretary Sevim.

"I'm glad you reminded me, Fofo. We must call Sevim Hanım too," I said.

"Why's that?"

"I think she was also hired to keep an eye on Sani. If we press her, we might find out more."

"You're suggesting that we should talk to her together?"

I nodded.

"So, we need to get hold of Sevim Hanım and Murat," said Fofo.

"Yes," I said.

Fofo got up and went to make some phone calls.

We met Sevim early that evening at the same Simit Sarayı. She explained at length that she wasn't at all happy about having to look for a job. She wanted to work in insurance, which was difficult because people feared another economic crisis was on the way and didn't want to take out insurance policies. She also wanted a job close to home. Fofo and I listened to her grumbling as she munched her way through a cream dessert, until I'd finally had enough.

"There's no way you'll earn the same sort of money you were paid at GreTur. You'll have to take a pay cut, whether you like it or not," I said.

"I didn't earn very much there," murmured Sevim.

"Maybe not, but with extras, perhaps—"

"What extras?" she interrupted, trying to gauge what and how much I knew.

"Let's not play games. Who was paying you to inform the Ankaralıgil family about what Sani was up to?" I said, intending to startle Sevim.

She was indeed startled.

"What?" she cried, going red in the face.

"Well, your sister and I certainly weren't the only people you told about Sinan," I said, sensing that it was time to be more hawkish.

"I haven't told tales about Sani Hanım to anyone," said Sevim, springing to her feet and grabbing her bag, which was dangling over the back of her chair.

"If you don't sit down, we're going straight to the police, and they might not be so patient," I said, having had enough of her waffle about searching for a job.

"Who were you doing it for?" asked Fofo.

"Look, I know you have a brother who needs constant care, and I know you need money. If you tell us everything, we won't go to the police," I said.

Sevim didn't look the slightest bit swayed by what I'd said. The game of good cop, bad cop needs to be consistent, otherwise it just causes confusion. Was I the good cop, or the bad?

"I don't know anything," she said, looking alarmed.

"Just tell us what you know," said Fofo.

Sevim sat down again, clutching the bag in her lap tightly.

"Sani Hanım wasn't killed because of me," she said.

"Who did you give information about Sani to?" I asked.

Sevim glanced towards the stairs, as if trying to calculate whether or not she could escape.

"You won't get away from us. We know where you live," said Fofo, throwing himself into the role with unusual fervour.

"They arranged for other people to monitor Sani as well," I said. "You weren't the only one, I can assure you."

"Who were the others, then?" asked Sevim.

Did she really think we'd tell her that?

"It's not important who they are. Their names are classified information. We won't give your name to anyone, either," I said.

"Really?" asked Sevim, looking as if she wanted to believe us and tell us what she knew so that she could get away as quickly as possible. That was what I was hoping, at any rate.

"Yes, really," I said. "Whatever you say remains between us three. No one else will find out."

"Honestly, I didn't do anything bad," said Sevim, before revealing everything.

As we left Simit Sarayı, I became aware that Fofo was angry with me and barely answering my questions.

"What is it, Fofo?"

"Nothing."

"Are you cross with me?"

"Hmm."

"Are you going to tell me why you're cross?"

Silence.

"For God's sake, what is it?"

The silence continued until finally Fofo said, "So Sevim told you about Sani's relationship with Sinan and you didn't bother to tell me?"

Whoops!

Whoops indeed. We continued to argue all the way home.

12

Pelin sounded ready to bite our heads off when we told her that yet again we wouldn't be at the shop that day. However, she soon pulled herself together. After all, we weren't out enjoying ourselves. Working for the benefit of the public meant that we had a right to expect a bit of support from those around us, didn't it? She would have to put up with it for a few days more. We were almost there, but just needed proof. And maybe Orhan Soner could help us with that.

"If he's not at home, we've come all this way for nothing," said Fofo, as we walked through the well-tended garden between rows of brilliant red roses that had obviously been planted in early autumn.

"Where would he go at this time on a Sunday?" I said, optimistically.

It wasn't long before the door opened, making me beam with pleasure at seeing my optimism rewarded. We found ourselves looking at a woman with shoulder-length hair swept back from her forehead and held in place by a hairband, making her look like a cartoon figure. It had to be Orhan's wife.

"Hello, we'd like to speak to Orhan Soner," I said.

"Orhan isn't here," said the woman. "Who are you?"

"We're investigating the death of your neighbour, Sani Ankaralıgil."

"What's there to investigate? I read that she died as the result of an accident."

"That's what the press said, but there are a few details that need checking out. Could we speak to Orhan Bey?"

She thought for a bit and finally replied, "What does this have to do with Orhan?"

"Well, since you're neighbours, he might have seen something," I said.

"Because Orhan's a neighbour? Or because he's her ex-lover?"

I didn't know what to say.

"Come inside. Orhan's out, but he'll be back soon," she said.

As soon as I sat down, I opened my bag and took out the magazine containing the photo of Tamaşa in her Valentino dress.

"Have you ever seen this woman around here?" I asked.

She glanced sideways at the photo.

"I don't think so," she said, shaking her head as if trying to brush away a fly. "Our front door opens on to the street, but we have no windows that side. The house was built to look out to sea rather than at the street, so we rarely know what's going on out there."

"Perhaps you could take another good look at the photo," I suggested. "Maybe, while watering the flowers in your front garden—"

"How many times do I have to look at it? I've already looked!" she said loudly, almost yelling.

Why the anger? I could have said something very crushing, but restrained myself because I still had a lot of questions to ask.

"You knew she was an ex-girlfriend of Orhan's, didn't you?" said the wife.

I didn't reply, and Fofo had already clammed up.

"Doesn't everyone have ex-lovers? All youngsters have them – even in the villages. I don't understand why you're making such a big deal out of this. So what if Orhan had a girlfriend all those years ago?"

235

Of course everyone had ex-lovers, but how many of them died in suspicious circumstances, especially if, in the whole of Istanbul, it happened in the house right opposite? However, I didn't pursue the point because, as I said, I wasn't finished and didn't want to upset her. Instead, I merely said, "We wanted to talk to Orhan Bey because your house is right opposite Sani's."

She didn't look convinced, but let the matter drop.

"Would you like some coffee?" she asked.

"If it's no bother," I said.

The woman disappeared.

Fofo and I sat alone for ten minutes in the sitting room. Perhaps we were meant to get up and leave. I'm sure that's what she hoped we'd do. However, neither of us were prepared to concede defeat just when we were on the home stretch, so we continued to sit there in forlorn silence.

Finally, a man entered, rubbing his hands together to get warm. Saved at last!

"Who are you?" he asked abruptly.

"We're investigating the death of Sani Ankaralıgil," I said, feeling sure that his manner would change on hearing these magical words. After all, she was both his former and his recent lover. Surely he'd want to know exactly how she died.

"Yes, my wife told me that much. What do you mean by 'investigating her death'? Are you the police?" said Orhan.

"We're private detectives."

"Private detectives?" said Orhan, pulling a face. "You must be very private indeed, given that you're here in my house on a Sunday evening."

I was beginning to get annoyed. True, we'd turned up at his door without phoning to make an appointment beforehand, but there was no need to be so rude. After all, the person who died had been his lover. He should have been more concerned than anyone that the cause of Sani's death was investigated properly.

"Get out of my house," said Orhan, pointing to the door. It was an awkward situation. We gathered our belongings. I knew that unless I said something to defuse the situation immediately, we might never get another chance to speak to this man, and it would be goodbye to getting to the bottom of Sani's suspicious death for us!

We were almost at the door when, as a last hope, I said, "Has Naz been in touch?"

"Naz?" he said, looking at us through narrowed eyes. "How do you know Naz?"

"Naz hired us to look into her sister's death," I said, lying without a qualm.

I reached out for the door handle. If Orhan didn't respond, we'd be out in the street within thirty seconds.

"Wait," he said.

"Yes?"

"Naz hired you?"

"I thought you weren't interested," I said, waving my hand dismissively.

"You should have told me that to begin with," said Orhan.

"To begin with? You didn't give us a chance to say anything."

"You're right," he said. How I love it when people are able to admit to being wrong, but he didn't need to know that. I opened the door, and even put one foot outside.

"Goodbye," I said. "Let's go, Fofo."

"Actually, there's no need for you to go," said Orhan.

"But I thought that's what you wanted," I said.

"Well...er..." he stuttered and murmured something unintelligible. I also love it when people realize they're cornered.

"Are we going or not?" asked Fofo, looking at me with admiration.

"Ask Orhan Bey," I said.

"Let's go back inside," said Orhan.

We returned to the chairs where we'd been sitting before. While Orhan lit a cigarette, I took the opportunity to look him up and down. Had I become less critical, or did Sani and Naz have exceptionally handsome male companions? Orhan was tall, with light brown hair and an athletic build. But that wasn't all. He exuded self-confidence in the way he moved and even sat, and seemed to radiate light. Yes, that was it. He radiated light in a way similar to Rembrandt's figures of Jesus. I couldn't help wondering what this man was doing with his cartoon wife. But that's real life for you. Married couples often seem mismatched.

"I believe you were abroad when Sani died," I said.

Orhan raised one eyebrow, clearly curious as to how I knew this.

"I'm working on several construction projects abroad at the moment," he said. "I'm away for two weeks of every month, sometimes three."

"In the Balkans?" I asked.

"The Balkans or Russia. What difference does it make?" he said.

"None at all," I said. "Except that I thought you might have some connection with the TLF."

I admit it was a strange link to make, but I was trying to startle him by posing questions that caught him off guard – a tactic that was usually successful, as you'll have noticed. However, if Orhan was startled, he gave no sign of it.

"In that case, anyone doing business in the Balkans is under suspicion," he laughed.

Why didn't he ask what the TLF was?

"Do you think the TLF might have been involved in Sani's death?" I asked.

"If you can explain your reasons for thinking that anyone at all was involved in Sani's death, I'll try to be of help."

Ah, of course, he thought Sani's death was the result of an accident, like everyone else. The ripples of that press statement had spread far and wide. I explained how she had died.

"So you're saying that someone was with Sani when she died," said Orhan, rubbing his temples.

"Who would you suspect, given the situation?" I asked.

"Definitely not the TLF," he said. "How did you find out about the TLF, anyway? Did Naz tell you?"

I shook my head in an ambiguous manner that could have indicated yes or no.

"It was Naz, wasn't it?" said Orhan. "Actually, it doesn't matter how you found out."

"Is the TLF involved in this?" I asked.

"Goodness, no," said Orhan, laughing as if it was a ridiculous idea. "I have no idea what you've been told about the TLF, but I can assure you that we're not a gang of murderers. If Naz suggested in any way that we could have been involved in Sani's death, then...Well, that would be very strange."

"But the TLF is a secret organization," I said.

"There's nothing secret about it at all. In fact, we're about to publish a journal, but Naz wouldn't know about that. The first edition's coming out next month," said Orhan, rummaging through a pile of magazines and papers on the coffee table. "There's a draft here somewhere. You should take a look at it. We're a group of professionals – architects, economists, doctors and environmental engineers and so on – and we all write under our own names. Do you think anyone intending to commit murder would write articles for such a magazine?"

"But a regional body like that..." I muttered, feeling very confused.

"If the people of Erzincan can have a Citizens' Association, why shouldn't the people of Thrace?" said Orhan.

"Did you always intend to publish a journal?" I asked.

"No, not exactly. Let's just say that, at one time, we got a bit carried away with our ideas and dreams of preserving our identity as Thracians."

"Mmm, dreams can..." I said and stopped, not knowing what more to say.

"I want to show you something," said Orhan. "Let's go for a drive."

We'd actually seen all there was to see and heard all there was to hear, so I had no wish to go out into the cold.

"Fine," I said.

We didn't speak again until all three of us were seated in the Audi parked outside Orhan's house. I sat in the front next to him.

"What are you going to show us?" I asked.

"Nothing, but I didn't want to discuss this in front of my wife," said Orhan. "All this hasn't exactly been good for our marriage."

Aha! Was this an admission of his relationship with Sani?

"I'm sorry. We shouldn't have come to your house," I said.

"Simin's aware of what's been going on, of course, but accepting it is another matter," said Orhan. "And it's better if the neighbours don't hear about it."

I nodded.

"So your relationship with Sani was back on," I said.

This time Orhan nodded.

"Since when?" I asked.

"A few months ago."

What did he mean by a few months?

"How many month ago?" I asked.

"It started around April or May."

So a few months meant five months.

"You arranged for Sani to rent that house, didn't you?" I asked.

"She had no money. When she left her husband, she was penniless and homeless. I offered to find her somewhere to live," said Orhan. "I searched everywhere and eventually found this house right opposite us. I didn't think anyone would remember that she was an ex-girlfriend of mine. How was I supposed to know that people have memories like elephants?"

"It's natural for people to be interested in the private lives, past or present, of people like the Ankaralıgils," I said.

"I realize that now."

"How did you meet up again?" I asked, out of curiosity.

"I wanted to speak to Sani in connection with the TLF," said Orhan. "Naz wasn't interested, but we thought we could get Sani onside."

"Was she with her husband at that time?"

"They split up a few months later," he said.

"Exactly how many months later?"

There was something strange about Orhan's use of the term "a few months".

"If I'm not mistaken, I spoke to her in February, maybe January," he said.

"Sani left her husband in March."

"It had nothing to do with me," said Orhan, obviously realizing what I was thinking.

Was this really credible?

"She was with someone else at the time."

"Who?" I asked.

"A young singer. But he wasn't the reason she left her husband," said Orhan. "Her marriage with Cem was an open relationship and Sani had a regular turnover of lovers. At least, that's what I was told."

It was the first time I'd heard anything about an "open relationship".

"Are you sure about this?" I asked.

"That's what Sani told me. They both had relationships with other people."

I turned to look at Fofo.

"Did she ever mention her husband's sexual preferences?" asked Fofo.

"Are you asking if I knew that Cem Ankaralıgil was gay?" asked Orhan.

"Did you hear it from Sani?" I asked.

"A lot more people knew about it than the Ankaralıgil family realized," said Orhan. "I told Sani that, but she insisted it was a big secret. They'd got married to conceal Cem's homosexuality."

"Sani told you that?" asked Fofo.

"Of course Sani told me. I have better things to do than waste my time in Istanbul listening to society gossip."

"Did she say why she suddenly decided to get a divorce?" I asked.

"Haven't you found that out yet?" said Orhan.

"She didn't talk to anyone other than you," I said.

"Sani didn't trust anyone. She was perfect material for that kind of marriage. Nobody could ever get a word out of her," said Orhan.

"Apart from you," I said.

"We'd known each other very well for a long time, which I regard as something of a privilege," said Orhan.

"Why did she want a divorce?" This time it was Fofo who asked.

"Sani had a cousin whom she cared for a great deal. He's called Tunca, and is the son of the uncle she grew up with," explained Orhan.

"The boy who was born after Sani went to live with her uncle?" I said, remembering that Naz had mentioned him to me.

"He's eighteen or nineteen now," said Orhan.

"Ah!" said Fofo. "Did Cem have a relationship with Tunca?" How had Fofo worked that out?

"A friendship would have been fine, but Cem came on to him," said Orhan.

"But everyone says what a good person Cem is," I said, closing my eyes and trying to digest this piece of information.

"You obviously haven't met Cem Ankaralıgil. He's like a child. Very naive and innocent," said Orhan.

"What kind of innocence is that?" I cried. Why did I have such difficulty comprehending situations since I'd given up smoking?

"If you ask me, his advances towards Tunca were a symptom of his naivety, because no normal person would behave that way," said Orhan.

"No, it wasn't normal, and nor would I regard it as innocent. I'd say he was being either bad-mannered or downright immoral," I said.

"If you knew Cem, you'd understand what I'm trying to say," said Orhan.

"How do you know him?" I asked.

"I went with Sani when she went to collect her belongings from their house," explained Orhan. "I talked to Cem a bit then. He wasn't like a mature adult. I certainly doubt whether he could ever run the company. I think he's just there for the sake of appearances."

"What was all that business about money? Why didn't Sani have any money?"

"She was so broke, she even sold her car," said Orhan.

"I thought she sold it to buy a newer model," I said, trying to remember what Naz had told me.

"Newer model? Where did you get that from?" asked Orhan.

"She didn't have a penny to her name. At first, I couldn't believe that she could have ended up so broke, but it was true."

Obviously, Sani had given no thought to her future.

"They say money gets its own revenge," said Fofo. "If people acquire money after living without it for a long time, they either spend it all, or stash it away for fear of being left penniless again."

"In either case, their relationship with money is never healthy," said Orhan the amateur psychologist.

Meanwhile, we'd been driven all round Paşabahçe and had returned to our starting point in front of the house. However, Orhan continued driving, without even slowing down.

"If Sani had agreed to marry Cem in order to conceal his homosexuality, don't you think she was entitled to some money?" I asked.

"Yes, and she was receiving it while she was married to Cem. But when it came to divorce... They were against divorce," said Orhan.

"*They* were against it? You mean Cem's family?" I asked.

"Sani had made a pact with Tamaşa Hanım, whom you obviously suspect had something to do with Sani's death," said Orhan.

I thought back over everything that had been said. Had I implied this in any way?

"How did you work that out?" I asked.

"You showed my wife a picture of her," said Orhan.

So Orhan's wife had recognized Tamaşa, even though she'd barely glanced at the photo.

"Do you know Tamaşa Hanım?" I asked.

"I've never met her, but I know that Sani didn't like her," said Orhan. "They had this horrid arrangement."

"Has your wife met her?" I asked.

"My wife? Leave her out of it," said Orhan sharply.

"Had Sani been threatening to expose the fact that Cem was gay?" I asked.

"She made all kinds of threats. It was very unpleasant," said Orhan.

"Have you ever seen Tamaşa Hanım anywhere near Sani's house?" I asked.

"It's not something I'd notice, to be honest. It's dark when I get home in the evenings, and I tend not to look at people's faces when I'm out in the street, anyway."

"When did you last see Sani?" I asked.

"Why do you ask?"

"It's a perfectly normal question, isn't it?"

"We met on Tuesday morning and my flight was later that afternoon," said Orhan, stopping to give way to a car coming from the right. "If you don't believe me, there's an exit stamp in my passport."

"So you went to Sani's house on Tuesday morning?" I asked.

"Her house? Of course I didn't go to her house. She lived right opposite us. I'd never have met her there," protested Orhan.

Clearly Orhan Soner and his wife did not have an open marriage.

"In that case, where did you meet?" I asked.

"Where we always met."

"Which was?"

"I have a little place in Beylerbeyi," said Orhan.

It was the first time I'd met a man with a pied-à-terre. I studied his face more carefully and cleared my throat in preparation for my next question, which wasn't easy to ask.

"Did you have sex?"

"That's got nothing to do with you."

"Sperm was found in Sani's underwear," I said. "If it belongs to you, then it's not only of concern to us, but also to the police."

Orhan didn't reply immediately. He was probably considering the ramifications of this.

"As far as I know, there's nothing in the statute books about adultery being a crime," he said eventually.

"Not adultery, but concealing information from officials—"

"You're not an official, and I know nothing," he interrupted.

"Are you certain about that?"

"What would I conceal from you?"

Indeed, what could he be concealing? I had no idea. He certainly didn't trust me. But why? Because of his fantasies about the TLF? Because he had a pied-à-terre? Then it struck me that it was because his wife had denied knowing Tamaşa from the photograph.

"We don't want to be involved in this," said Orhan, clenching his fist and banging the steering wheel.

We don't want... First person plural. Meaning him and his cartoon wife. Hmm.

"I'm sorry, but you're already involved," I said.

"We don't want to be involved!" cried Orhan.

Owners of Mercedes and Volkswagen automobiles say they aren't what they used to be. However, Audis are still very good, something I was reminded of when Orhan suddenly slammed on the brakes halfway down a hill. It was here that the fiction stopped and Orhan started telling us everything he knew.

I wanted to call Batuhan on the way home, but Fofo stopped me. "You can talk to him more comfortably at home," he said.

"You're right," I said, stretching contentedly. "Let's enjoy ourselves first. We're not a bad team, are we, Fofo?"

"Not bad? We're marvellous! Mar-vel-lous!" he laughed. "Bloody marvellous!"

*

While dear Fofo made some green tea to warm us up, I settled myself comfortably on the sofa and dialled Batuhan's mobile.

"What's happening? Where are you?" I asked.

"Don't ask. I'm in Yedikule, with an unidentified corpse," said Batuhan.

Poor bloke. And in that weather!

"Batuhan, we've solved it. Call in on your way back and we'll explain everything."

"You've solved it?" he cried. "Have you spoken to Orhan Soner?"

"Actually, his wife—"

"I knew that man was involved," said Batuhan, ignoring me and making it clear that his money was on Orhan. "Was his trip abroad all fiction?"

"No," I said. "That's not it. His wife saw Tamaşa Hanım getting out of a taxi in front of Sani's house on Tuesday evening."

"Tamaşa Hanım? What did she have to do with it?"

"Ah!" I said. "She had everything to do with it."

Turkish mothers treat their sons like infants even when they reach seventy, and Tamaşa was no different.

"Was she protecting Cem?" asked Batuhan.

"Exactly," I said and took a deep breath.

"Good God!" he said. "Mothers!"

Epilogue

*A matelassé It Bag by Miu Miu head designer Miuccia
Prada, and a perfume created for Audrey Hepburn*

The attorney was persuaded to issue a search warrant for Tamaşa
Ankaralıgil's house based on Simin Soner's evidence. After that,
matters took a dramatic turn. Tamaşa was sleeping peacefully in
her nice warm bed when the police arrived at her door. However,
the paparazzi were wide awake. The following day, photos of
Tamaşa being escorted by officers to a police car outside her
house appeared on page one of all the papers under headlines like
Mother-in-law's Revenge, Scary Mother-in-law and *Brides Beware!*

During her first interrogation, Tamaşa admitted that she'd
been to see her daughter-in-law to discuss alimony and the
divorce proceedings but denied all charges, claiming that when
she left the house Sani had been very much alive, and had even
escorted her to the door.

It wasn't the evidence of the trainers, which were found in her
wardrobe and which matched the footprints on the floor of Sani's
sitting room, that led Tamaşa to confess. Which was interesting,
don't you think? She never denied being at the house. Tamaşa's
downfall was brought about by something we hadn't really
touched on during the investigation: the brown dye under Sani's
fingernails, which had been mentioned in the autopsy report. This
turned out to have come from a brown bag produced by Miu Miu
for the 2006 summer collection. Apparently, when poor Sani fell,

she'd tried desperately to cling on to her mother-in-law, but had grabbed hold of her bag instead.

And why did this monstrous mother-in-law make no attempt to get rid of any evidence that might implicate her when she learned that Sani had died after she'd left her unconscious on the floor? I guess she was unable to bring herself to sacrifice her priceless Miu Miu bag. In my opinion, Tamaşa's problem was that she didn't read crime fiction. If she had, she would have destroyed everything she'd been wearing or carrying as a precaution, even if she was unaware that the Turkish police now used ultraviolet photography.

It was of course Tamaşa who took Sani's laptop from the house. She'd learned from her son that Sani kept a diary and had taken the laptop, thinking it might contain damaging information about her relationship with Cem. I had no way of knowing what Sani had written in the diary, but it must have been sufficiently bad for Tamaşa to send her chauffeur and his brother-in-law to steal the GreTur computers from the office. These poor men were given light sentences, since neither had any previous convictions. Tamaşa also claimed that Cem's arrangement with the nightwatchman to keep an eye on Sani's house had been her idea, though I couldn't help thinking Cem at least had a hand in this.

The matter of the mysterious stopper that Naz had found at Sani's house and which I'd absent-mindedly thrown into my bag, turned out to be rather unfortunate – for us, at any rate. We learned that it was indeed the top of a bottle, and that it must have rolled under the table and escaped Tamaşa's notice when Sani clutched at the Miu Miu bag, causing its contents to spill on the floor. By the time I'd handed over the stopper to Batuhan, it was covered with our fingerprints, and couldn't be used as evidence. As you can imagine, I was subjected to a lengthy sermon about the necessity of putting any object found at a crime scene straight into a sealed container without touching it by hand. As an expert in crime fiction, I was of course well aware of this fundamental rule. But hey, sometimes people just get caught up in the heat of the moment.

You're probably wondering about the bottle that the stopper had come from, and so you should. I learned from Jasmin Gil that Tamaşa had used the same perfume ever since her youth. It was L'Interdit, a perfume created for Audrey Hepburn by Givenchy in 1957. Since only limited amounts were produced, it was hard to find. The perfume was a mixture of spices, pepper, rose, jasmine, sandalwood and hibiscus (this information came from the Internet). Batuhan didn't bother to look to see if there was a bottle of L'Interdit without a lid in Tamaşa's house, because evidence contaminated by our fingerprints was of no use to him.

Jasmin Gil called a few days ago to say that she was returning to Bodrum, and thanked us for all that we'd done. I said that there was nothing to thank us for, and that we'd merely been doing our duty. Jasmin had met her father after Tamaşa's arrest and was optimistic that their relationship could be restored, even after so many years. I certainly hoped that would happen. With Tamaşa's true nature revealed, there was nothing to prevent it.

Batuhan said he was very grateful for our help in "closing this file" (his exact words), and that he would nominate us for one of the medals handed out by the Istanbul police to members of the public whose assistance has led to an arrest. Hearing this made me feel as if I'd been doused with boiling water, whereas Fofo could hardly contain his excitement at the thought of claiming his medal, until I brought him to his senses. When receiving such an award, it was obligatory to shake the hand of Istanbul's Chief of Police, and having close contact with one member of the police force was quite enough for me.

I know you're curious to know what happened with Sinan. We met up again, and I told him in the kindest possible way that there could be nothing between us and that he should find someone his own age. After all, I had more important things to do than chase after boys, such as paying off my bank loan and stashing away a few pennies for a rainy day.

And Selim? I still find my hand reaching for the telephone. Who knows what might happen?

A KATI HIRSCHEL MYSTERY NOVEL

HOTEL BOSPHORUS

Esmahan Aykol

Kati Hirschel is a foreigner and the proud owner of the only
crime bookshop in Istanbul. When the director of a film starring her old
school friend is found murdered in his hotel room, Kati cannot resist the
temptation to start her own maverick investigation. After all,
her friend Petra is the police's principal suspect, and reading all
those detective novels must have taught Kati something.

This suspenseful tale of murder features a heroine who is funny, feisty
and undresses men in her mind more often than she would actually
admit, even to herself. The men are too hot to handle, but is she too
cool to resist? Sharp observation and wry, sexy humour expose Western
prejudices about Turkey as well as Turkish stereotyping of Europeans.

PRAISE FOR *HOTEL BOSPHORUS*

"A wonderful novel about Istanbul. The Turkish way of life,
prejudices, men, politics, corruption – Esmahan Aykol
writes about all these with a light and humorous touch."
Petros Markaris, author of *Che Committed Suicide* and *Zone Defence*

"Told in a light, chatty style that is likeable and best compared to
the contents of a personal diary we get a varied slice of personal life
that includes pathos, bathos and sexual revelation. As a portrait of a
fascinating city, *Hotel Bosphorus* paints an intriguing and humorous
picture. The further exploits of this feisty heroine suggest a promising
future for what is intended to be an ongoing series. I look forward
to more tales of strong Turkish coffee and cigarettes." *Crime Time*

£8.99/$14.95
Crime Paperback Original
ISBN 978-1904738-688
eBook
ISBN 978-1904738-718

www.bitterlemonpress.com

A KATI HIRSCHEL MYSTERY NOVEL

BAKSHEESH

Esmahan Aykol

In her second novel Esmahan Aykol takes us to the alleys and boulevards of cosmopolitan Istanbul, to posh villas and seedy basement flats, to the property agents and lawyers, to Islamist leaders and city officials – in fact everywhere that baksheesh helps move things along.

Kati Hirschel, in her thirties, is the proud owner of Istanbul's only crime bookshop. She has learned the corrupt ways of her adored city and soon takes possession of an apartment obtained with the help of a generous bribe to a government official. All is well until a man is found murdered in her dream apartment and Kati becomes the police's primary suspect.

PRAISE FOR *BAKSHEESH*

"In Aykol's impressive second Kati Hirschel mystery set in Istanbul (after 2011's *Hotel Bosphorus*), Kati, a German expatriate 'who loves reading detective stories and has a shop specializing in crime fiction'... once again turns amateur sleuth with aplomb." *Publishers Weekly*

"When you want to be more than a pretty wife, you may have to go above and beyond the call of duty. *Baksheesh* is a mystery following Kati Hirschel, a Turkish wife of a powerful lawyer who runs a store specializing in mystery books. With characters all around her putting the pressure on her, she pushes herself to keep her independence, until her interest becomes her business in more than one way. *Baksheesh* is a strongly recommended pick for lovers of international mystery, highly recommended." *MBR Bookwatch*

£8.99/$14.95
Crime Paperback Original
ISBN 978-1908524-041
eBook
ISBN 978-1908524-058

www.bitterlemonpress.com

DATE DUE